The
Water
and the
Wild

The Water and the Wild

K. E. Ormsbee

chronicle books · san francisco

Library of Congress Cataloging-in-Publication Data:

Ormsbee, Kathryn, author.

The water and the wild / by Kathryn Ormsbee ; illustrations by Elsa Mora.

pages cm

Summary: Lottie Fiske is a lonely twelve-year-old orphan, who lives in a boardinghouse, and her only friends in the world are Eliot, a boy who is very sick, and the mysterious letter-writer who sends her birthday gifts—so when a strange girl steps out of a closet and insists that Lottie follow her down the roots of the apple tree in the yard to another world, which may hold a cure for Eliot, Lottie has to go.

ISBN 978-1-4521-1386-9 (alk. paper)

1. Magic—Juvenile fiction. 2. Orphans—Juvenile fiction. 3. Friendship—Juvenile fiction. 4. Adventure stories. [1. Magic—Fiction. 2. Orphans—Fiction. 3. Friendship—Fiction. 4. Adventure and adventurers—Fiction.] I. Mora, Elsa, 1971– illustrator. II. Title.

PZ7.O637Wat 2015

[Fic]—dc23

2014013372

Manufactured in China.

Design by Amelia Mack.

Typeset in Jannon Antiqua.

The illustrations in this book were rendered in cut paper.

10 9 8 7 6 5 4 3 2 1

Chronicle Books LLC
680 Second Street
San Francisco, California 94107
www.chroniclekids.com

To Lindell and Susan Ormshee
You taught me my first and best lessons.
You taught me to love words.
This bundle of words is for you.

References to poems are marked with a ✦.
Find a complete list of the poems referenced on page 431.

Come away, O human child!
To the waters and the wild
With a faery, hand in hand,

for the world's more full of weeping than you can understand.

—W. B. YEATS, "THE STOLEN CHILD"

CHAPTER ONE

The Finch and the Apple Tree

A GREEN APPLE TREE grew in the heart of Thirsby Square. Its leaves were a sad emerald and its apples a cheery peridot, and the passersby all agreed amongst themselves that it was the strangest sight in an otherwise respectable neighborhood. None of the neighbors knew why the late Mr. Dedalus Yates III had planted the tree in his garden or why his son, the late Mr. Dedalus Yates IV, had kept it alive. It was decidedly out of place on their posh street.

Perhaps the tree would be more forgivable if Mrs. Hester Yates were a kindly old widow who used the apples to bake strudel that she delivered to orphans, vagabonds, and other persons in the direst of circumstances. But Mrs. Yates did not make any such strudel and, in fact, was not a kindly widow at all. The word "dour" is very apt here. Mrs. Hester Yates was a dour widow. Appropriately for a dour widow, she had the squinched face of a crow that had rammed its beak into one too many windowpanes. Inappropriately, she also had a little girl.

If Mrs. Yates could have had her druthers instead of a girl, there would have been no children whatsoever in her neighborhood and certainly none in her boardinghouse. In her opinion, children belonged to a noxious class of furless, yippy house pets that did nothing but make noise at inconvenient times and crash into her potted gardenias. She had, in fact, been instrumental in placing a notice in the square common that read:

NO PETS, NO FOOTBALL, NO NOISY BEHAVIOR.

Unlike his wife, the late Mr. Dedalus Yates IV had a tremendous knack for doing nice things, and one of those nice things had been to insist on taking an orphaned, lemony-haired baby into his home. The late Mr. Yates had also insisted on doing a lot of other nice but highly impractical things that had put the Yateses, a rich and respectable family, into a very unrespectable amount of debt. On the day that five angry creditors came calling at Thirsby Square, Mr. Yates inconveniently fell nose first into his porridge and died, leaving Mrs. Yates to clean up the mess in the kitchen and at the bank.

Mrs. Yates discovered that creditors don't get any less angry just because the man who owes them money has died before so much as taking his morning Darjeeling.

She decided that the best way to repay the creditors was to let out her home as a boardinghouse. It was a good plan. In two years, Mrs. Yates had paid off her husband's debts. Then, since she had gotten so used to the setup, she went right on putting up respectable boarders with no pets, no footballs, and no noisy behaviors.

At first, Mrs. Yates thought that the otherwise good-for-nothing orphan might finally turn out to be useful. She decided to assign the girl simple tasks like cooking and cleaning. A week later, Mrs. Yates found the boardinghouse kitchen in a billowing swirl of blue smoke while the girl frolicked in the back garden, shaking pepper and paprika out of their shakers and shouting, "Begone!"

to imaginary goblins, oblivious to the burnt goose in the oven. That night, Mrs. Yates resigned herself to the fact that Dedalus Yates IV had only ever brought misery into her life and that the orphan girl was no exception. Then she hired a cook.

"Maddening," Mrs. Yates would say at least twice a day. "That child is positively maddening. Mind like a sieve."

The respectful residents of Thirsby Square all agreed with Mrs. Yates. The girl was maddening, or quite possibly just *mad*. She was very likely the maddest girl not just in Thirsby Square but in the entire town of New Kemble and very likely in all of Kemble Isle. She did not belong in town any more than that ridiculous green apple tree did; in fact, suggested some neighbors, it would be best if the girl were simply shipped off the island altogether, where the Bostonians would know what to do with her. Mrs. Yates, however, had made a promise to her husband to care for the girl, and so the girl had to stay.

The girl had a name. The teachers who read roll at Kemble School called off Charlotte G. Fiske, though she preferred to be called Lottie and, out of respect for her wishes, that is what the author will call her, too. Unlike Mrs. Yates, who had prematurely wrinkled and stooped like wilted spinach, Lottie looked much younger than her twelve years. She had grown up to have a tangled mess of lemony hair, a face smattered with freckles, and gray eyes that frightened the locals.

Of all the things that made Lottie Fiske's gray eyes brighten, there was only one that did so every morning, when she would open the curtains of her window looking onto Thirsby Square: it was the green apple tree.

From the first feathery recollections of her life in the boardinghouse, Lottie could remember her apple tree. It was constant, sure, and always peeking into the panes of her window. It grew tall with her, though she could never quite catch up with it; it lost branches as she lost baby teeth; it tapped her window throughout the day to say hello. It was alive and odd, and so was Lottie Fiske. Camaraderie was inevitable.

The green apple tree was also where Lottie had chosen to hide her copper keepsake box. At the tree's base, just where the knotty nub of a root peeked out, there was a small, copper-box-shaped hollow, and it was here that Lottie kept every scrap of paper and every trinket that she held dear. Papers and trinkets were the only things Lottie could hold dear, because they were the only clues she had ever gotten about her past. On the subject of Lottie's parents, Mrs. Yates had remained, as on most matters, silent. There were dim rumors in Thirsby Square, however, that Mrs. Fiske had been a foreigner and responsible for passing on her bright gray eyes to her daughter.

Everything that Lottie knew about her parents could be found in an envelope that she had received on her sixth birthday. Inside the envelope was a letter written in very poor handwriting. It informed Lottie of her parents' names, deaths, and undying love for her. Also enclosed in the envelope was a picture, now faded and folded from years of Lottie's incessant gazing, of a man and a woman, both freckled and laughing. On the back of the picture there was a note, scrawled in the same bad handwriting as the letter's:

If you should ever need anything, write back.

Six-year-old Lottie took the note seriously. She wrote back right away to the mysterious letter-writer, asking for a new set of hair bows, please and thank you. Then she asked Mrs. Yates to mail her note, at which point

Mrs. Yates sat Lottie down and explained that it is impossible to send correspondence without a name or an address. Since Lottie's mysterious letter did not provide either, a reply was impossible, and Lottie could forget about those silly hair bows. So Lottie, saddened and rather confused about postal matters, took back her unaddressed letter, folded it up with her mystery letter, and went to have a pity party underneath the green apple tree. That was when she found the copper box in the copper-box-shaped hollow, and that was when she first placed her treasured letters inside.

A year later, on Lottie's seventh birthday, a letter appeared in the mailbox of the boardinghouse at Thirsby Square. It was much lumpier than the first one, but it was addressed to Lottie in that same terrible handwriting. Inside were the most marvelous white taffeta hair bows that Lottie had ever seen. Attached was the same note as before:

If you should ever need anything, write back.

Mrs. Yates was dumbfounded. She decided to teach Lottie that day what the word "coincidence" meant. But

Lottie didn't need a big word to explain what had happened. She knew a far simpler, far better one: *magic*. Her apple tree was *magic*. Lottie wrote back every year without fail and received a present on her birthday each following year. She stored her letters and her trinkets in the copper box. It was only on Lottie's ninth birthday that she decided to really push her luck and ask for a parakeet. (Penelope Bloomfield, the most popular girl at school, had gotten a parakeet for *her* birthday.) Instead, on her next birthday, all she got was an old, frayed book by a man named Edmund Spenser with a note attached to the cover that read:

This is better.

Lottie thought that the book was exceptionally boring. She decided not to ask for anything too extravagant in the future.

Not, that is, until Eliot Walsch got very sick.

Lottie and her green apple tree may have been comrades, but it did get lonely talking to a tree, if for no other reason than that the tree never talked back. Even Mrs. Yates was helpful enough to suggest to Lottie that she should make friends with the kids at her school. The problem with the kids at Lottie's school was that they never talked back to Lottie, either. Lottie did not enjoy chattering about lip gloss and magazines, like the most popular girls. As a result, Pen Bloomfield (of parakeet fame) had called her Oddy Lottie in the fourth grade, and the name had stuck. Lottie's lemony hair didn't help matters much.

Eliot Walsch didn't mind lemony hair. In fact, he quite liked it and made a point to tell Lottie this the day they met at Kemble School. Lottie and Eliot had been best friends ever since. Eliot was odd, too. He liked to paint. He also lived atop a shop his father owned called the Barmy Badger, and it was common knowledge at Kemble School that you couldn't possibly fit in if you lived in a place called barmy or badger, let alone both. The third strike against Eliot, and the one that now kept Lottie Fiske awake at night, was that he was almost always sick. Eliot had been born sick and he had remained sick, no matter how many doctors Mr. Walsch took him to see.

"The strangest thing," the doctors said at first, "but we've seen worse."

"Let's run some tests," others said.

"Let's try this remedy!" still others cried.

But now, twelve years later, Eliot Walsch only ever got one response:

"Incurable," said the doctors, sadly shaking their heads. "The disease is *incurable*."

There was only one doctor across the Atlantic who was willing to keep trying, and he said, "Five hundred thousand pounds."

Mr. Walsch did not have that sort of money in pounds sterling or dollars, so Eliot stayed incurable. He began to get sicker. Much sicker. So sick that he began to miss school. So sick that, on Lottie's twelfth birthday, she wrote through lonely tears and angry sniffs:

> *I won't ask for anything else ever again, but please cure
> Eliot Walsch of the Barmy Badger, New Kemble.
> He's my best friend.*
>
> *Sincerest of sincerelys,
> Lottie Fiske*
>
> *P.S. And don't you dare send me another book by that
> Spenser guy! Thanks.*

Lottie stuffed the letter into the copper box beneath the green apple tree.

Then she waited.

Six months had passed, and Eliot was still sick. Nothing had changed. Nothing except for the bird.

The morning after she had locked away her tearstained request in the copper box, Lottie had woken up to the chirp of a bird outside her window. It was not a parakeet. It was a finch, and it was perched on her green apple tree.

The finch had feathers of the purest white, like crisp sidewalk snow before the shovelers get to it. This, however, was not the most remarkable thing about the bird. Every so often, the finch would appear, perch on the green apple tree, and sing songs that Lottie was almost sure she recognized. It would, in fact, oblige Lottie with a song whenever she opened her window. This habit had begun to result in confrontations between Lottie and Mrs. Yates, who did not approve of any of her boarders (orphans included) opening their windows on rainy days and letting in the wet.

On the rainy September Tuesday on which this story truly begins, Lottie's window was wide open, and she was getting ready for school to the twittered tune of what sounded a lot like "Here We Go 'Round the Mulberry Bush."

Lottie had just pulled her tweed coat over her school uniform when Mrs. Yates, as was her custom, threw open Lottie's door without a knock. Mrs. Yates looked at the open window. She looked at Lottie. She marched to the window, slammed it shut, and informed Lottie that a prospective boarder was coming over that night for a tour and that Lottie should at least *attempt* to behave decently if sighted on the premises, but that it'd be best if she wasn't sighted at all. Lottie blinked, sneezed, and nodded. Mrs. Yates left the room. This was the extent of Lottie Fiske's relationship with Mrs. Yates.

Lottie sneezed again. There was something about tweed that made her nose itch, but she refused to wear any coat other than this one. It was periwinkle, Lottie's favorite color, and periwinkle was hard to come by around Thirsby Square.

Lottie Fiske, like most sharp and odd persons in this world, was having a miserable school experience. She had the audacity to not be very pretty or rich or even stupid, and at least one of these qualities was essential for a girl in a place like Kemble School. She actually answered questions when called on by her teachers, and though her answers weren't always right, the awful thing was that Lottie *cared*. You could not care at Kemble School and get away with it. Girls like Pen Bloomfield would sniff you out, usually by the school bike racks, and call you things like Oddy Lottie.

On the days when Pen sniffed her out, though, Lottie reminded herself that she had a plan. She and Eliot had made it on the catwalk in the rafters of the school auditorium, while the other kids had been auditioning below for the school musical.

"Look here," Eliot had said over Bert Sotheby's squeaky attempt to reach a glass-cracking note, "you're smart as tacks, Lottie, and all I want to do is paint. If we get good grades here, we could get into any school we want to. We could go to a university far away from here."

They had spat and shaken on it. They were going to get scholarships, they were going to study in Boston first thing out of Kemble School, and they were never going to look back at their school days except to say, "Remember when that old hag Pen Bloomfield didn't take us seriously!"

That future all depended on Eliot. He and Lottie had made this pact together, and they were going to see it through together. His sickness was not going to change the plan. But where *was* Eliot? Lottie looked around anxiously in her first class of the day, but Eliot was not in his seat or anywhere else to be found.

"Walsch, Eliot. Absent."

Mr. Kidd, Lottie's English teacher, marked the last name off of roll. *Absent.* For the fourth time this month. It was the sickness. Lottie scribbled on the tip of her notebook paper as Mr. Kidd rumbled on about Irish poetry. The sickness had to go. It was ruining everything. Ruining their plans, ruining Eliot's laugh, ruining Eliot's life. Ruining her concentration! What *had* Mr. Kidd been chanting?

"Come away, O human child!
To the waters and the wild
With a faery, hand in hand,
For the world's more full of weeping than you can understand."

Lottie looked at the penciled spirals and squares on her notebook paper. No notes. She wasn't going to get good grades this way. *"Come away, come away,"* repeated Mr. Kidd's voice in her head, even as the last bell of the school day clattered out its shrill song down the Kemble School hallways.

Lottie had ridden her bike to school in the rain that morning because Mrs. Yates had been too busy knitting to drive her. It was still drizzling outside when Lottie left school and got to the bike racks. Pen Bloomfield was already there, leaned up against Lottie's bike. A few other girls were twittering around Pen; when they saw Lottie they hushed. They had been waiting for her.

"I was just telling the girls," Pen announced, "how sad it is that some girls have to ride their bikes in the rain. I feel so *sad* for you, Lottie, how you don't have *real* parents to take care of you."

Pen had learned a new way to be mean over the summer break: she said the same old mean things, but now she said them *sympathetically*. She'd discovered that pity and a tearful sniffle could make nasty remarks even nastier.

Lottie's eyes frowned at Pen, but her lips smiled. That was how things were done at Kemble School. Girls smiled when they were angry, and they pretended to be concerned when they were really being cruel.

"I'd like to get my bike, *please*," Lottie said politely, though she felt more like kicking a puddle of rainwater onto Pen's perfectly pressed uniform, "and you're in the way."

Pen moved out of the way, but as she did so, she caught Lottie by the shoulder. Leaning forward, she placed her lips to the curl of Lottie's ear.

"*Hushed-up* parents," she whispered, "make for *blushed-up* girls." Pulling away, Pen asked, "Do you know what that means? It means nothing good ever comes from filth."

"My parents," Lottie said, "were not filth."

"Everyone knows that your mom wasn't an islander," said Pen. "She was from the mainland. Maybe even *Canada*. Doesn't get much filthier than that."

Anger had been growing in Lottie like rising dough threatening to spill over the sides of its pan, and she knew what would happen if the dough did spill: she would have another one of her bad spells. Lottie called them bad spells, even though she knew that the real term for them was "panic attacks." It was an ugly adult term that she had heard the doctor use at her last checkup.

Lottie had gotten the bad spells since she was a little girl. First, they had only come at night, when she woke from bad dreams about her parents. They came oftener and oftener now. She didn't need to feel frightened or inadequate anymore for them to brew up, just angry with Pen Bloomfield.

"So," Pen went on, "where's your friend, Sir Coughs-a-Lot?"

"Why?" Lottie's hands trembled as she unlocked her bike chain. "You don't care about Eliot."

"No," said Pen, "I don't. I was just hoping that he'd gone ahead and"—she snapped her fingers—"already." It's getting so tedious to have to listen to lectures over his wheezing. I'm pretty sure it wasn't Napoleon Coughaparte who was exiled to Elba, but that's what I've got in my notes."

"Take better notes." Lottie stuffed the bike chain into her backpack.

"Come on, Oddy Lottie," Pen snorted. "Can't take a joke? I thought you'd be relieved to know that there's someone more pathetic at school than you: that stupid Walsch boy."

Lottie turned calmly around. Then she rammed her head into Penelope Bloomfield's gut.

Pen's friends shrieked in horror. Lottie felt dizzy but satisfied. She scrambled to get ahold of her bike just as Pen's fist flew up and caught the side of Lottie's mouth, knocking soundly into her teeth. Lottie ducked against the pain and pushed her bike out of the circle of girls.

"Don't you ever," she sputtered, recklessly mounting her bike, "*ever* breathe another word about Eliot!"

"Well, I won't have to, will I?" Pen shrieked after Lottie, staggering back to her feet with the help of her friends. "Not for much longer! Not once he's *dead*!"

Lottie did not wait to hear more. She pedaled away.

The sky had begun to clear. Lottie could feel patches of sun warming the back of her head in between the tangles of her hair, but even the fresh sunshine could not rid the chill shooting down her legs as she pedaled. She could feel something wet trickling down the side of her mouth. She pressed her hand against her jaw, and when she lowered it to the handlebar, there was a bright splotch of blood staining the lines of her knuckle notches.

A horn blared and tires squelched. Lottie glanced up and swerved her bike, just missing an oncoming car. Trembling more than ever, she pedaled on and turned into a narrow street crowded with pedestrians. Up ahead was the familiar sight of a pale yellow storefront, over which a blue-lettered banner read: THE BARMY BADGER.

Mr. Walsch, the owner of the Barmy Badger, was a plump, simple man with a face full of white whiskers who specialized in engraving and calligraphy. Though Mr. Walsch was not clever, he was kind, and Lottie liked his stories about his rough days as a cannery boy in Newfoundland better than any novel on her shelves back home. Today, though, Lottie wanted to know only one thing from Mr. Walsch when she burst into his office.

"How is he? How's Eliot?"

Mr. Walsch gave a squeak of surprise. He sprung up in his chair, upsetting his carefully calligraphing hand. Black ink spattered on his button-up shirt in a dozen tiny pinpricks.

"Oh, dear," said Mr. Walsch, scratching his nose with his inky pen. "But that's all right. I'd just begun. No harm done. No harm at all."

He did not look at Lottie, which she knew could only mean one thing: Eliot was worse. Something pricked behind Lottie's eyes, wet and unwelcome. She gulped down air and swallowed the salty scratch of unshed tears.

"What can I do?" Lottie said, blinking fiercely.

"He's still sleeping," said Mr. Walsch, pulling out a fresh sheet of white paper, "or else you know what I'd recommend. There's no one who can cheer up my boy like you, Lottie."

Lottie wished that Mr. Walsch would look at her, but she supposed that this was his way of warding off a cry, much like her own extra gulps of air. She left him to his calligraphy and trudged back to the front door.

"Lottie?"

Lottie turned around. Eliot stood at the top of the staircase. He looked as pale as a freshly opened package of flour, and by the time he reached the bottom of the stairs, he was out of breath.

"I thought I heard you," he said, taking Lottie's hand in his hot one and towing her up the stairs. "Come on, come see! I've been painting."

Eliot was always painting. Even when he had started to get the headaches in second grade and the nausea in fifth, he still painted. Every few weeks, Eliot had a new master-piece ready to frame, but since Mr. Walsch couldn't afford any frames, Eliot had just hammered the paintings onto every spare inch of wall he could find in the Barmy Badger. Eliot's first work of art, a big purple blob that he claimed was an elephant, rested atop the kitchen cabinet with utmost reverence. His most recent work, a skyline of spires and steeples and a setting sun, hung proudly in the stair-well; Eliot planned on submitting this one to the Kemble School art exhibit at the end of the year.

Lottie looked around Eliot's room for a new canvas, but there was none to be found.

"Well?" she said eagerly, after her third circle around the room. "Where is it?"

Eliot grinned. He pointed up. Lottie followed his fin-ger to the bedroom's slanted ceiling. Above, painted blues and yellows swirled into clouds and blurry stars. The stars circled around Eliot's skylight, which was known to the two as "ye ol' porthole." Eliot's telescope was propped beneath ye ol' porthole, ready for stargazing.

"It's terrific," said Lottie. "A masterpiece!"

Eliot surveyed his ceiling with pride. "I had the inspiration last night, looking out of the porthole. You can't see the sky on cloudy nights like we've been having this month. I thought, what's the use of ye ol' porthole if you can't see the sky? That's when I decided to bring the sky *inside*. Now we'll be able to see the stars no matter how nasty the weather gets."

Eliot took a good look at Lottie.

"Your mouth is bleeding," he observed. "And you've got a toe sticking out of your shoe."

Lottie looked at her feet. Eliot was right. Her big toe was sticking straight out of her right loafer. She supposed that ramming into Pen Bloomfield and pedaling to the Barmy Badger like a mad hamster had something to do with her battered condition.

"Here," Eliot said. He heeled off his green sneakers and nudged them Lottie's way. "Take my shoes for the ride home. After today, I don't think I'll be needing them anytime soon."

Lottie stared at Eliot. "What does that mean?"

"Dad and I visited the doctor this morning. He said I've got to stay home all week." Eliot shrugged. "He's just overreacting. It's only a cough."

"You, on the other hand," Eliot went on, pointing at Lottie's chin, "could die from loss of blood if we don't staunch the wound!"

Eliot grabbed one of several tissue boxes resting by his bedside and offered it to Lottie. She took a tissue and dabbed the side of her mouth. Then she kicked off her shoes and began to lace on Eliot's worn but sturdy sneakers.

"Thanks, Michelangelo," she said.

Eliot beamed. "Don't mention it."

When Lottie looked back up, a piece of candy was flying toward her nose. She lunged to claim it, one-handed, and tucked the neon green sweet-so-sour into her coat pocket. That day on the catwalk, when she and Eliot had made their great plan for the future, they had also come to the definite conclusion that sour candies were the solution to any trouble.

"They give you something *else* to cry over," said Eliot. "Your eyes start watering from the sour, not the bad, and you start to forget what was so awful in the first place."

Since then, Eliot and Lottie always kept a stash of sweet-so-sours around for swaps.

"Nice catch," said Eliot before sprawling on the ground. He patted the dusty floor beside him. "Why exactly are you all bloody?"

"I got into a fight," Lottie confessed.

"With Pen Bloomfield," guessed Eliot. "About what?"

Lottie stared down at her new shoes. She wasn't about to tell Eliot that it had been about him.

"My parents."

Eliot did not say anything, but his chest heaved. Lottie could hear a dull sound of *hrm, hrm, hrms*. He was covering up his cough.

"You're not getting better, Eliot," she whispered.

Eliot frowned. "Sorry. Can't hear you."

Lottie sank to the floor next to him, tucking her hands behind her head and gazing up at the muddied sky through ye ol' porthole.

"I said, I missed you at school today."

"I'm really sorry. I guess I've just worn myself out from too much painting, is all. I'll be better faster than the doctor thinks." He nudged Lottie's ankle with his bare foot. "What about your parents?"

Lottie grimaced. She had hoped that Eliot would drop that subject.

"The same things," she said. "Pen called them filth. It doesn't matter. I know she's wrong, and one day I'm going to find someone who can prove it."

"You mean the letter-writer."

Eliot knew all about the letters and the gifts that Lottie kept in her copper box. He did not know about Lottie's most recent request, however, and Lottie did not mean for him to find out.

"I don't see," said Eliot, "why you don't just ask the letter-writer about it. He sent you your parents' picture. He's got to know something about them."

"I don't want to bother him," said Lottie. "He has to be a very busy person if it takes him a full year just to send back a birthday gift."

Though not the one birthday gift she wanted most.

"Anyway," she went on, "I already know what my parents were like. Mom was terribly beautiful and smart. Canadian, I think, and she could speak the most butter-melting French you can imagine. She met Dad while he was studying on the mainland to be a world famous chef. They had big dreams. They just died tragically together in a subway accident in New York before they had the chance to live the dreams out."

Eliot coughed. "But Lottie, you made that whole story up. Not to mention, it's different every time."

"It could just as well be true as not!" said Lottie. "Pen's wrong. They weren't filth."

"How can you know that, though?" Eliot said slowly. "What if that isn't the way it happened?"

"Are you siding with Pen Bloomfield?"

Eliot readjusted his glasses. "I'm not taking sides. I'm just saying, what good is all your storytelling if you only see what you want to see?"

Eliot closed his eyes and drummed his fingers slowly, one by one, on his chest.

"Maybe you're afraid," he said quietly. "Maybe you're afraid of what the letter-writer might tell you, because it won't be the story you want to hear."

Lottie sat up, crumpling her bloodied tissue. "You're one to talk about seeing only what you'd like to see."

Eliot's tired face flushed. "What's that supposed to mean?"

"You're broken, Eliot," Lottie said. "*Broken*. You're not getting better. You're painting when you should be resting, and you're missing school because you're getting sicker. You say we'll still go to Boston, that nothing's going to stop our plan, but the truth is, you're—"

The anger that had been in Eliot's eyes turned fearful.

Lottie could not say the word.

None of the doctors knew how to fix Eliot's sickness, and not even the letter-writer could give her a cure for a birthday present.

Lottie only now realized how strongly the room smelled of paint.

"That fight," said Eliot. "It wasn't about your parents, was it?"

"Don't even think it was about *you*!"

The room went silent.

"Why don't you leave?" Eliot suggested in a whisper.

"Yes," snapped Lottie. "Why don't I?"

She leapt to her feet and ran from the room, leaving the sound of Eliot's hoarse, barklike coughs behind her.

She took the stairs three at a time, heading straight for the door.

"Lottie!"

Lottie stopped on the bottom landing and brushed away an angry tear. Mr. Walsch stood in the doorway of his office.

"How is my boy, do you think?" Mr. Walsch asked.

"Well," Lottie whispered, "he's still painting. I think that's a good sign, don't you?"

Mr. Walsch smiled sadly and nodded. "You've been a true friend to him, dear. That's why I feel you ought to know."

Lottie clung to the banister. "Know what?"

"Eliot had his appointment with the doctor this morning," said Mr. Walsch. "The test results weren't good. The doctor said that there are two, maybe three weeks."

Two, maybe three weeks of what? Lottie thought. She didn't understand what Mr. Walsch was trying to say, or why he was looking at her in that strange way.

"I should go," she said, confused. She opened the door, and a harsh gust of wind blew in the first chill of autumn. "Take care, Mr. Walsch."

She heard a timid "goodbye" as she slammed the door shut, and the warm glow of the Barmy Badger disappeared.

CHAPTER TWO

In Which Oddities Begin to Occur

LOTTIE PEDALED QUICKLY down the wet streets. She took the route from the Barmy Badger to Thirsby Square so often that she could have biked it blind, and in the current weather she might as well have been. The rain had picked up again and now drove so savagely into the pavement that the raindrops seemed to be bouncing straight back up into the sky. Lottie didn't realize immediately that she was crying. When had she started crying?

Sickly yellow streetlamps had begun to zap on, and with each new flicker of light came a new bite of remorse in Lottie's gut. She had not meant to lose her temper with Eliot, and now—*two, maybe three weeks.* Tomorrow, Lottie decided, she would bike early to Eliot's and apologize. That would fix their friendship, but it would not fix Eliot. Only the letter-writer, if anyone, could do that, and so far the letter-writer did not seem to care.

Lottie sped past a stalled taxicab and cut into Skelderidge Park, where the trees would soften the rainfall. Her hands had gone raisiny, and Lottie braked to let out a shivery sneeze. She wiped her wet sleeve across her wetter nose and looked around. The park was empty because of the dark and the rain, but Lottie thought for a moment that she had heard voices. They were muffled, like voices coming from the earpiece of a telephone, but they were close.

"Anyone there?" was what Lottie was going to call, but it turned into another sneeze.

Then she heard a sound—not voices, but a rough, inhuman noise. It sounded at first, Lottie thought, like a cracking egg. Then a cracking whip. Then a cracking *tree,* which was, in fact, what it turned out to be. The tall, gnarled tree under which Lottie had stopped her bike gave a great shudder and then, with no consideration as to where Lottie happened to be standing, it began to heave toward her.

Lottie, like any red-blooded girl, had been taught to get out of the way of things like speeding convertibles and masked men with guns, but she had never expected to have a run-in with a homicidal *tree*. More than that, and what confused Lottie most, in the split second she had to realize that she was about to get smashed to smithereens, was that she had not seen any lightning. If she was going to be killed by a falling tree, Lottie thought in that last moment of cognizance, she wished it would have at least had the decency to get struck by lightning first. That would have been a much more dramatic way to go.

Lottie's hands were iced to the handlebars in panic. She closed her eyes, and a rushing sound filled her ears. She could feel the wet hair that had been plastered around her face blow back in a windy shock. Lottie thought of her green apple tree, of Eliot, and of her parents' photographed, freckled faces. A hand clamped around her right arm. Then she heard one last thundering *crack*.

❧

A familiar smell tickled up Lottie's nose. It smelled of home. She opened her eyes. She was not home. She was slumped against the cold iron of a park bench. It was still

raining. Across from her lay the hulking silhouette of a
fallen tree and, from where she sat, Lottie saw a glint of
metal peeking out from under one of the tree branches. It
took her a long, stupid minute to realize that the metal was
all that remained of her bicycle; the rest of it had gotten a
thorough pancaking.

But I'm *not pancaked!* Lottie thought, shaking her
legs out. They seemed fine. The only pain she felt came
from her left arm. Lottie pulled back the sleeve of her
periwinkle coat to see just how bad a bruise she had
gotten.

But there wasn't a bruise. Where a bruise should have
been, there was a handprint. A deep black handprint covered the crook of her elbow, and from it pulsed a hot, tight,
uncomfortable feeling, like someone had tied a steaming
tea bag too tightly around Lottie's skin.

A merry chirp shook Lottie's attention, and she
looked up from the strange mark on her arm to catch
a sight stranger still: a white fluttering of wings. A lone
white finch was flying away, up into the nighttime rain,
until Lottie could not distinguish it from the glaring
white raindrops themselves.

Lottie did not want to think long on why her bike was under a giant tree trunk and why she was not. Instead, she pulled herself off the park bench and began running. That is, she meant to run but ended up doing more of a lollop-stagger instead. She stumbled on something round and slick—an apple—and realized that this had been the familiar smell of home. The tree that had fallen had been an apple tree. The scent of apples grew too strong and sour in the time it took Lottie to get her wits together, and she had to stop lollop-staggering a second time when her stomach lurched and she found herself vomiting an entire school lunch behind a shrubbery at the Skelderidge Park entrance.

Lottie left the park. The rain had slackened to a drizzle so that she could just make out signposts at the park corner. She did not recognize the street names. Lottie felt her stomach clenching again. Her legs screeched, her brain buzzed, and a dry, cottony creep was working its way around her tongue, her lips, and the roof of her mouth. She was so thirsty.

Lottie willed her feet across the street, toward a low hum of voices. She heard laughter, shouts, and tipsy-pitched singing. When she looked up again, she realized just where she was. Those shouts were coming from New Kemble's only pub, the Flying Squirrel. The warm pulse of the pub's frosted windows shone beneath its sign, a splintered gray squirrel raising a chalice in its paws. Mrs. Yates would murder Lottie on the spot rather than see her set foot in such an establishment. But Mrs. Yates was not here, and Lottie had just had an encounter with a lethal apple tree. Surely she was entitled to a glass of water.

A peeling sign that hung from the front door informed Lottie that no one under the age of twenty-one was permitted. Lottie did not look twenty-one. She hardly looked her real age of twelve. But Mollie Browne worked at the Flying Squirrel, and Mollie was one of Mrs. Yates' old boarders and had babysat Lottie as a little girl. Mrs. Yates had eventually evicted Mollie for playing an electric guitar at three o'clock in the morning and "forgetting" to pay her rent three months in a row. Mollie still liked Lottie, though, and she would always blow a kiss from the window when Lottie biked past the pub.

Lottie crossed both sets of fingers for luck, hoping that Mollie would be on shift. Then she went in, nudging into a mass of sweaty bodies swathed in a cheery, orange glow. If she were not so dazed, Lottie would have relished feeling wickedly rebellious. At the moment, though, she only felt wickedly sick.

"Excuse me!" Lottie piped up, trying to get the attention of a scraggly-faced man behind the bar counter.

The bartender didn't acknowledge her. Lottie tried to speak again, but a man who smelled of sauerkraut stepped on her foot and knocked her back against a metal stool.

That was when the bad spell began. At long last, one had caught up with her.

Lottie knew the symptoms very well. First came a sensation like her chest was folding in over itself like a bedsheet, again, again, and again. Next came a tingle in her brain, her ears, her fingers. She choked in short, staggering breaths and closed her eyes, fighting hard against the pain. It would be over soon, she told herself. Bad spells always ended, no matter how bad they got, just so long as she fought back. She grasped on to the rough edge of the bar counter, trembling.

"Oi! All right there?"

Lottie's eyelids snapped open. She could breathe again. She gulped a few more times and nodded at the scraggly-faced bartender, who had just shoved a handful of peanuts into his mouth and did not look nearly as concerned as he had sounded.

"Could I have a glass of water?" Lottie asked.

Scraggly Man blinked blankly at her before revealing a crooked row of browned teeth. He snorted and jabbed a girl with dreadlocks standing next to him.

"Did you hear that, Molls? This little lost mouse has taken a wrong turn. Thinks we might be giving away free water at this high-class establishment."

Lottie blushed furiously. The girl turned around. It was Mollie Browne, who looked just as shocked to see Lottie as Lottie was to discover that Mollie now wore dreadlocks.

"Shoo," Scraggly Man barked at Lottie. "You're too young to be in here."

"For the love of Hendrix," Mollie huffed, tossing the bartender the glass she had been drying and swinging her legs over the counter. "Can't you tell she's dog sick?"

Mollie rested a firm hand on Lottie's shoulder and stooped to look into her eyes.

"What're you doing here, Lottie?" she said. "Does Mrs. Yates know where you are?"

"I fell off my bike," explained Lottie, "and I'm feeling sick. I didn't think I could make it back to Thirsby Square without some water. Could I just have a glassful? I promise I won't be any trouble."

Mollie bit down on her pierced lip, giving it some thought. "We've got an employee break room in the back. Let's get you back there, yeah?"

Lottie hadn't expected for Mollie to grab her, let alone swing her up onto her shoulders and barrel right past the man who smelled of sauerkraut.

"Out of the way, fellows!" she shouted, shimmying past burly baseball fans and shoving through a door marked EMPLOYEES ONLY. The door swung shut, and the grizzled shouts of the Flying Squirrel disappeared into the dim dank of the break room.

"A bike accident, huh?" Mollie said, setting Lottie back on her feet. "Well, you look all right, just a little shaken up. Sure you're just thirsty? I can find a first-aid kit, if you need one."

"I'm fine," Lottie said, trying to smile. "Scrapes don't bother me much."

Mollie grinned tiredly. "Yeah, I remember that about you, Lottie Fiske. That's what you said when you fell out of that apple tree."

"Thanks for helping me."

Mollie waved Lottie off. "I would stay, but I'm walking a thin wire with the boss as it is. If he found out I let in a kid like you, I'd lose my job."

She pointed out a couple of cabinets with towels and glasses and then disappeared in another swoosh of the break room's swinging door. The room was small and poorly lit, but it had what Lottie needed. Lottie rinsed out a dusty glass under the sputtering tap water and finally raised a glassful to her lips. She chugged the water greedily, and another glassful after it. Then she began to wash off her numb, muddy arms.

She gasped at the sight of what was on the inside of her left arm. The handprint was still there. Unlike a bruise, the mark was not an uneven patch of brown, blue, or purple— just a thick black that ran against her skin in the perfect outline of a palm and five fingers. Though *no,* there weren't five fingers after all. Where the imprint of a pinky had been before, there was now only the slightest sliver of black.

As Lottie stared dumbly at the mark, she heard a commotion from outside, in the bar. She jerked off the faucet, the handprint momentarily forgotten, and peered through the slatted window of the break room door. There were shouts of anger and surprise as the crowd parted for a sight that Lottie could barely make out. It looked like one figure supporting another, and those two figures were making their way past the rowdy crowd straight toward —the break room door.

Getting discovered meant getting Mollie Browne into trouble, and that was no way to repay a favor. Lottie ducked down and frantically crammed herself into a forest of employees' coats that hung in a wooden alcove by the door. Just as she had swatted a prickly scarf away from her face and hugged her knees up to her chest, the door swung open. Shouts from the pub swam in with the sweet, sickly smell of beer. She heard footsteps, followed by the scraping of chairs. Then there were voices. Mollie was the first to speak.

"Well! She must've skipped out already. Poor girl. You kids have got a knack for getting scratched up tonight, haven't you? Never rains, but it pours."

Lottie heard a dull thud and the sound of labored breathing.

"Ugh," said Mollie. "He's a wreck. Gang brawl, was it? Serves him right. Who lets you kids carry around switchblades, anyway?"

"I wouldn't know," said a boy's distracted voice. "Do you have any clean towels?"

"In the lower cupboard over there. I expect to get repaid for bloodied-up linens, though, got that? And this place better not look any worse for the wear. You're lucky I'm feeling like such a humanitarian tonight. Be grateful."

"Oh. Right! Yeah, sorry, I am."

There was the shuffling of feet, the creaking of door hinges, a momentary burst of pub shouts, and then nothing but the muffled sounds from inside the break room. By now, Lottie had worked up enough courage to peek through the folds of the coats. She immediately wished that she hadn't. A body was sprawled out on the table in the middle of the room, and its bloody arm hung just a few feet from Lottie's nose. Meanwhile, a boy was crouched by the cupboards, pulling out an armful of white towels. The body on the table coughed.

"Thanks, doctor," said the voice of the body, and it sounded like it belonged to a boy no older than Lottie.

Despite the phlegm and pain in the voice, Lottie could swear that the injured boy sounded like he was making a *joke*. Apparently she was right, because two laughs followed, one soft and wary, the other strangled. Lottie shirked back into the coats as the other boy passed by and turned on the tap.

"I thought we were goners for sure," he said. "Just think, a few seconds later, and we would've been trapped inside that tree for all eternity."

"I think," said the voice from the table, "that was the general idea."

"You mean, you don't think it was an accident?"

"I don't know, but Father sure won't."

"So, you think it was worth it?" The faucet turned off, and the boy-doctor returned to the table.

"She's safe. That's what matters."

"And Ada can take care of the rest."

"If anyone can, Ada can."

The boys laughed again. Then there was a sharp wheeze of breath, the kind Lottie had made growing up when Mrs. Yates had pitilessly cleaned up her scrapes with rubbing alcohol.

"Sorry, mate. I know it hurts."

"Stop flavoring, Fife. You can just tell me how bad it is."

"Your arm's pretty mangled, but nothing's broken. It'll look nasty more than anything else."

"Right." A pause. "Thanks. I know you didn't have to get yourself involved in this."

"Don't be an idiot. Someone's got to clean up after you. Now shut up. I've got to disinfect it, and all I've got is this stinging human stuff. Just remember, no touching. I don't want any new tattoos tonight."

There was the sound of wet towel hitting skin, followed by a scream from the boy on the table. Lottie clutched her stomach, woozy from the smell of antiseptic and blood. The injured boy let out another shriek. Lottie felt herself getting sick again—horribly sick. She couldn't stay crouched in the coat closet any longer. Anything, even the risk of getting caught as an eavesdropper, was better than puking all over Eliot's green sneakers.

Lottie counted to one—two—three, then leapt up, sprang from the coats, and pushed out through the break room door. She ran, ignoring a shout from behind her.

Out in the pub, the injured boy's screams were swallowed up in the blare of the baseball game and the yells of drunken men. She burst out the front door and into the blisteringly cold rain. It was still three blocks to Thirsby Square. Lottie looked at her wristwatch, which she was relieved to find had survived the accident. It was past eight o'clock, her curfew, and Mrs. Yates would be irate if she found Lottie's bedroom empty.

Lottie passed under a maple tree and shivered. To be so close to death, and for someone to pull her out of the way! Now that Lottie had time to think about it, this was the only explanation for why she hadn't been smushed in Skelderidge Park: someone must have yanked her away from that falling tree. Then, that someone had just--disappeared. Lottie tugged up the sleeve of her periwinkle coat and looked again at the handprint on her arm. The sting had gone away, but just looking at the mark, she felt sick. Lottie decided that she was never going to wander into a pub ever again. She felt worse now than she had when she had first gone inside.

Lottie opened the wrought iron gate of the boarding-house at Thirsby Square. But she didn't go inside. Not yet. Instead, Lottie crawled under the shelter of her green apple tree. She ran her fingers lovingly down its sturdy trunk, then stooped at its roots. The ground was runny with mud, and Lottie's fingers went slick as she dug up her copper box. She sat down on the root notch and opened the lid, though only by a crack, so as to shield the box's contents from the rain. She breathed deeply, and quite suddenly the cold and the rain couldn't reach her at all. When Lottie opened her copper box, the world outside—with its Pen Bloomfields and Mrs. Yateses and incurable illnesses and falling trees—bled away like watercolors under the tap.

When her box was open, Lottie could pretend that it was the magic of the letter-writer that was real, not the rules at Kemble School.

Lottie peered inside at the worn photograph of her parents, and her heart squeezed up her breath in a painful hitch. Unbidden, Mr. Kidd's recitation from English class winked in her mind:

For the world's more full of weeping than you can understand.
"CHARLOTTE!"

Lottie slammed her box shut and whipped around. Mrs. Yates stood on the front porch, her arms folded.

"What *are* you doing? Get in this house at once!"

Lottie shoved her copper box back beneath the tree root. She tripped up the front porch, face burning. Mrs. Yates would ground her for this. She would keep her inside for the weekend. She wouldn't let Lottie visit the Barmy Badger, not even to apologize to Eliot.

"I—I—" Lottie began.

But Mrs. Yates held up a hand to silence her. "You're grounded."

"I'm wet," Lottie replied stupidly.

Looking over Mrs. Yates' shoulder, Lottie noticed that they were not alone. A man dressed in a fancy pinstriped suit was sitting in the parlor.

"This is Mr. Grissom, Charlotte," said Mrs. Yates, waving Lottie into the parlor. "He's that nice prospective boarder for our third floor that I was telling you about."

The only thing that Lottie could remember Mrs. Yates telling her about a prospective boarder had been that morning, when she'd warned Lottie to stay out of sight. There was no chance of that now, though, as Lottie was as in sight as she could possibly be.

"Hello," the man said, inclining his head toward Lottie. "You must be the little lady of the house."

Lottie frowned. She did not like the way that the man looked at her, as though she were five years younger than she really was.

"I'm not a lady," corrected Lottie. "I'm just Lottie."

"You *are* wet," said Mrs. Yates, who had apparently not believed Lottie until now. "Careful, child! Don't drip on the Oriental."

Lottie edged away from the ugly, puce-colored rug so that she could more conveniently drip on the bare floor.

"Now, Charlotte, what happened?" Mrs. Yates said. "I was just explaining to Mr. Grissom that I have a strictly enforced curfew for all guests, no exceptions." She turned to Mr. Grissom. "This *usually* doesn't happen."

"I got attacked by a tree," Lottie explained in what she thought was a very calm, adult manner. "It crushed my bike, but I escaped. Someone pulled me out of the way just in time."

Mr. Grissom made a gurgling sound, and Lottie wondered if he was choking. Finally he said, "That's quite an imagination the young lady has."

"Excuse us, Mr. Grissom," said Mrs. Yates, grabbing Lottie's arm and dragging her out of the parlor.

"You're lying," hissed Mrs. Yates just as soon as they were out of earshot of the man. "Here I am, trying to make a good impression, and you waltz in, a flagrant liar and a curfew breaker! Now tell me what really happened."

"I just *did* tell you," said Lottie, trying to pull free from Mrs. Yates' pincer grasp. "A tree attacked!"

"That's as silly as your notions about goblins and magical boxes," Mrs. Yates said. "Don't think that ridiculous story is going to save you from punishment. I've a guest to entertain, and you may not look up to an explanation now, but believe me, I'll expect one in the morning. In the meantime, you're absolutely forbidden from setting one foot outside this house without my express permission."

With that, Mrs. Yates sent Lottie straight upstairs without dinner. The lack of food was all the same to Lottie, who was exhausted and had no appetite after puking up five fish sticks' worth of lunch in Skelderidge Park. But to be grounded the whole weekend through? She *had* to see Eliot. She had to apologize. If there were only two, maybe three weeks left, every day counted.

She would just have to go back tonight.

Mrs. Yates would be busy with Mr. Grissom downstairs. All Lottie had to do was sneak out the kitchen door.

It would be a long run back to the Barmy Badger, but she knew all the best shortcuts. It was a risk, and it might mean a punishment of a whole *year* full of grounded weekends. But tomorrow Mrs. Yates might lock Lottie's door, as she'd done many times before. Tonight, Lottie still had a chance.

Lottie barreled into her bedroom. She grabbed an umbrella from under her bed. Then she tossed off her periwinkle coat and threw open her closet to find a dry shirt and shorts good for running.

What she found instead was a girl.

CHAPTER THREE

Down and Up

THE GIRL BLINKED ONCE. "You have the strangest taste in clothing," she said.

Lottie stumbled backward. In the dimness, she could only just make out the outline of the girl emerging from the closet. She was approaching Lottie softly (impossibly softly!) with arms raised as though to show she was harmless. Lottie fumbled with the switch of a nearby lamp. In a *snap,* soft light filled the room. When Lottie's eyes adjusted, they met a pair of blazing blue ones.

"How did you get in here?"

"The window," chirped the girl.

Lottie looked at the window that Mrs. Yates had slammed shut that morning.

"The window's closed."

"Not anymore, it isn't," said the girl, who walked to the window and flung it open. She turned around, leaning against the ledge and letting out a noisy yawn. "Shall we go?"

"Get *out*, would you?" Lottie said, her face growing hot. "What do you mean by barging in here?" She paused and frowned. "And go where?"

Then Lottie realized something. "Are you wearing my clothes?"

The girl flung a scarf, *Lottie's scarf,* over her shoulder with flourish. "What a silly question to ask at a time like this!"

Lottie had had too long a day for this. She glared. "Are you going to leave on your own, or should I give you a nice shove out that window?"

The girl clung fiercely onto the ledge. "Don't even think about it! I've come here for you, Lottie Fiske, and I don't mean to leave without you."

Lottie opened her mouth, then shut it, then opened it again. "How do you know my name?"

"Oh, I know a lot more than that," the girl said. Her eyes twinkled in a way that made Lottie want to pop her in the nose.

"Like what, exactly?" Lottie asked instead.

The girl tugged off Lottie's scarf and tossed it back toward the closet. "Such an ugly shade of green," she remarked to herself. "Like a rotten avocado."

Then she held out a slip of paper. "Here."

Lottie snatched the paper out of the girl's hand. In familiarly bad handwriting, it read:

This is better.

Lottie read the note three times. Then she looked up. "*You're* the letter-writer?"

"Me?" The girl snorted. "Of course not. It's from my father."

Lottie held the paper up. "What does this even mean? *What's* better?"

"I don't know," the girl said thoughtfully. "Me, I guess. You're supposed to come back with me."

"Why," said Lottie, "would I go anywhere with you?"

"Look," said the girl, taking a step closer to Lottie. "You believe in magic, don't you?"

Lottie did, but she did not want to say that aloud. She only admitted that to herself when she was under her green apple tree and her copper box was open. She nodded cautiously.

"Well, what if I told you that my father, the greatest healer on the island, is making a medicine that will cure anything?"

Lottie frowned. "That's not magic. That's science."

"I thought you said you believed in magic."

"I believe in magic within reason," amended Lottie.

"Magic within reason wouldn't be magic," said the girl. "Now, are you coming or not?"

"Out the window?" asked Lottie.

"Yes," the girl said seriously.

It had to be a dream, Lottie thought. She must have already passed out on her bed hours before this, only to dream up a girl in her closet with all the answers to her problems. *Well!* she thought, *Isn't it better? Isn't anything better than waiting for two, maybe three weeks to go by?*

"All right," she said. "I'll come."

The other girl was already out the window and balanced on one of the green apple tree's branches.

"I knew you'd agree," she said. "Now, give me your hand."

"Hang on," said Lottie. "I've got to get my coat."

Lottie peeled her wet, periwinkle coat off the floor. Then, because the breeze blowing through the window felt particularly chilly, she scooped up the green scarf that the other girl had discarded and shoved it in her coat pocket. She braced herself against her window ledge.

Then the girl grabbed Lottie's arm, and Lottie suddenly found herself sliding most uncomfortably down a tree branch.

"I'm Adelaide, by the way," the girl said, winging her legs down to the next branch.

Lottie heard the dull thuds of apples hitting the ground below as the girls' descent knocked them loose. Lottie supposed that, had anyone across the square been watching, it must have looked like a ridiculous spectacle—two girls dropping from tree branch to tree branch, the girl named Adelaide in three graceful swings and Lottie in many more clumsy ones.

Lottie hit the damp grass with a solid *pomp*. A shower of apples gave their thudding applause at her successful landing.

"Do you think Mrs. Yates heard us?" she asked.

"Not a chance," said Adelaide, who was rustling in the folds of her billowy skirt. "You people have atrocious hearing."

"Where are we going? Do you live in town?"

"No," said Adelaide. Then, "Well, yes."

The girl pulled something from her pocket. Lottie gasped. A lavender finch was perched on Adelaide's finger. Not only that, but Adelaide was whispering something to it. The finch gave a single chirp, then fluttered up and alighted on the lowest branch of the apple tree.

"As to where we're going," said Adelaide, hopping up so that both of her hands grabbed ahold of the branch where the finch had landed, "you might call it going down. Or up, depending on your perspective."

The branch Adelaide hung from bent reluctantly and then swung down to the ground with a terrific screech, like brittle fingernails grating against metal. What had once been the dull brown bark of the apple tree trunk now began to shine and glint like silver in the moonlight. With a great creaking shudder, the branches, leaves, even the trunk itself started to shift and shake. One moment, the apple tree looked like the dear friend that Lottie had known and loved her whole life. The next, the tree's trunk had whorled into a splintery, human-sized opening.

Adelaide let go of the branch, wiped her hands on her skirt, and gave a low whistle. The lavender finch flitted back to her hand.

"What did you just do?" Lottie whispered.

"Pulled the silver bough," said Adelaide, as naturally as she might say that she had eaten peas for supper.

She tucked the lavender finch into her pocket.

"But—you can't do that to a bird," Lottie said stupidly.

Adelaide looked confused. "Of course I can. Lila *lives* in my pocket. Doesn't yours?"

Yes, this must be a dream, Lottie decided. It was all pretend. Until now, all of that pretend had been neatly locked in her copper box. But her copper box was shut tight; Lottie could see it even now, winking out from under the tree roots. How had she managed to let the magic out?

"My what?"

If Adelaide had heard Lottie, she did not bother to reply. She pushed her aside and looked the tree over, up and down. Then she marched right up to the dark opening, motioning for Lottie to follow.

"In we go," she said.

Lottie shook her head. "I'd rather not," she said. "Trees and I aren't on good terms right now."

Adelaide rounded Lottie and nudged her forward. "It's perfectly safe. How do you think I got here?"

Lottie wondered. It now seemed very likely to her that Adelaide had escaped from Hopewell Manor, the lunatic asylum on the mainland. Then again, Adelaide wasn't the only one seeing doors in trees. But before Lottie could further contemplate her own sanity, Adelaide had given her a firm shove into the tree and hopped in after.

"Wait!" Lottie cried, but Adelaide was already crowding in.

The bark door closed in on them, and they were cast into darkness.

"By the way," Adelaide said, "this might hurt."

"What might—?"

There was great groan, followed by a *snap*. The tree shuddered. Suddenly, it felt like lead weights were pressing in on Lottie from her sides, her kneecaps, her fingertips, her toe tips, and even her ear tips.

"What's going on?" she choked out to Adelaide. "Make it stop!"

The pressure grew heavier, as though Lottie were being condensed into a jar. The bridge of her nose tingled, and her ears filled up with a gauzy dullness. She was being pressed, pressed, *pressed*. But just when Lottie thought that her brains would be shoved down into her small intestine, the pressure stopped as quickly as it had started. There was a short silence. Then there was a rush of wind. Lottie's wet, stringy hair whipped up on her face. Her feet left the floor of the tree—or was it a tree anymore?

"What's happening?!" she shrieked.

"We're going down, of course," called Adelaide, who sounded perfectly calm. "The tree's shooting us down, and then back up. Down and up."

"It only feels like *down* to me!" Lottie called back.

It was just then that Lottie's toes whipped up past her nose and over her face. She tumbled up into a heap on the ceiling. She tumbled down into a heap on the floor.

Then the pressure, the wind, and the flipping stopped. A single flame, encased in a glass lantern, flickered to life above Lottie's head. She looked around to see who had lit it, but there was only Adelaide, who was still standing, arms folded, looking quite at ease.

"All right?" Adelaide smiled.

"No!" said Lottie. "And I'm not going to be all right until you tell me what's going on."

"I told you." Adelaide sighed. "We went down through your world. Now we're going up through mine." Adelaide clasped her hands neatly in front of her. "I much prefer *my* half of the ride."

This tree-room had to be like an elevator, then, Lottie decided. A sort of underground, topsy-turvy elevator that connected the front garden of Thirsby Square to—

"Your world?" repeated Lottie. "What do you mean, *your* world?"

"You'll see for yourself in a minute," Adelaide said, offering Lottie a hand to help her to her feet. "Better now? I told you it might hurt. You get used to it after a while, once your body's accustomed to root shooting."

"Excuse me?"

"Root shooting. Shooting through the roots. What we just did."

Lottie glared at Adelaide. Lottie wasn't stupid, and she didn't appreciate Adelaide looking at her as though she were. Still, Mrs. Yates had taught her once that politeness was the best response to rudeness.

"I never really introduced myself," she said, extending her hand for a shake. "I'm Lottie Fiske. But I guess you already know that."

Adelaide shook Lottie's hand with mock formality.

"Yes," she said. "Yes, we know."

❧

The rest of the ride was silent. If Adelaide had not told Lottie that they were going up, Lottie wouldn't have thought that she was moving in any direction at all. The "elevator," Lottie found on closer inspection, was covered in peeling Victorian-style wallpaper. A soot-spotted mirror hung on one of the walls.

A shuddering sound broke the silence. Then, quite suddenly, one of the elevator walls began to warp and splinter, revealing a little crack of light at its center. The crack grew larger and larger, filling the elevator with more and more bright light until suddenly the opening was big enough to walk through.

"*Now* you may step out," said Adelaide. "Go on. It just takes a little adjusting, that's all."

Lottie stepped out, shading her eyes. They were indoors, and they were standing in the grandest foyer that Lottie had ever seen. The floor was made of glinting black-and-ivory-checkered marble, and to Lottie's left, two giant fir trees—far more exciting than the fake ficus plants that Mrs. Yates kept in the boardinghouse—guarded a stone archway. The light came from a great silver chandelier that hung from a domed ceiling overhead, and that ceiling was carved in a way that reminded Lottie of a certain type of flower—an iris, she thought it was.

A breeze was sweeping through the room, as though someone had left a window open. In the breeze sung a faint, sweet smell of garden. Lottie turned back to see where she and Adelaide had come from. There was her green apple tree, but it was horribly out of place; its branches were stuffed and spiraled inside a small closet.

Lottie turned to Adelaide.

"How did you stuff my apple tree in *there*?"

Adelaide gave Lottie the same look she'd been giving her all this time, as though Lottie were dense. "That's not *your* apple tree. It's ours. Obviously. It's in *our* closet."

"Who keeps a tree in their closet?"

"Who keeps atrocious periwinkle coats in *theirs*?"

Adelaide didn't catch the scowl that Lottie gave her. She was too busy pulling the lavender finch named Lila from her pocket. The tiny creature gave a high, blithe *twipper!* and fluttered to a perch in one of the foyer's great fir trees. Then Adelaide smiled smugly at Lottie.

"Welcome," she announced, "to Iris Gate, home of the Wilfers."

Only now did Lottie really look at Adelaide. The girl turned out to be quite a lot taller than Lottie was. Long, straight, acorn-colored hair framed her radish-shaped face. She had high and full cheeks, and when her front teeth slipped out from her smile, Lottie noticed that one of them was chipped.

Adelaide tugged Lottie across the great foyer to a velvet settee outside a set of wooden doors.

"I'll be back," Adelaide said, opening one of the doors. "I need to let someone know you're here."

"Your dad, right?" said Lottie. "The one who can cure Eliot."

But Adelaide had already slipped out of the foyer.

Lottie sat on the settee, chin propped on her knees.

To her right loomed a spiraling marble staircase and to her left a wall of floor-length doors made entirely of glass. One of the doors was wide open to the night beyond, and that, Lottie guessed, was the source of the nice garden scent in the room. Just ahead of Lottie was the stone archway, which looked unsettlingly like a great big gaping mouth, opened wide to devour the rest of the room, herself included. She shivered and hoped that Adelaide would hurry up.

When Lottie leaned back, she discovered that a row of portraits hung on the wall, circling her with a host of somber, oil-painted faces. When she set eyes on the picture just above her, Lottie jumped out of her seat. A portly man with finely combed whiskers and unforgiving black eyes glowered down at her. He gave Lottie a distinct impression of black licorice. Underneath his pair of grotesque buckled shoes read the name *Quincy Francis Eugene Wilfer*. Lottie cracked a smile. With a name like that, the painted man was not half so frightening. Lottie made an equally ferocious face up at Mr. Quincy Francis Eugene Wilfer to see what he would do about it.

"It's a nice collection, isn't it?"

Lottie whirled around, a snarling expression still stuck on her face. A boy stood before her wearing the most curious of expressions himself. He looked somewhat shy and somewhat sly, and he had bright, blazing blue eyes. One of the boy's arms was bandaged up from wrist to elbow, and that curious face of his was badly bruised along the right cheekbone. His voice was familiar, though clearer now than the last time Lottie had heard it. She sank back onto the settee, blushing. This was the injured boy from the break room of the Flying Squirrel. Lottie was sure of it.

"You're Adelaide's brother," Lottie guessed. "You've got the same eyes."

But the moment she said it, Lottie realized that she had been wrong. The boy's eyes weren't blue at all. They were—yellow? Yes! A dirty yellow, the color of honey mustard.

"Your eyes," Lottie began. "Weren't they just—"

But the boy interrupted.

"I'm Oliver," he said. "Oliver Wilfer."

"How d'you do?" said Lottie, offering her hand to him.

Rather than take it, Oliver squinted, and Lottie was sure of it this time: the boy's eyes were *changing colors*. Now they were neither blue nor yellow, but a dull gray—just a shade deeper than her own.

"Do you mind if I join you?" the boy asked, nodding toward the settee.

"Yes. No! I mean no, I don't mind." Lottie's blush grew deeper.

Oliver sat down cautiously on the very edge of the settee, his peculiar eyes never leaving Lottie.

"Are you all right?" he asked.

"I'm Lottie," she said hurriedly, in place of an answer.

She was busy wondering just how hideous that Quincy Francis Eugene Wilfer impression of hers had been. Mrs. Yates had taught her that first impressions were everything, and now she was afraid that this Oliver boy was going to forever think of her with crossed eyes and a flipped lower lip.

"Oh, I know who you are," said Oliver. "My face in thine eye, thine in mine appears, and true plain hearts do in the faces rest."

"Beg your pardon?" Lottie sputtered. It sounded like the boy had switched, midsentence, into a foreign language.

"It's poetry," Oliver said matter-of-factly.

Lottie did not know how to respond to *that*, so she tried another question.

"Where are we?"

Oliver frowned and scratched his ear. "Where do you think we are?"

"In a dream," Lottie said. "Or maybe . . . maybe I'm dead. Maybe the tree killed me after all."

"The apple tree didn't kill you."

"How do you know?" said Lottie, looking up at Oliver, whose face had grown slyer.

Rather than answer, he pointed to the row of glass doors.

"If you'd like to know where you are, why not take a look?"

Lottie got up, and Oliver followed her to the open door. The scent of flowers grew stronger on the night air, and so did new smells of pine, of smoke, and of fresh-fallen water. She was standing on a terrace in the middle of a dim garden full of irises. Oliver pointed Lottie's gaze to a higher point, beyond the garden. She peered into the light of the half moon, and slowly images came into focus:

rows of cobblestone streets, wooden roofs, and flickers of lamplight; and towering over all of these things were trees, hundreds and hundreds of trees. Lottie had never seen so many trees in one place except in pictures from her geography textbook about places like the Black Forest and the Cascade Mountains.

"It's nice enough," she told Oliver, "but I still don't know where we are."

"You really don't recognize it? It *is* your own backyard."

Lottie looked out again, then back to Oliver.

"No, it's not. I live in New Kemble, on Kemble Isle. That"—she swept her arm out toward the lights and trees— "is not New Kemble."

"Myself unseen," said Oliver, "I see in white defined, far off the homes of men."

Lottie frowned. "Was that poetry again?"

"Yes."

"Well, it didn't make sense," Lottie informed him. "Don't you think I know what my own home looks like? If this is New Kemble, where is St. George's Church? Where is the old bell tower? You can see those things from any street in New Kemble, and that's a fact. Even if it weren't, there's definitely not a whole forest growing in the middle of the city."

"Well," Oliver said in a very rational tone of voice, "it's not my fault that your people are worse landscapers. Or that you cut down all of *your* trees."

Lottie let out a squawk of exasperation. "Why are you and Adelaide talking like that?"

"Like what?"

"With *yours* and *ours* and *ups* and *downs*? I just want to know where I am!"

"You're in New *Albion*," Oliver said. "It's your city, only in *our* world. I don't know how else to explain it to you."

Lottie narrowed her eyes at the boy named Oliver. Nothing he said made sense, so of course this all still had to be a dream. Lottie left the terrace and plopped back down on the settee inside. Then she squeezed her eyes shut and poked herself in the ribs, hard, in an attempt to wake herself up.

"What are you doing?"

Lottie's eyelids fluttered open. Oliver had followed her back inside.

She stared at him. "Nothing," she said, and she stared some more.

Despite the bruises splotching it, Oliver's face was a nice one, framed by curly hair the shade of bronze. Lottie was sure that if Oliver attended Kemble School, he'd be a prime topic of swooning and giggling for Pen Bloomfield and her crowd. Lottie noticed that the boy's eyes had changed color again, this time to a pinked shade like fresh salmon. Lottie noticed, too, that Oliver was standing quite far from her, like she was about to sneeze and he didn't want to get covered in the snot. *Perhaps*, she thought miserably, *Mrs. Yates was right about first impressions, and now Oliver is afraid I'll pull another face on him.*

"So, how'd you hurt your arm?" she asked at last, pointing to his bandaged elbow.

"Same as anyone does," said Oliver, but he was looking at Quincy Francis Eugene Wilfer, not her. "I had an accident."

"Oh, did you?" An urge was bubbling up Lottie's throat, threatening to pop loose. Suddenly, it did. "And were any *flying squirrels* involved in your accident?"

Oliver was quiet for a moment.

"What makes you say that?" he asked.

"I was there at the pub," said Lottie, "when you and your friend—Flute, or something—came into the break room. You were all bloody. I know it had to be you, so don't deny it."

Oliver's eyes had gone bright blue again. "So *you're* the one who went running out of the coats."

Lottie nodded.

"Father didn't say you'd be so nosy," Oliver muttered, and this would have hurt Lottie's feelings, except that she thought she saw Oliver smiling when he said it.

Suddenly, the wooden doors by the settee flew open, and Adelaide came leaping out.

"Lottie, you can—oh! Hello. Sweet Oberon, what happened to your arm?"

Oliver shrugged.

But Adelaide wasn't waiting for an answer. She had turned her attention right back to Lottie. "Father will see you now."

Lottie cast a glance at the portrait of Quincy Francis Eugene Wilfer. Was the letter-writer going to be like *that*? Pompous and ugly and intimidating?

"He," faltered Lottie, "is a good person, isn't he?"

"Ugh," groaned Adelaide. "Stop asking so many questions."

"Be nice, Adelaide," said Oliver. "She's just naturally nosy."

He *was* smiling.

"Go on, go on," insisted Adelaide, pushing Lottie toward the double doors. "Of course he's nice, he's my father. He'll answer your questions. He might even ask you some, too. After all, he's curious about you."

"We all are," Oliver said.

"What?" said Lottie. "What's that supposed to mean?"

But Adelaide only shooed at her impatiently. Lottie, reasoning that this was certainly not the strangest thing to have happened to her tonight, walked past the doors. They closed behind her with the faintest of clicks.

CHAPTER FOUR

Otherwise Incurable

LOTTIE FOUND HERSELF in what looked a lot like the abandoned laboratory of a mad scientist. The ceilings were high here, but there was not a window in sight. The floors were caked with so much dust that Eliot's green sneakers made an impressive *poof!* with each step that Lottie took. Hundreds of vials of all shapes—squares and ovals and diamonds and wonky pyramids—lined shelves running so high up the walls that Lottie could not see an end to them. There were even more colors in the vials' insides than there were shapes on the outside.

Maybe it was just the dust getting to Lottie's brain, but it seemed to her that each of those colors had a very personal feeling, all to itself, and that each of those feelings was obvious at a glance: the sapphire blues were wistful and those were not *just* blacks, but mournful blacks, and those the most content of violets. Beakers, candles, and other strange contraptions lay on the two long, brass-clawed tables that lined the room. This place looked nothing like the rich, spotless foyer outside, but it was just as overwhelming.

As fascinating as the laboratory was, Lottie was still looking for the letter-writer. The trouble was that there was no letter-writer in sight.

"Hello?" called Lottie, her voice bouncing back in distorted echoes.

She tucked her hands into the pockets of her tweed coat and walked carefully onward. Then she heard a trickling sound, followed by a long hiss. A scent, strong and chemical, wafted past her, stinging the edges of her nose. Just as she was about to call again, she saw something move by one of the tables. She hurried toward the movement.

"Ex-excuse me?" she called.

The figure stopped moving. Then it began to grow larger, and Lottie realized that this was because the figure was a man who had been stooped over a fizzing beaker and was only now straightening up to face her. The man lifted a pair of large, silver-rimmed goggles from his eyes and set them atop his head. He took a long look at Lottie. Lottie took a long look back at him.

The man's face was grooved, stubbly, and tired. The hair around his ears was thin, and his eyes were squinty. He dropped his goggles back on his face and squinted harder at Lottie through them. Then he removed the gloves from his hands.

"Moritasgus Horatio Wilfer," said the man. "It's a pleasure."

His voice shook, but he smiled. That was a relief. He was nervous, and he was nice. Nothing at all like a Quincy Francis Eugene Wilfer.

"And you are, I presume," Mr. Wilfer continued, "Miss Charlotte Grace Fiske."

"Lottie," she corrected, shaking his hand. "My name's Lottie, and I've got to get that cure for my best friend."

Mr. Wilfer let go of her hand. "My! You don't lose a minute, do you?"

He shook his head and laughed. It was the sort of laugh that Lottie heard adults make every so often, to themselves, as though they were in on a private joke from their past. Lottie didn't like it; that laugh always made her feel left out.

"*Lottie* Fiske," Mr. Wilfer said, turning back to his place at the table and setting aside some jars. "You're very grown up. More than I was expecting."

"I'm not grown at all," said Lottie. "Mrs. Yates' friends say I look too young for my age."

Mr. Wilfer laughed the same laugh again. Lottie grimaced.

"Excuse me," said the man, checking himself and wiping his hands on an apron tied around his waist. "I've forgotten my manners. Would you be so good as to join me in my study?"

He led Lottie farther into the room, past more rows of vials, beakers, and strange instruments. At the end of the laboratory was another set of double doors. Mr. Wilfer flung them open, onto a snug, tidy room as different from the laboratory as the laboratory had been from the foyer before it.

It was dim inside the study, but a fire was crackling in the fireplace, and its light waltzed on the rug beneath Lottie's feet. The ceiling was shorter here, and sloped, producing a cozy effect. Mr. Wilfer motioned for Lottie to take a seat, as he took his own chair behind a mahogany desk. Lottie's chair sagged dangerously, and as soon as she was stuck in its velvet cushion, she began to panic about whether she would ever get *un*stuck again.

Just before her, on Mr. Wilfer's desk, was a silver abacus strung with beads that looked like fresh-cut flower buds. Next to the abacus sat a massive leather-bound book that looked too thick to be a dictionary, yet too thin to be a proper encyclopedia.

Mr. Wilfer harrumphed and lit a pipe that quivered between his lips. The dusky smell of tobacco crept into Lottie's nostrils, and it reminded her of being much younger, when Mr. Yates had been alive and had smoked a pipe religiously, three times a day. Lottie shook her head of the faint memory and tried her best to sit up straight in her chair.

"Are you the letter-writer?" she asked.

"I am."

Lottie looked at the rumpled old man uncertainly. *This* was the source of her birthday presents?

"Well, then, Mr. Wilfer," she began, "I'm not sure where this is or how I got here. I only came because Adelaide told me that you have a medicine to make Eliot better."

Mr. Wilfer released a puff of smoke. The firelight glinted off his goggles, so Lottie could not tell whether he was looking at her.

He spoke quietly. "You've always had a very firm idea of what you want, Lottie Fiske, ever since your first letter. I trust all of your previous presents arrived in good condition?"

"Oh!" Lottie whitened. She was, she realized, being exceptionally rude. The letter-writer had given Lottie many presents over the years. "Um, yes. Of course. Thank you very much. They were all nice presents. That is, except for that one book about the fairy queen."

Mr. Wilfer raised an eyebrow over his goggles. "You don't like fairy tales?"

"Should I?" she asked.

"It would be helpful if you did," said Mr. Wilfer, "as I'm a fairy myself. A *sprite,* to be precise. We sprites and your Earth's fairies share old blood."

Lottie blinked.

"But you can't be something magical," she said sensibly. "You're a doctor."

"I'm a healer, yes," said Mr. Wilfer, standing up. "And that is, currently, the most important point of our conversation."

There was a glass case resting on the study's mantelpiece, and it was to this case that Mr. Wilfer now directed his attention. He turned his back to Lottie, and she heard the sound of a key opening a lock. Mr. Wilfer returned to the desk and sat down. In one hand, he still held his pipe. The other hand he extended to Lottie. He uncurled his fingers to reveal a squat, square vial in his palm. It was filled with a liquid colored the most anxious of reds.

Lottie scooted her chair closer. On the vial was a label written in thin, scrawling script: *Otherwise Incurable.*

Lottie read the label out loud and looked up. "Does it really work?" she whispered, reaching out. "Does it cure incurable things?"

Mr. Wilfer retracted the bottle before Lottie could touch it. "I'm afraid the whole matter still requires . . . time."

"But," Lottie said, "Eliot doesn't have time. He's only got weeks left!"

"Medicine," said Mr. Wilfer, "is like magic. You cannot rush it. You cannot pinch it off and tie it up, clean and neat. You cannot make it behave. This potion"—he tapped the vial—"has become my life's work, and much as I've tried these past months to expedite the process, I am still missing one important ingredient."

"What sort of ingredient?" asked Lottie.

Mr. Wilfer raised a hand. "There are things I still need to explain to you."

Lottie did not see what else needed explaining. If one missing ingredient was all that kept Eliot from getting better, nothing else could possibly matter. Then again, Mr. Wilfer was the one with a medicine in his hand. She nodded begrudgingly.

"What's this?" she asked, poking her finger against the spine of the massive book on his table. "Does this tell you how to make your medicines?"

"That?" said Mr. Wilfer. "It does, in fact, tell me how to make *one* medicine. I have hundreds of notebooks like these."

Mr. Wilfer opened the book and pushed it across the table. Lottie wiggled to the edge of her saggy chair to get a better view. It was neither a dictionary nor an encyclopedia.

"It's a-—*scrapbook?*"

Lottie scrunched her nose in distaste. The only people she knew who made and kept scrapbooks were Mrs. Yates and the sneer-lipped ladies who came over for tea.

"A *note*book," Mr. Wilfer corrected her.

The pages of the book were ragged and uneven with pasted pictures of plant diagrams, an article on cloud condensation, and what looked like a recipe torn from a cookbook. Around the pasted scraps, every spare sliver of paper was covered with thin-edged words and symbols. It looked like two pages full of nonsense. Lottie turned the page. Two *more* pages full of nonsense. Only these two held a clump of dried flowers and twigs, a poem, and a checked-off checklist.

Lottie looked up. "What is all of this?"

"This," said Mr. Wilfer, "is my best guess for how to concoct a cure for foot blisters. Medicines take years of inquiry and research. Long nights of experimentation, decades of case studies and careful observation—all to compile what you see in a book like this. My notebook for the Otherwise Incurable is nearly twice as thick."

"You mean, this is how you're going to save Eliot? With dried flowers and photographs?" Lottie looked at the book with more scrutiny. "And recipes for lemon chess squares?"

She chewed her lip anxiously. What had she gotten herself into? Mr. Wilfer wasn't a real doctor at all. He thought he could heal Eliot with nothing more than a giant, nonsensical scrapbook!

"Medicines aren't made like that," she said at last. "Medicines are made from precise measurements and chemical reactions. It's a very scientific business."

"Is that how they do it where you come from, Lottie?" said Mr. Wilfer. He didn't look offended, only curious.

"Yes. Everyone knows that's what medicines are. Especially doctors."

"Ah," said Mr. Wilfer. "But what about your healers?"

Lottie wavered. "We don't have those. Not like you. Not that I know of, anyway."

Mr. Wilfer looked genuinely surprised. "None? No healers at all in New Kemble?"

"No healers *anywhere*," said Lottie. "Not even on the mainland."

Mr. Wilfer spent a full, silence-stuffed minute pondering this information.

"Well," he said, "that is sad but believable news. Healers are a rare enough breed here. Only ten of us in all of Albion Isle. Healers are doctors, yes, but we are not so backward as to discount the great uses of intuition, of the art of the soul, of *magic*."

Lottie gulped. "You mean . . . you're a magician?"

"Oh, no, that's quite a different thing. There are no easy recipes or chemical formulas or magic spell books on hand here. Each one of my cures I extract from experience, from music, from poetry, from the wilds of this world, from—ah! I can tell from that face that you don't believe a word I'm saying."

Lottie was thinking of her green apple tree. She was thinking of her copper box. Magic had been so tidy back home. Each year, she had closed up her wishes in a box and every following year she'd received her reply. Magic stayed in the box. But Mr. Wilfer was talking like magic was—well, was *at large*.

"Mr. Wilfer," Lottie said at last. "I don't mean to sound ungrateful. I really don't. But where I come from, you don't get rid of the flu by . . . scrapbooking."

"You would like proof," said Mr. Wilfer.

Lottie thought about this. "Do you have any?" she said dubiously.

"Dear girl! Magic may not be reasonable. It may not be tamable or even reliable. But it does provide plenty of proof."

Mr. Wilfer reached into his desk drawer and handed Lottie a vial, thin and fragile, filled to the top with a suspicious-looking gray liquid.

"That is a cure that took me a year to perfect. I had to capture ten laughs on a rainy day and all the ingredients of eggs Benedict. Then I had to quote a full book of sonnets at it. Go on, try it. It's for the cut across your forehead."

Lottie raised a hand to her eyebrow and found that there was, in fact, a nastily scabbed cut there, which must have come from her bicycle accident. She looked suspiciously at the medicine, and it looked suspiciously gray back at her. She unstoppered the vial, and the prettiest smell of hot omelet drifted out. Lottie raised the vial to her lips, looking all the while at Mr. Wilfer, and took the tiniest of sips. A prickle fizzed across her forehead and a sound like a *snap!* smacked around the walls of the room. At first, Lottie thought her head had exploded and how stupid she had been to taste a strange potion from a strange man! But her head was still very much intact and in much better shape than it had been a second before. Her cut had healed. Lottie rubbed her finger along her smooth skin and set the vial back down.

"It worked," she said.

"It worked," said Mr. Wilfer.

Lottie was still rubbing her forehead. Trees that were elevators, doctors that weren't human, New Kembles that weren't New Kembles, and now medicines made from eggs Benedict! It was all a bit much to take after a full day of school.

"You don't believe me yet," Mr. Wilfer said. "I understand. This is hardly the ideal way to tell you everything, all at once. I hadn't even intended for you to root shoot until your sixteenth birthday."

"Did my letter change your mind?"

"That," said Mr. Wilfer, "and something else. Something complicated."

Lottie wasn't much in the mood for complications. Eliot was what mattered.

"All right," she said. "Say I believe you, Mr. Wilfer, and all of this business about cooking up medicines. If it's true, then I can't go back to Thirsby Square. Not until I've got a cure for Eliot."

"That is what I expected," said Mr. Wilfer. "I've made all the arrangements to have you stay with us for however long it takes."

"It can't take long," Lottie whispered. "There isn't much time."

Mr. Wilfer looked Lottie straight in the eye. She had never seen a man—not even Mr. Walsch on his worst day in the calligraphy office—look so tired as Mr. Wilfer did at this moment. Still, Lottie could not help but ask the question.

"What's the final ingredient for the Otherwise Incurable?"

"It is late," said Mr. Wilfer, "and both you and I are weary. Adelaide will show you to bed. In the morning, we will revisit this conversation."

"But—" protested Lottie.

"This," Mr. Wilfer assured her, "is better."

🌰

When Lottie emerged from the laboratory, Mr. Wilfer instructed a waiting Adelaide to take their guest to a bedroom on the second floor, at the tip-top of the foyer's spiral staircase. Oliver was nowhere to be seen, which was disappointing. Even though his poetry quoting and eye color changing were more than a little strange, Lottie had decided that she liked the sly-faced boy. She also would have much preferred Oliver to Adelaide as her guide through the house called Iris Gate. The entire journey up the stairs, Adelaide spouted off boring facts and corrections as though she were preparing Lottie for a short-answer quiz at Kemble School.

"The banister is very old," she said solemnly. "The wood was a gift from the Southerly Court to our great-great-grandfather as a token of friendship. So don't clutch it so hard, please. Oh, and be careful walking on the hall rug. It's fine wisp-weaved, practically antique. I should've asked you to take off your shoes. You clomp so carelessly. I guess that's a human trait."

Lottie was annoyed, but she said nothing. Mr. Wilfer was offering her a chance to save Eliot, after all, and she *was* a guest in Adelaide's house.

The guest bedroom was smaller than any of the other rooms that Lottie had seen, but it was still terrifyingly large for a bedroom, and Lottie had begun to suspect that perhaps she had shrunk during her bumpy tree ride here. The room's vaulted ceiling towered over a lush-carpeted floor, and a marble fireplace yawned in one corner next to a big canopied bed.

"Father said you might be coming one day soon," Adelaide said, tugging down the bed's duvet, "so I made some arrangements. You should sleep like a changeling."

She pointed out a neatly stacked pile of clothes. "Those are mine. They'll be a little long on you," Adelaide eyed down the good six-inch difference between her and Lottie, "but they're still better than what you've got on."

Lottie did not particularly like having her wardrobe under attack. She put up with enough of those remarks from Pen Bloomfield without Adelaide's contributions.

"That's so *awfully* good of you," Lottie said in a very awful way.

Adelaide blew a puff of air through her lips and rolled her eyes.

"It was a thrill," she said, sounding anything but thrilled. "There's an adjoining bathroom just there, and if you need anything, I'm the next door down."

Lottie nodded, already certain that she would much rather do without something than ask her snotty hostess—who was *still* lingering in the doorway.

"All right, thanks," said Lottie, hoping that Adelaide would take the hint and leave.

But still Adelaide stood in the threshold, hard-faced.

"Lottie," she said, the venom-sweetness gone from her voice, "do you really need that medicine?"

"I told you I did," said Lottie. "That's the whole reason you brought me here, isn't it?"

Adelaide shook her head. "You don't understand. Father hasn't been making it for you. He's been making it for someone else. Someone more important than you."

"Who?"

"King Starkling," Adelaide whispered, her voice chilled. "He's the ruler of the sprites. Ruler of the Southerly sprites, that is—and they're the only sprites that really matter. If Father gives the medicine to you instead of the king, he'll be in the worst sort of trouble."

"That doesn't make any sense," said Lottie. "If some king wants it, then why would Mr. Wilfer tell me—"

"Because he's a good person!" cried Adelaide. "And because you're a Fiske."

"What does that mean?" demanded Lottie. "What's so fantastic about being a Fiske?"

Adelaide wrinkled her nose. "Don't you know?"

Lottie shook her head. Adelaide sighed. Her eyes dropped, her shoulders slumped, and Lottie knew that she had won the argument. She just didn't know what the argument had been about.

"Look," said Lottie. "I don't want to get anyone in trouble. I just want to save Eliot. Then I'll leave you alone, I promise."

Lottie thought this would make Adelaide happy. Instead, Adelaide stiffened.

"Fine," she spat. "Go ahead and do it. Take the medicine. You're so selfish!"

With that, the door slammed shut. Lottie stared at it for a full minute. Numbness, like a worm, had inched into her ribs, coiled its way around them, and now prevented Lottie from feeling anything.

She peered into the adjoining bathroom, which looked just like a normal bathroom from back in New Kemble, except that the faucet was lined with pearls and a glass chandelier hung directly over the toilet. Though she was tired, even more so Lottie felt dirty from hiking in rain all day, avoiding death by tree, and traveling underground or upground, or however it was that she'd gotten to this place. She peeled off her clothes and climbed into the shower. As the hot water streamed down on her, the numbness began to unwind itself from Lottie's ribs, and she began to properly think and feel again.

Could she really believe any of it? That she had fallen down a tree into another world? Lottie looked at herself in the bathroom mirror. She pressed her thumb to her perfectly smooth forehead, which showed no trace of a scab or a scar. Mr. Wilfer's medicine had made that wound better. He could make Eliot better, too. Whatever else she believed, Lottie had to believe there was a cure.

Lottie tried on the nightgown that Adelaide had left her. It pooled past her toes and cinched her at the waist, and the frills along the cuffs and collar scratched her skin. She grunted and pulled the gown off, deciding she preferred her old clothes, dirty and damp as they were.

Lottie fell back onto the giant canopy bed, but she could not possibly sleep at a time like this.

There were questions that Mr. Wilfer had left unanswered, but that didn't mean Lottie couldn't try to answer them for herself. She laced Eliot's sturdy green sneakers back on and then sat down by her door, counting off minutes and listening closely for any movement outside. Each time she thought it might be safe to crack the door open, though, she swore she heard a rustle or a scamper or a flitter in the hallway, and she would have to start counting over. Perhaps she was so tired that she was simply hearing things, but Lottie didn't want to risk getting caught.

At last, convinced that it had been dead silent outside her room for more than an hour, Lottie stretched out her tired legs, creaked open the door, and, after glancing left and right a total of five times, crept out. It was so dark in the corridor that she could not make out the end of the hallway. Deep shadows hit her feet as she padded down the passageway to the spiral stairs.

Then Lottie felt something rush by. The air went cold beside her, and *something* ever so slightly brushed her cheek. She bit the inside of her lip, trapping in a yelp, and scampered all the way down the winding staircase. The foyer was empty, and that gaping archway at the end of it looked larger and more like a hungry mouth than ever. Lottie wanted very much to run back up the stairs and jump back into that comfy canopy bed. She simply couldn't, though, because she'd already come so far and was now only a nose's breadth away from the laboratory doors.

Lottie glanced around, swallowed, and tried a door handle. It was locked. She cursed under her breath. The foyer echoed the bad word back, making Lottie blush. Steeling herself, she tried the handle of the other door. This one obligingly gave way. Lottie slipped inside the laboratory. She walked briskly down the long, drafty room, careful not to sneeze at the clouds of dust circling her or to look around at those looming vials and instruments lest she frighten herself. At last, she reached the second set of doors and, remembering her previous luck, tried the left door first. The handle slipped down, the door creaked open, and Lottie was back in Mr. Wilfer's study.

The room was far less cheery now that the fire had died out, but moonlight streamed in from a row of curtainless windows, and its light was bright enough to show that the study was a wreck. Since Lottie had last been there, desk drawers had been opened and dozens upon dozens of papers scattered on the floor. There were discarded vials, too, some broken, some unstopped, and all of them empty.

There was one vial, however, that remained unstopped and unbroken. The vial marked *Otherwise Incurable* sat inside the glass case on the mantel of the darkened fireplace. Lottie crept closer, staring at the anxious red liquid in the medicine vial. She found that if she looked very closely, the liquid almost seemed to be looking back at her, like it was waiting for something to happen, waiting for her to do something.

She reached for the glass case.

"Looking for something?"

Lottie's breath hitched. She turned around. There, on Mr. Wilfer's desk, sat Adelaide Wilfer, blue eyes cold as windowpane frost.

"Come to steal Father's medicine, have you?"

"I—" stammered Lottie.

Adelaide jumped from the desk and approached Lottie with frightening speed. "You've got a lot of nerve," she hissed. "I knew you were no good the moment I set eyes on you!"

Lottie backed away. "I just wanted to look around!" she insisted.

Adelaide's eyes narrowed. "You could be charged before the Southerly Guard for snoopery and attempted thievery!"

"I'm not a thief!" Lottie shouted. "And so what if I'm snooping? What would you do if your best friend was—*dying*?"

She'd done it. She'd managed to say the word. *Dying.* That's what was happening to Eliot. Now that she'd said it, though, Lottie didn't feel any sense of accomplishment, just a sensation like her heart was being shredded by a cheese grater.

"*I'd* act with a little more dignity," said Adelaide. "That's what I'd do. Father has shown you nothing but kindness. Who's the one who sent you all those birthday gifts? Who promised to help your stupid friend? Who welcomed you into our house? Who's putting his life in danger for you? And how do you repay him? By stealing. Disgusting! Do all humans have as little self-respect as you?"

Lottie searched for words, but none came. She'd told Adelaide the truth, and even if she could come up with another explanation, Adelaide wouldn't listen.

"You followed me," Lottie said, remembering the brush of cool air on the stairwell. "How could you have heard me? I was so quiet."

"No," Adelaide said. "You weren't."

Neither she nor Lottie said anything more. Adelaide only took Lottie by the arm and, with a grip much stronger than Lottie expected, pulled her back through the house, all the way up to the guest bedroom.

"Just because Father trusts you doesn't mean I do," hissed Adelaide, pushing Lottie into the guest bedroom and slamming the door shut. "Just try stealing from us now!"

Lottie heard the telltale *click* of metal slipping against metal. Adelaide had locked her inside the bedroom. Even though Lottie knew that pounding her fist against the door would do nothing to unlock it, she still pounded, each time harder than before.

"Adelaide, let me out! I'm not a thief!"

Adelaide did not answer.

Lottie began to feel an all-too-familiar tightening in her sides. She was getting a bad spell. She sank to the ground, setting her head down between her knees, and hugged her ankles tightly, willing away the white splotches that appeared on the insides of her eyelids. *Fight it*, thought Lottie. *Don't give in. Fight . . .*

CHAPTER FIVE

Fife

THWOCK.

THWACK.

THWOCK.

Lottie opened her eyes to a room full of pale light. The first thing she became aware of was that her arm, the arm she had slumped atop when she had drifted to sleep on the floor the night before, was horribly sore. The next things were that a window was open, its shutters were *thwack-thwocking* in the wind, and on the window ledge sat a boy who was grinning at Lottie.

"Hallo," said the boy before somersaulting onto the floor.

A shock of black hair, green eyes, and a mad grin were now just a foot from Lottie's nose.

"Are you a robber?" asked the boy. Then he stuck his tongue out at Lottie. Though he wasn't exactly sticking his tongue out *at* her; he was just sticking his tongue *out,* as if he expected to catch a falling snowflake upon it.

"I'm not a robber," Lottie said.

"That's good news. Always a smart idea to check. Nice to meet you, then." He clapped his hands and then offered one of them to Lottie. When she didn't take it, his eyes darted between his hand and her face. "Oh. I see you've met Ollie."

"How do you know Oliver?"

"He's my best friend," said the boy, jolting up so that he was squatting on the balls of his feet. "Anyway, you haven't met *me*. I'm Fife Dulcet."

"Lottie Fiske."

Lottie wondered straightaway if that had been wise to say. *She* might not be a robber, but who was to say that this boy wasn't one—or something worse? Mrs. Yates had taught her not to give her name to strangers. But then,

Lottie had been doing a lot of things lately of which Mrs. Yates would not approve.

Fife, in the meantime, had fallen onto his backside. He let out a low, wondering whistle.

"A *Fiske!*" he cried, "From Earth!"

"I'm from New Kemble," Lottie tried to explain.

Fife didn't seem to be listening. He leapt over Lottie and jiggled the door handle.

"What's this?" he asked. "Who's locked you in?"

"Adelaide," grumbled Lottie, wiping sleep from her eyes and stumbling to her feet.

Fife guffawed. "*Ah-del-aide,*" he said in an upper-crust drawl. "So you've met her, too."

"Yes, and I wish I hadn't," said Lottie. "She's awful."

"You're not alone in that sentiment, Lottie Fiske," Fife said, patting her on the back. "Ada's a few airs short of a charmer."

"She called me unrefined."

"Oh, she calls me that all the time," Fife said with a dismissive wave. "Consider yourself in good company."

"Does she criticize your clothes, too?"

"Constantly," Fife said, looking around the room and settling his sights on the window. "There are a few rules to keep in mind when you come to play at the Wilfers: (a) Don't roughhouse with Ollie, and (b) Don't take anything Adelaide says personally. Simple as that." He frowned in contemplation. "Well, I might add (c) Don't ever combine beet root with pure extract of wishful thinking. It might cure a headache, but it gives you some ghastly bloating."

"Oh." Lottie nodded uncertainly.

"Mm. Well, enough of that. I bet you're itching with cabin fever. Lucky for you, I've got us an escape route."

He pointed to the open window.

"What?" Lottie shook her head. "Oh no. No, *no*. I've had enough of going out windows."

"Tush," said Fife. "I'm sure it's just that you haven't done it properly. Not like *this*."

Fife ran toward the window and leapt right out of the room and out of sight.

Lottie shrieked. She dashed to the ledge, afraid that she was going to find little bits of Fife scattered all over the garden path below. Instead, she bonked foreheads with the boy, who was hovering cross-legged just beneath the windowsill.

"Ow." Lottie rubbed her head. Then her stomach rumbled, and she remembered that she hadn't had supper last night.

The window didn't look quite so bad as it had before. Fife was smiling at her, and she ventured a smile back.

"Judging from your awed reaction," said Fife, "I'm guessing Ada didn't do anything like *that*."

"No," Lottie said. "We climbed down a tree in Thirsby Square."

"What?" cried Fife. "Climbed down a tree with your bare hands? How barbaric. You're much safer with me. C'mon."

Fife reached up and caught a fistful of Lottie's hair.

Lottie yelped. "What do you think you're doing?"

"I've got to hold on to you for it to work. Don't worry. It's perfectly safe."

"Why don't you take this instead," Lottie suggested, wiggling her fingers at him.

"*Now* she gives me her hand," sighed Fife.

Fife let go of Lottie's hair and instead folded his fingers through hers. Then he pulled her straight out of the window. Though the guest room was only on the second floor, the two of them had a considerable distance to go down (the house did have very high ceilings, after all), and down they went.

It was a thrilling descent for Lottie. First of all, she'd never floated through midair and, second, no boy—not even Eliot—had ever held her hand quite so tightly as Fife was holding hers now. They sped closer and closer to the ground until, not quite knowing how, Lottie found her nose buried in a flower bed of irises.

"*Mermph!*" she coughed, spitting out soil and gravel.

"Did I promise safety?" asked Fife, looking guiltily over at Lottie and shaking gravel out of his hair. "My mistake."

"It *was* more exciting than tree climbing," Lottie admitted, rubbing her nose.

This seemed to satisfy Fife. "Don't we do things better in our world?"

Lottie nodded hesitantly. Then she paused. Then she shook her head. "Oliver told me this place is supposed to be my city."

Fife yanked an iris out of the ground and began brandishing it in the air like a conductor's baton. "Hmm, yes," he said dazedly. "Of course it is."

"But it's *not* my city."

"No," Fife said, tilting his head curiously at Lottie, "of course it isn't. Your city is in Earth. Our city is in Limn. Haven't you ever been taught geography? Our cities are piled on top of each other like layers of a cake. The apple trees are what connect them."

"You mean," said Lottie, "that Earth is connected to your—what did you call it?"

"Limn," said Fife. "Yes. That's where you are."

"Then, when Adelaide took me down that tree, she was really taking me—"

"Between Earth and Limn!" said Fife, waving his iris baton under Lottie's nose. "Simple. See?"

Lottie nodded slowly.

There was something about Fife that made Lottie want to believe. Maybe it was the floating.

"So, is this the only city in, uh, *Limn,* or do you all have your own Kemble Isle?" Lottie asked.

"Kemble Isle?" Fife stopped his conducting midwave and dropped the flower, looking confused.

"The island," said Lottie. "The island where you live. Where I come from, we call it Kemble Isle."

"Oh." Fife laughed. "We call ours *Albion* Isle."

Lottie thought about this. "I like your version better."

"So do I," said Fife.

Lottie looked around the garden where they sat. Irises bloomed in thick clumps and sprawled out toward a spindled silver fence, and beyond that fence Lottie could see the rooftops of stone houses and the tips of trees. These houses weren't like those from back home. Their stones looked older and their windows more weathered, but the roofs were high and the windows large. Lottie knew what that meant back where she came from: these houses were old, but they were also expensive.

"This is a nice neighborhood, isn't it?" said Lottie.

"It's the center of town," Fife said. "Only the wealthiest sprites live here. Mr. Wilfer, he's the Head Healer. That's why he's got such a nice place. The king gave it to him."

"So not everyone here is as rich as the Wilfers?"

Fife shrugged. "Southerly sprites are rich no matter where you go. That's why there's that saying, you know: don't arrive at a Southerly's with a full stomach; don't leave without one."

At this news, Lottie's stomach grumbled. She clutched it, embarrassed, but Fife grinned.

"I've got a cure for that," he said, and before Lottie had time to blink, Fife had shoved something in her hands.

"Chocolate?" Lottie asked, enraptured.

Fife, who had taken a bite of the stuff before handing it to Lottie, coughed and swallowed.

"Thank you," said Lottie, biting off a piece of chocolate herself so that her reply sounded more like "Hank wu."

"Good, isn't it?" said Fife, finishing off his piece. "That's 'cause it's from the North. Though don't let on that I told you that, or you'd put me in a nasty way with the Southerly Guard."

Lottie blinked. She hadn't understood half of what Fife had said, only that the Southerly Guard was, apparently, bad news.

"C'mon," Fife said. "Let's get out of this dirt."

Lottie finished off her chocolate and, with Fife's help, got up—more than up. Fife was floating again, and this time he floated the both of them right through an open window on the first floor of Iris Gate. He plunked Lottie down on a window seat and lighted his feet on a nearby stack of books.

They were in a library. The room was enormous. Rows and rows of tall bookcases stretched before Lottie, each one chock full of shelf upon shelf of books. It was a sight glorious enough to make her forget for a moment that she was alone there with a strange, floating boy.

Fife, however, appeared to be busy with something entirely unrelated to Lottie. He began to poke about shelves and race around the corners of the room so quickly that the sight of him became little more than a blur.

"What're you doing?" she called.

"Looking for Ollie, of course," said Fife. "He and Ada are usually in here for their daily tutorial. I've come to thwart their scholastic pursuits!"

"Scholastic pursuits" was what was going to get Lottie and Eliot out of Kemble School and into a good university, provided Eliot was well enough to go.

"I don't think you should sound so pleased with yourself about that," said Lottie. "Schoolwork is important."

"Oh, don't tell *me* about the merits of schoolwork," said Fife. "I want to be a healer myself, just like Mr. Wilfer. He's promised me that if I study hard and read diligently, he'll give me an assessment when I'm sixteen. If he thinks I'm good enough, then I'll get to be his apprentice."

Fife stopped his searching and hopped onto the window seat next to Lottie. "Sorry if I scared you up there, by the way. The guest room's usually empty. I always sneak in through there because if Adelaide catches me coming in from the foyer . . ." Fife grabbed his neck with his hands and made a choking noise. "Now, there's a sprite that'll spook you out of your skin."

"Sprite," repeated Lottie. The word still sounded strange and tinselly in her ears. "Can all sprites do what you do?"

"Do what? This?"

Fife floated up a few inches from where they were sitting, fluttering his hands with dramatic flourish.

"Yes, that."

Fife smiled broadly.

"No sprite can do that," he said, returning to his seat. "Just folks like me."

"But if you're not a sprite—"

"Who said I wasn't a sprite?" interrupted Fife, whom Lottie noticed was sticking his tongue out at her again.

"But you just said—"

Fife raised his eyebrows.

"Oh, never mind," said Lottie. "I only ask because I'm not sure I even believe it."

"Believe what? In sprites?"

"Well," said Lottie, "I know that there's *something* weird going on here, and Mr. Wilfer expects me to believe it's magic."

"But you don't believe that?"

Lottie thought for a good minute. How could she explain flying out a window? Or the silver-boughed tree? Or how she no longer had a cut upon her forehead? Those were things too big to keep in a copper box.

"Maybe I do," she said.

Fife looked at her strangely. The very tip of his tongue protruded from his lips. "Do you mean to say that no one ever told you anything about Limn?"

Lottie shook her head. No one told her much of anything back home. She was lucky if Mrs. Yates informed her that a boarder was coming to stay in Thirsby Square.

"Should someone have told me?" Lottie asked.

"Well, only just about every Southerly sprite since the beginning of time has gotten the history of Limn pounded into their little Southerly brains."

"You've said that word before," said Lottie. "Southerly. What's that mean?"

"Southerly," repeated Fife, licking his lower lip. "As in, the opposite of Northerly."

He pulled back the sleeve of his shirt and held his right hand up, close to Lottie's nose. Inked just below the knobby bone jutting from his wrist was a tattoo of a black diamond. Lottie's eyes widened. She'd never met a boy with a tattoo before.

"See that?" Fife asked. "The black diamond. That's the mark of the Northerly Court. All the Northerlies have got one."

"Do Southerlies have one, too?"

"It's so lame," Fife snorted. "They call it the white orb, but 'orb' is just a fancy name for 'circle.' Anyway, that's the mark of the Southerly Court. It's the mark that people like the Wilfers have got."

"Why the difference?" asked Lottie.

"Because," said Fife, leaning back against the window-pane, "the Northerlies live in the North and the Southerlies in the South. The two courts hate each other. It's about something that happened a long time ago."

"But," said Lottie, "you don't hate Oliver. You said that Oliver was your best friend, and he's a Southerly. *And* you said that you weren't even a sprite!"

"Really," said Fife, smiling. "Did I say all that?"

Lottie didn't have the chance to get upset with Fife. Someone else already was, and that someone had just flung open the doors of the library.

"FIFE DULCET!"

Adelaide stormed toward both of them, looking quite ready to set Fife's floppy black hair on fire with her glare alone. Oliver was hurrying up behind her.

"How dare you!" Adelaide shrieked, close enough now to draw her hand back as though to smack Fife's shoulder.

Fife shot up and over Adelaide and landed on his feet next to Oliver.

"School over so soon?" Fife asked conversationally.

"I had Tutor dismissed the minute I heard you," said Adelaide, whipping back around. "What do you mean by—"

"By breaking out your prisoner?" interrupted Fife. He lolled his head toward Lottie. "It's not very nice to lock up your guests, Ada."

"Lottie is not my prisoner!" snapped Adelaide, scowling in Lottie's direction. "She's just not trustworthy."

"Adelaide," said Oliver, his eyes turning a startled lime color, "is that true? You locked Lottie up?"

"I had a good reason to lock her up, and she knows perfectly well why," huffed Adelaide, glaring at Lottie. "And I have just as good a reason for telling *him*"—she pointed at Fife as though he were a bug that she'd just found under her shoe—"to leave Iris Gate immediately."

"No you haven't," said Fife. "Lottie and I have become good friends while you've been away, haven't we, Lottie Fiske?"

Adelaide gasped. "You know who she is?" She turned to Oliver. "*He knows who she is?* Father told us it was a secret. How could you tell *him*?"

"Fife's my best friend," said Oliver, and this seemed to be as much of an introduction to Lottie as it was an answer to Adelaide.

"Where's Mr. Wilfer?" asked Lottie.

Adelaide, Oliver, and Fife suddenly seemed to forget their bickering. Three gazes turned to Lottie.

"Sorry to interrupt," said Lottie, who wasn't really at all sorry, "but I've got to see him. He said he'd explain more to me in the morning, so . . ."

"Father," said Adelaide coolly, "is out of town for the day. He told Oliver and me that he had urgent business to attend to, and he left us with strict instructions to watch out for you when you'd woken up. And for your information, it's not morning."

"It's nearly suppertime," said Fife, patting his stomach.

Lottie blanched. The pale light outside those library windows was not dawn, but dusk. She had slept a whole day. She'd slept away precious time to save Eliot.

"Did Mr. Wilfer say what the urgent business was?" Lottie asked. Maybe he had already gone out without her to find the one missing ingredient: a poem or a laugh or whatever that special scrapbook required.

Adelaide and Oliver exchanged glances.

"Father was pretty shaken up about something late last night," Oliver said quietly. "He just left us a note."

"Did he say when he'd be back?"

"Why?" sniffed Adelaide. "It's not like you care about Father's urgent business. This is just about getting your hands on that medicine."

Lottie narrowed her eyes at Adelaide. "So?"

"Hey," Fife laughed nervously, glancing from Lottie to Adelaide. "Air's getting a bit thin in here, eh? Maybe we should open another window, get some ventilation . . ."

But neither Lottie nor Adelaide paid attention to the offer.

"I wasn't trying to steal anything," said Lottie.

"You were *snooping*. Refined sprites don't snoop," Adelaide said, tilting up her chin in a haughty glare. "And what strange things did Father tell you, exactly? That you're nothing but a halfling? That you and all Fiskes are nothing but a disappointment? That you and your stupid birthday wish could cost Father his life?"

"Adelaide!" Oliver's eyes had turned a wild amber. "Don't talk to Lottie like that. Can't you see she's still adjusting?"

"Yeah," Fife said, nodding in agreement. "For some-one as refined as you, Ada, you really know how to—"

"SHHH!" Adelaide held her finger to her mouth and waved for the boys to be quiet; and quite unlike Lottie had expected, both of them obeyed.

"What is it?" whispered Oliver. "What do you hear?"

Adelaide shook her head and kept her finger pressed to her lips. Her face paled. She looked at Lottie, then at her brother.

"Father's back," she whispered.

"Well, thank Titania!" laughed Fife. "That solves all of our problems."

Fife floated over to the library doors. Adelaide leapt in front of him.

"No, you idiot!" she hissed, shaking her head fiercely. "Listen to me. Father's back, and *he's not alone.*"

Lottie could finally hear the voices that Adelaide was talking about. They were coming from just outside the library doors.

"They're headed this way," said Fife, shoving Adelaide and Lottie into a nearby aisle of bookshelves. Oliver slinked in after them, just in time. The library doors swung open, and Lottie heard the heavy tread of marching boots.

"Bring him in," boomed a man's voice. "We won't be seen through the street windows in here. Now drop him."

There was a thud, and from where Lottie was uncomfortably squished against a row of uneven book spines, she saw a man drop to the floor.

"You will tell us where it is," the booming voice continued. "Then you will tell us where the girl is. If you do not comply, you know as a Southerly citizen what your due punishment will be."

The stooped man raised his goggles-clad face, and Lottie gulped down a gasp. It was Mr. Wilfer.

"I told you, it is not ready," Mr. Wilfer said in a hoarse voice. "Starkling knows this. I need more time. No one in my practice can rush such a process."

"Perhaps that is why so few in your practice are still alive," said the voice, and at last the man to whom it belonged stepped into view.

Lottie stifled another gasp. She knew this man, too, the one speaking the cruel words. He was so easy to recognize because he was looking at Mr. Wilfer just the same way he had looked at Lottie in Thirsby Square. It was a bored and unforgiving look, and it belonged to Mr. Grissom, Mrs. Yates' prospective boarder.

"You have been given deadline after deadline with no results," he barked, circling the kneeling Mr. Wilfer. "And now you've betrayed the king."

"You don't have any proof of that," said Mr. Wilfer.

"You underestimate me, Moritasgus. You always have. You were suspicious that I was tracking your movements, I'll give you credit for that. But you were a fool to send out your own children, thinking that I wouldn't track *them*."

Mr. Wilfer looked up. "What did you do?"

"*I* didn't do anything." Lottie could hear a smile in Grissom's voice. "You know as well as I do that your son and his little halfling friend shouldn't have been root shooting from an unauthorized tree in Albion Park. Whose fault would it be if they were inside when the Guard chopped it down? Who sent them?"

"You could have killed them." Mr. Wilfer's voice was low, and it pricked gooseflesh up Lottie's arms.

"They managed. But, my dear sprite, you can't pull

the wool over my eyes. I saw the Fiske girl in person. One moment she was in Earth, and the next she wasn't. We both know why that is, Moritasgus. You and I were the only ones privy to the king's plan, so that means that one of us has turned traitor. And it wasn't me."

"No," said Mr. Wilfer. "It wasn't you. You wouldn't have had the courage."

Grissom grew very still. Then he struck Mr. Wilfer across the face. Adelaide let out a cry before hiding her face in her hands. Fortunately, it seemed that the echoing *whack!* of Grissom's slap had drowned out the cry, because Grissom did not look their way. Mr. Wilfer, however, did. Lottie was almost positive that he *smiled* at them—a short, sad smile. Then he dropped his eyes back to the ground.

"You have the girl," hissed Grissom. "She is either here or somewhere close by, being harbored by Northerly sympathizers. The Southerly Guard will be here soon to find her. It will be easier on her and on you, however, if you simply tell us where she's hidden."

Mr. Wilfer bowed his head. The shadows of dusk slanted over his stooped form. He did not speak.

"Very well," Grissom said after a long silence. "We will smoke her out. As to the other matter. Starkling is losing his patience, not to mention his faith in you as Head Healer. He's deemed it best that you work under careful supervision from now on, to hurry things along, as it were."

"I have told him, and I have told you, the process cannot be rushed."

"It can, and it will. Just as you can and will fetch what you've made so far of the Otherwise Incurable, and you can and will accompany us back to the Southerly Court, where you will finish the king's medicine in three days' time."

More silence followed, during which Lottie could hear the impatient tap of Grissom's boot and the raspy hitch of Mr. Wilfer's breathing.

"Very well," Mr. Wilfer said at last. "My children have already lost their mother. I do not wish for them to lose their father, too. The medicine is upstairs. I keep it in my bedchamber."

Grissom's boot stopped tapping. "Good."

He motioned to two other boot-clad men, who dragged Mr. Wilfer back to his feet.

"Take him upstairs," Grissom ordered.

The guards clomped out of the room, hauling Mr. Wilfer behind them. For a long, silent moment, Grissom watched them leave. Slowly, a satisfied smile curled up his mouth. Then he, too, left the dusk-darkened library.

CHAPTER SIX

Fire and Temper

FIFE LET OUT a rattled breath. Adelaide was crying quietly. Oliver stood apart from the others, head bowed against a stack of books. His eyes had gone a solemn, tar black. Lottie felt that she had stumbled onto something very awful and private and sad. Worst of all, she felt as though it was somehow her fault.

Adelaide had been right the night before: Mr. Wilfer was in some sort of trouble with the king. He was in trouble because of the Otherwise Incurable, and he was in trouble because of *her*. Why?

Suddenly, Adelaide stopped up her crying and whipped her head out of her hands with a gasp. "Father is buying us time. Don't you see? He's buying us time!"

She looked entreatingly at the rest of them. "The medicine isn't in his bedchamber. Father never takes any of his experiments out of the laboratory. The Southerly Guard mean to confiscate it, but Father means to buy us the time to steal it from his study and run!"

"Sweet Oberon, Ada," said Fife. "I think you're right."

"Of course I'm right," snapped Adelaide, stumbling to her feet and brushing tears from her face. "He knew we were in here. He looked at us that once, didn't you notice? No wonder he was in such a tizzy last night. Father *suspected* that this might happen. He wants us to take the medicine and escape."

"Not just the medicine," said Oliver, whose eyes had turned from black to a cautious yellow. "He wants us to take Lottie. You heard what Grissom said. The Guard is coming for her. She's not safe here anymore."

Adelaide nodded brusquely in Lottie's direction. "But we have to *hurry*!"

"Fife," said Oliver, "take Lottie back to the guest bedroom so that she can get her things. Only be careful;

we don't know what sort of keens those guards have. Adelaide and I will get the medicine from the study and meet you in the back garden, behind the mulberry bushes."

Fife nodded and grabbed Lottie's hand. Before Lottie had time to open her mouth, Fife had pulled her up, up, up, and out of the library window to the second floor. With a startled *"Umph!"* she tumbled through the guest bedroom window.

"Quick," said Fife, glancing around nervously. "Get whatever you need."

Lottie pulled on her tweed coat, which was the only belonging she had to fetch.

"Who's the Southerly Guard?" she whispered, buttoning the coat up to her neck.

Fife wet his lips. "Let's hope you don't have to find out."

He took Lottie by the hand and they floated off again. This time, they made a smoother landing. Lottie's feet hit the gravelly garden path, and Fife righted her balance. From here, she could see back through Iris Gate's glass windows into the foyer. There was a flash of movement inside, and through the window she saw Oliver and Adelaide stumble out of the laboratory. Oliver bounded for the French doors, but Adelaide was running the other way, toward that gaping, hungry archway.

"Ada!" Fife shouted.

Somehow, Adelaide heard him through the glass. She turned around, made a motion with her hands that Lottie could not understand, and ran off again, away from them.

Oliver caught up with Fife and Lottie in the garden. "Keep going," he puffed. "Adelaide's coming."

They scampered down the garden path until they reached the dark, tall arms of mulberry bush branches. Oliver crouched down and motioned for them to do the same.

"That Grissom guy," said Lottie, "is one of Mrs. Yates' boarders."

"He was following you," said Oliver. "There's been a rumor for weeks in the Southerly Court that you exist. He was going to kidnap you last night. Luckily, we got to you first."

"Luckily," Lottie repeated faintly. "He's got to be really powerful if he's allowed to treat your dad like that."

"He's the Southerly King's left-hand sprite."

"Who's his right-hand sprite?" asked Lottie.

"Father," Oliver whispered. "Or, at least, Father *was*, until just now."

"What's Ada still doing in there?" said Fife. "She's going to get caught."

Oliver only shook his head and motioned for them both to be quiet. Suddenly, Adelaide's pale, freckled face appeared from behind a mulberry branch.

"YAH!" Fife shrieked.

"Shut up," Adelaide's hissed, smacking Fife's ear. "I could hear you breathing all the way from the kitchen, you oaf." She stooped down, dropping a big satchel at her feet. "I just needed to get some things."

"Do you have the Otherwise Incurable?" Lottie asked.

Adelaide shot Lottie one long, icy stare. "Is that all you can think about? No, I haven't got it. Oliver has."

As proof, Oliver held up the square vial labeled *Otherwise Incurable*.

Lottie, however, had become distracted. In the fuzzy edges of her periphery, she had caught sight of two pure white eyes with pinprick silver pupils. They were staring out at her from the mulberry leaves at her back. She could feel something warm and damp next to her neck, and she realized in sudden horror that the dampness was coming from a mouth and that this mouth was attached to the same face that held those eyes. The mouth was breathing softly, slowly, against her ear, in a low growl.

"The Heir," it snarled. "The Heir of Fiske."

At that, Lottie had the presence of mind to tumble away from the mulberry bush.

"There!" Lottie shrieked. "That! Look!"

She pointed at the bush. The pinprick eyes had disappeared.

Fife crawled over to Lottie and cautiously plucked her back up. Lottie reddened at how her limbs trembled in the process. She was ashamed of herself, and she was also surprised that Fife, whose lank body looked weaker than a flower stem, was more than strong enough to pull her right side up.

"There, what?" Fife said. "Nothing's there. Shoo, Lottie. You can't scare us like that. We're already on the run. Tense times as it is!"

"But I saw, I heard—" Lottie broke off at the blank looks the others were giving her.

There was no sign of the eyes or mouth or voice. Lottie shrunk in on herself and shook her head. "Never mind," she mumbled.

"They're going to take Father away," whispered Adelaide. "The moment they find out he's lied to them and the medicine is gone, they'll take him to the Southerly Court."

"And then they'll send the Guard after us," said Fife.

"We can't just hide out back here forever," Adelaide said, "and going back to Iris Gate is as good as turning ourselves in."

"So where do we go?" whispered Lottie.

Oliver, whom Lottie had thought had not even been paying attention, spoke.

"Ingle," he said quietly. "Mr. Ingle, at the old inn. He's one of Father's oldest friends. He'll know what to do."

"Then we'll go to the inn," said Adelaide. "Mr. Ingle will know how to help Father, and we can stay with him until we know it's safe to come back to Iris Gate."

It was about that time that Lottie again saw something that the others did not; only this time there was no chance that she could have imagined it. It was too big and too terrible a thing to imagine. A great big bluish blast of light had shot up from Iris Gate and hung, for just a moment, bright and dazzling in the air. Then the light began to change, writhing into hundreds of long flames that curled into the darkening sky like serpent tongues, and then shot down, fast and frantic, back onto the roof of Iris Gate. Lottie's ears filled with a thick, crackling sound. A rush of heat swept across her face, prickling her skin. Then the roof was suddenly a spectacle of white flames and black smoke. The fire began to lick down the sides of the stone house and toward the garden. The thick tongues of flame turned into thinner, fiery cords, and those cords weaved and crossed a path from the walls of the house down to the silverwork of the garden fence.

Lottie was not the only one staring now.

"By Puck," whispered Fife. "Grissom wasn't kidding about smoking us out."

There was a smell in the air that Lottie liked very much under normal circumstances. It brought to mind autumn, early nights, cider, patched-up coats, and crunchy leaves. It was the smell of burning wood, but tonight it did not come from a snug fireplace or a friendly bonfire.

Iris Gate was burning.

Sparks shot from the unnatural white flames, catching fire to ivy and shrubberies. In the harsh, orange light, Lottie saw the bent silhouettes of hundreds of irises wilting. Tendrils of blue flames licked down the garden path, eating up more irises still, then wisteria, then mulberry leaves. The fire was crawling quickly, greedily toward them.

"Enchanted fire," said Fife. "Grissom thinks we're still here. He's trying to trap us."

"Then we've got to get out!" said Adelaide.

"Can't you float us out of here?" Lottie asked Fife.

Fife shook his head. "Not carrying three other people."

Oliver looked as though he'd gone into a trance, his eyes the color of coal. "From what I've tasted of desire," he whispered, "I hold with those who favor fire."

"This is no time to be quoting!" shrieked Adelaide. "Run for the back gate. Just run!"

Adelaide took off, her satchel clutched to her chest. Lottie stumbled after, toward the back garden gate. Her eyes stung, leaking tears across her toasted cheeks. Her hair grew wet with sweat, sticking to her ears and chin. She could feel the fire growing hotter and hotter at her back. Lottie ran faster, keeping her eyes on Adelaide's feet in front of her. Just a few more steps. Three, two—through the gate, and with one great swoosh, Lottie was free from the garden. They were out, all four of them, in a cobblestone alleyway, staring back at the flaming garden of Iris Gate.

"Everyone all right?" asked Oliver.

"Well enough," coughed Fife, floating back to the ground. One straggly clump of his hair was glowing.

"Watch it!" Adelaide cried, licking her fingers and closing them over the crackling hair.

"Guh," said Fife, shrinking back. "Sprite spit."

"You're welcome," said Adelaide.

"Which way?" Lottie asked, wiping sweat from her cheek.

"Up the hill," Oliver said. "We'll have to use the main road. Just stay in the shadows and out of sight."

Oliver led them out of the alleyway. Blue turrets of flame crowned the high walls of Iris Gate. The crackle of burning greenery followed them as they slipped onto the main road. The road was cobblestone and lined with tall old lattice-worked buildings and gaslit lampposts whose dim, sweet smell mixed with the stench of burning flowers. A large crowd had already gathered around Iris Gate, muttering loudly, gasping, and coughing from the smoke that billowed into the streets. Lottie and the others skirted around the crowd, away from Iris Gate and up the beginnings of a steep hill.

"Hurry," said Adelaide. *"Hurry!"*

But Oliver had stopped running and was staring back at the house.

"Something's happening," he said.

Something *was* happening. The clamor of the crowd had softened, and Lottie could just make out the sight of a man dressed in a long red cloak, who was shooing away those nearest the house. He turned toward the crowd and raised his hands in a silencing gesture. Lottie supposed that this must be an important man, for the crowd hushed immediately, and the only noise that followed was the insistent sizzle of burning garden. The man lowered his hands. He then produced something from his cloak that looked like a scroll. He uncurled the scroll and cleared his throat.

"By order of his most revered majesty, Starkling, King of the Southerly Court, Healer Moritasgus Horatio Wilfer of Iris Gate has hereby been revoked of the title Head Healer!"

A ripple of murmurs trembled through the crowd. The messenger raised his voice as he continued.

"Healer Moritasgus Horatio Wilfer is hereby banned from his private practice and has been taken into custody of the Southerly Court!"

Louder whispers spread through the crowd. Lottie saw Adelaide clench her fists. Oliver was staring at the cobble-stones, and Fife looked ill.

"The Wilfer Estate of Iris Gate is hereby ordered to be strictly guarded. It is suspected to be the haven of a great enemy of our most illustrious Southerly Court."

The crowd booed.

"Should the public enemy not be recovered from within Iris Gate," the messenger went on, "the menace shall be duly apprehended. All apple trees within New Albion shall be strictly monitored. Houses may be searched. Any sprites who aid or abet these wanted souls will be tried to the full extent of Southerly law. Report all suspicious activity to your nearest Southerly Guard official."

In the silence, a nearby streetlamp guttered and popped, followed by the shriek of an unhappy baby. Coughs peppered the crowd. The man in red lowered his arms.

"End of dictation."

A burly man on the outskirts of the crowd stooped to pick up a loose cobblestone. Lottie's mouth dried in horror as she watched him raise the stone above his head and hurl it toward the house. A window of Iris Gate shattered.

"Good riddance!" shouted the stone thrower. "Down with the traitor, Moritasgus Wilfer!"

A few other hoarse voices of approval rang out. The messenger, encouraged, raised his fist in the air.

"Down with all traitors of the Southerly Court!" he shouted.

"*No,*" Oliver whispered.

Adelaide gasped and grabbed Lottie's elbow. Then she realized what she had done and quickly let it go again.

The crowd erupted into agreement with the man in red. More windows shattered. The crying baby began to squall, and the guttering lamplight gave way to the dark of night. Lottie was cold. She wanted nothing more to do with this place. She wanted to go home.

"This is *your* fault!"

Lottie stumbled back. Adelaide had lunged at her, grabbing the collar of Lottie's tweed coat.

"We're not the guilty ones," she shrieked, "you are!"

"Hey, get off her!" said Fife, wrenching Adelaide loose. "Lottie didn't know. She couldn't have!"

"You and your stupid ancestors!" Adelaide spat at Lottie, shrugging Fife from her shoulders. "We wouldn't have any trouble at all if it weren't for you Fiskes."

"Wh-what?" Lottie stammered.

"Father taken away," Adelaide went on, "Iris Gate burned up, and the Guard trying to take us away. What are we supposed to do now?"

Adelaide sank to the cobblestone, sobbing into her folded knees.

Lottie was trembling. "We can't just stand in the middle of the street, can we?" she asked Fife, who seemed the likeliest to hear her out. "You heard what that messenger said. Something about duly apprehending and—and important orders and all that. They're sending people to look for us, aren't they? Bad people."

"Yeah," said Fife. "We're marked sprites now, I guess. Aiders and abettors and all that, huh, Ollie?"

Oliver had knelt next to Adelaide and was whispering words to her that Lottie couldn't make out. He now looked up and wiped a trickle of either sweat or tears—Lottie could not tell which—from his cheek.

"Others," he said, "I am not the first, have willed more mischief than they durst. If in the breathless night I too shiver now, 'tis nothing new."

Lottie groaned at Oliver's first rhyme, but by the end of it all, she found that the words had made a strange sort of sense. To Fife, at least, the poetry worked like a proper answer.

"Then it's settled," Fife said. "We've got to get to Mr. Ingle. And fast." He touched his tongue to the side of his mouth and crouched in front of Adelaide. "Listen, Ada—"

"Don't you *dare*!" Adelaide cried, slapping him away. "Don't use your keen on me! I don't need your special attention."

By now, the swarm of spectators had had their fun taking out every window of Iris Gate with loose cobblestones and were disappearing into the bends, gates, and alleyways off the main street. Nearby, a group of hiccuping, singing boys had begun to straggle up the cobblestone hill.

"C'mon, Ada," said Fife, still crouching. "We've got to move, unless you want to get trampled on by your boyfriend and company."

"*Don't* call me Ada," snapped Adelaide, though she looked genuinely terrified when she saw the group of rowdy boys approaching them. "And Hagen Marplemeyer is *not* my boyfriend!"

"Sure, he's not," Fife conceded, helping to hoist a wriggling Adelaide to her feet. "But he still knows who you are, doesn't he?"

"Of course he does. Every sprite in this city knows who I am. I'm a Wilfer."

"Well, every sprite in this city is going to be looking for a Wilfer. Didn't you hear? You're criminals now."

"I bet you're just relishing that," growled Adelaide, shoving Fife back again.

"Both of you, cut it out," said Oliver, whom Lottie had assumed had just been lost in another poetic trance. "Let's *go*."

With that, Oliver started briskly up the hill, and Lottie and Fife followed. Adelaide, however, clenched her hands to her hips and stomped in the opposite direction, down the hill, toward the gaggle of laughing boys.

"Hagen Marplemeyer, you *fiend*!" Adelaide screeched into the group.

Hagen, a stout, long-haired boy, whistled up at her. "Well, if it isn't Miss High-and-Mighty herself! Not so proud to be a Wilfer now, are you?"

"I saw you smash *my* bedroom window with that rock!"

Hagen grinned. "And what are you going to do about it, huh? Sic your freak brother on me? Have him turn my skin all the colors of the rainbow?"

Lottie couldn't make out what happened next, but when it was over, Hagen Marplemeyer was howling on the ground, and Adelaide was steaming up the hill with two clenched fists, one of which was spattered in something reddish-black. When she caught up, she whipped her hair toward Fife in a defiant swoop.

"Hagen Marplemeyer," she said triumphantly, "is *not* my boyfriend."

Then Adelaide turned back to the boys and yelled, "Don't you ever breathe another word about Oliver!"

In that moment, Lottie wondered if Adelaide Wilfer might not be so very different from her after all.

Ingle Inn sat at the very top of the cobblestone hill. It was a narrow, wooden building with boarded-up windows, lodged like a splinter between two brick walls. Its garden was overgrown with thistles and rotting cabbages and moldering pumpkins. There were signs that there had once been steps leading to the front door, but those steps were now gone, and Lottie could only climb onto the front landing with the help of Fife's outstretched hand.

When she had been younger, Lottie had been forced to trail Mrs. Yates about the Isle's countryside to visit old, important, and fantastically boring houses. As they had puttered about, taking flashless pictures with their cameras, Mrs. Yates and the other tourists would often say things like "Can you sense it? This place has a life of its own!" Lottie had thought these remarks to be very stupid.

If houses really did have lives of their own, though, Ingle Inn's life had left it long, long ago. Lottie felt less like she was walking through the front door of an inn and more like she was slipping into the mouth of a shriveled corpse.

Plaster and sawdust peppered Lottie's periwinkle coat as she followed Oliver and Fife into a lamplit corridor.

There were drafty holes in the wood-paneled walls, and something screeched from under the floorboards. Lottie nearly toppled back onto Adelaide when she saw a many-legged thing scuttle at her feet.

"Sorry," she said in a whisper, which seemed like the appropriate way to speak.

Adelaide merely sniffed and pushed past Lottie to join the others, who were now whispering to someone at the inn's front desk.

Lottie sat down on the only straight-backed chair in the corridor that was not missing one of its legs. The others could work things out with this Mr. Ingle, but she preferred to be near the door in case this dead inn decided to give it up entirely and cave in on itself, necessitating a quick exit.

From where she sat, feet propped up on the chair rung to keep clear of any more scuttling things, Lottie could just make out Oliver whispering the words "arrest," "Father," and "Fiske."

Lottie looked down at her soot-stained green sneakers and wished more than ever that she had gone back to the Barmy Badger and apologized to Eliot while she'd still had the chance.

"Charlotte Fiske?"

Lottie looked up. No one called her Charlotte except for her schoolteachers and Mrs. Yates. She half expected the next words to be a geography problem or an order that she go to her room without supper.

The man from the front desk was approaching her. He was bald, and his face resembled a walnut; it looked as though his eyes, nose, and mouth had been crammed into the creases and wrinkles of his face. Lottie would have been frightened if the man's eyes didn't look so kind.

"Blessed brass buttons," said Mr. Ingle, hobbling toward Lottie. "Charlotte Fiske. I never thought I'd see you again, not in my lifetime."

"Charlotte," snorted Fife, peeking out from behind Mr. Ingle. "Is that your real name?"

Lottie reddened. She would have preferred it if Fife had never found out her full name.

"How do you know my name?" Lottie asked Mr. Ingle.

"How?" said Mr. Ingle. "Why, dear child, I was there when Bertram and Eloise chose it."

Lottie straightened up. Bertram and Eloise were the names of her parents, the names that had been scribbled on the back of the black-and-white photograph she had received from Mr. Wilfer all those years ago. Lottie had never heard those words spoken out loud by anyone other than herself, and then only in a whisper very late at night, under her bedsheets.

Mr. Ingle gave a phlegmy sigh. "Hard to believe how the years have passed. Yes, that was at the end of the brighter days. Back when I was a rich, busy man. Back when these walls"—Mr. Ingle smacked a wood panel, causing a concealed mouse to squeak— "housed lords and ladies from the most illustrious Southerly and Northerly houses! You wouldn't ever imagine that of me and my humble inn nowadays, would you?"

"I can imagine a lot, Mr. Ingle," Lottie said.

Mr. Ingle grinned toothily at her. "Yes. I could smell that on you."

"Mr. Ingle," said Oliver, "perhaps you'd like to tell Lottie about our plan."

"Ah!" Mr. Ingle clapped his hands together. "Yes. The plan. Oliver's told me about your troubles, and I must say that I've never been so outraged in my life!" Here, he hit the wood panel again, causing an owl to hoot from somewhere in the room. "Moritasgus and I go back, far back. He helped me in my own hard times, and any assistance I can provide to his family and to Eloise's is a kindness well spent."

"Mr. Ingle says he'll let us spend the evening here," said Fife. "You know, harbor us like the wanted criminals we are. Like fugitives!"

"Titania's sake," groaned Adelaide. "We are not fugitives."

Fife made a kissy-face at Adelaide. Mr. Ingle raised an eyebrow at this little exchange, but he went on.

"As I was telling your friends," he said, "there is only one way that this tragedy might be averted, and that is to make a formal plea at the Southerly Court. That is how these things have been dealt with time out of mind, when one believes a party to have been wronged by the Southerly Court. An advocate from the wronged sprite's house must make a petition before the king."

"That means," said Oliver, "that Adelaide and I can petition for our father. If we can make it to the Southerly Court in time, the king will have to listen to our plea."

"But where exactly is the Southerly Court?" Lottie asked.

"A good two days' journey from here," Mr. Ingle said. "It is not an easy trip. More than that, I suspect that you are all worn from the night's events. I suggest, then, that the best thing to do is take rest and nourishment here while you can and set out first thing in the morning."

"And once we've reached the court," said Lottie, "we can plead or grovel or whatever it is that one does at court, and they'll set Mr. Wilfer free, right? We've just got to get him back. He's the only way that Eliot's medicine will be ready in time."

Adelaide made a shrill noise that sounded like a dying ferret. "Of course it doesn't matter that he's my father and he's in mortal danger!"

Lottie turned on Adelaide. "Well, of course that matters!"

As she yelled it, though, Lottie realized that she had been thinking all this time about Eliot. The fact that Mr. Wilfer could really be in serious danger had not even crossed her mind. Now, for the first time, Adelaide's situation struck Lottie a little more clearly: Adelaide's father had just been kidnapped, her home had been condemned and smashed up, and now she had to deal with Lottie, who, for a reason Lottie had yet to figure out, seemed to be responsible for all of these problems.

"It matters," Lottie repeated, this time more softly. "I know your dad must mean everything to you. Don't you think I know what it's like to not have parents around?"

"You don't know anything about it," Adelaide said thinly. "I've *just* lost my father. You never even knew your parents."

Fife looked around uneasily. "Uh," he coughed, "on a cheerier note, the Southerly Guard will probably be prowling around for us any second."

"Shouldn't be surprised if they haven't sent out the Guard," said Mr. Ingle, nodding. "All the more reason to stay out of sight tonight. As it is, you can leave at dawn and still be outside the court walls the next evening."

"But," said Lottie, "isn't there a quicker way to get there? I mean, can't you travel by . . . apple tree or something?"

Adelaide made a gritty snort that could mean one thing and one thing only, and that was that Lottie was a complete and utter imbecile.

"What Adelaide's saying so sweetly," said Fife, "is that travel by tree is only for trips between worlds. We're painfully old-fashioned when it comes to public transportation. We use a system called 'by foot.'"

"There is one way to travel quicker," Oliver said, "by Royal Piskie Dust. But that's royal, of course, and very rare. Only the king and the Guard can use it."

"Which means," said Fife, "that Grissom has already got Mr. Wilfer locked up at the Southerly Court, and we've got to spend all this time just catching up with them."

"So shouldn't Lottie just stay here?" said Adelaide.

Lottie looked up sharply. "What?"

"You're half human," Adelaide said. "You'll only slow us down. Anyway, this is about our father. There's no need for *you* to come along. Or Fife, for that matter."

Fife sputtered.

"Fife is coming," Oliver said firmly. "He's my friend, and more than that, he knows the wood better than the two of us combined. You know that, Adelaide."

"But what good is *she* to us?" Adelaide protested, pointing at Lottie. "She can't plead for Father. She just wants him to finish the medicine for her stupid friend."

"But I can't stay here!" said Lottie, realizing in a panic that this was true. "You heard that Grissom man. People are searching for me, here and back home. I won't be safe."

"You won't exactly be safe with us," Oliver pointed out.

"But I'll be *doing* something," Lottie said. "I'll be doing something for Eliot. I'm not just going to wait around for you all. I'm going, too."

Fife folded his arms and smirked at the others. "Lottie has spoken. She knows what she wants."

Adelaide began to protest again, but Lottie shot her a cold look. She'd had enough of Adelaide Wilfer tonight.

"I'm coming," she said in a steely voice.

Slowly, Oliver nodded. "She's coming."

"We set out first thing in the morning, like you say," said Lottie. "Or sooner."

"First thing," agreed Fife.

"Or sooner," said Oliver.

Lottie smiled at the boys. Maybe, just maybe, they were going to get along. Adelaide only crossed her arms and rolled her eyes. Mr. Ingle, meantime, was shifting his weight from boot to boot, causing the floorboards of the inn to creak tremendously.

"Then it's settled!" the old man cried. "Excellent. I can't say how much good this does my old heart. It's been ten years since I've had a proper guest."

He pounded the wood panels for emphasis, and a cockroach hissed.

CHAPTER SEVEN

At Ingle Inn

MR. INGLE PROMPTLY scooted his guests into a musty dining room in which Lottie tried to choke down what Fife told her was flower-bulb soup. All the while, she gazed at a wall-sized, moth-eaten tapestry that depicted an argument between a winged queen and king over a jewel-eyed baby boy.

After supper, with a gas lamp in hand, Mr. Ingle showed his guests up flight after flight of wheezing stairs to the sixth floor of the inn, where there were three empty bedrooms. One, he explained, belonged to him; the other two, which were set aside for the occasional guest, could be split amongst the four of them.

When Lottie asked why Mr. Ingle chose to live six floors away from his front door, he answered, "The smell, dear child! The smell. I simply couldn't sleep with all the scents of the street wafting under my nose!" Lottie, as she had gotten into a habit of doing recently, pretended to understand. Then, after taking a deep breath, she asked if she could speak with Mr. Ingle alone.

"What for?" said Adelaide, snapping to attention. "There's nothing to tell Mr. Ingle that you can't tell all of us."

"Or that Adelaide can't hear," said Fife.

Adelaide gave Fife a dirty look.

"I just want to ask Mr. Ingle something personal," Lottie said crossly. "It's my own private business."

"Right, then," said Fife, stretching his arms between Lottie and Adelaide in a peacemaking gesture. "Let's not get worked up. You, Ollie, and I can have our own secret conversation, can't we, Ada?"

Adelaide aimed a kick at Fife's shin, but his feet left the ground just in time for her to miss and lose her balance. It looked like Adelaide was working up a shout, and Lottie seized the lull to push Mr. Ingle into his room and shut the door behind them.

"My!" said Mr. Ingle, smiling as he toppled inside. "The apple doesn't fall far from the tree, does it?"

"See! That's exactly why I want to talk to you, Mr. Ingle," Lottie said.

"About apple trees?" Mr. Ingle looked confused.

"No," said Lottie. "Because you said that you knew my parents, Bertram and Eloise."

From outside the door, Lottie heard Fife say in a voice that was extra loud for her benefit, "Well, I guess we'll just go and have our own deliciously secret conversation! Did I mention that it's going to be *deliciously secret*?"

Mr. Ingle took a seat on a tattered, spring-pocked sofa. He motioned for Lottie to do the same.

"Moritasgus locked up in the Southerly dungeons," he said, shaking his head. "Poor fellow."

Lottie took a seat on the sofa. "Mr. Ingle," she said, "is it my fault that Mr. Wilfer was taken away?"

"No," said Mr. Ingle. "That is the Southerly King's fault. Don't let anyone else tell you otherwise."

"He doesn't seem to me to be a very good king," said Lottie. "Back where I come from, you can't just go around burning up gardens and throwing people into dungeons. At least, not anymore."

"Ah, where you come from . . ."

Lottie waited for Mr. Ingle to finish that thought, but apparently Mr. Ingle thought it was finished enough. He looked entranced, like he'd just spotted a distant ship on the horizon.

"Mr. Ingle?" Lottie pressed, attempting to reel in his attention.

Without a word, Mr. Ingle got up from the couch, opened the door, and left the room.

Lottie was afraid that she had offended the innkeeper in some way. Mr. Ingle returned, however, in a minute's time. By the looks of his tousled hair and heaving chest, it seemed he'd made an effort to retrieve whatever he now held.

It was a birdcage.

"Do you know what this is?" Mr. Ingle asked, setting the birdcage in front of her.

Lottie squinted at the cage. It was simply designed—a small, silver-barred dome with a single perch. What had captured Lottie's attention wasn't the birdcage at all but what was inside it.

A small bird sat inside, on the perch. Its head was tucked down, its body completely still. Its feathers were a deep, inky black.

"Is it—*alive*?" Lottie whispered.

"I've held him in my keeping for far too long," said Mr. Ingle. "Eloise told me that you would be back for him one day, and blow me down if she wasn't right. Now, if you'd be so good as to wake him up?"

Lottie frowned at Mr. Ingle. Then she frowned at the small, still bird.

"It's sleeping?"

"For more than twelve years now." Mr. Ingle hesitated. Then, quietly, he asked, "You *do* know what this is, don't you?"

"It's a bird," Lottie said, though she guessed that Mr. Ingle was expecting another answer, and something inside Lottie told her that she knew what this answer was.

Mr. Ingle unlatched the cage door and motioned for Lottie to lean closer. "Put out your hands," he instructed. "Both of them. Form them like a bowl. Then ask him to wake up. He knows your voice."

Lottie didn't see how a *bird* could possibly know her voice, let alone a bird she'd never seen before. Still, she did as Mr. Ingle asked and placed her cupped hands at the birdcage's open door.

"Um," she said. "Wake up?"

Nothing happened for a long moment. Then the little mound of feathers began to quiver. Then it rustled. Then the bird untucked his head from his breast and opened his eyes. Suddenly, he gave a great, fluttering jump and landed in Lottie's cupped hands. She gave a cry of surprise.

The bird stared up at her. He chirped.

"What kind of bird *is* it?" Lottie whispered.

"He's an obsidian warbler, if we're being specific," said Mr. Ingle. "Even more specifically, he's a genga."

The bird opened his slate-gray beak and piped out another tweet. It was a soothing sound that put Lottie in mind of wind chimes on a late April day.

"I've seen one of these before," said Lottie. "Adelaide keeps one in her pocket."

"The pocket is customary. You can use your own pocket if you'd like. Or you may choose a satchel or a hat. Anywhere close by. Gengas don't like to be separated from their sprites."

Lottie blinked dumbly at the chirruping bird. Then she understood.

"It's *my* genga?" she whispered.

Mr. Ingle nodded. "Look. He knows you."

The warbler had fluttered to the edge of Lottie's hands and perched precariously on her fingertips, his head tilted to one side and black eyes glinting curiously at Lottie. Then, in one great go, he hopped from Lottie's hands and landed on her knee. He bent his head and scrunched his feathers up in a cottony poof, and then he sprung into an upward swoop. He circled about the room, skimming the edge of the crown molding with his wings. At last, he settled back on Lottie's knee and gave a low, content warble.

Cautiously, Lottie outstretched her forefinger and brushed it along the genga's wing. The bird cooed and rubbed his downy face against Lottie's fingernail.

"He's beautiful," she whispered. "How can he have been asleep this whole time?"

"Gengas only respond to their owners' voice," said Mr. Ingle. "They're extremely delicate creatures, you understand. That is why Eloise entrusted yours to me. Any being that lives outside of his or her own world is bound to grow weak. But gengas are especially fragile. Your parents had decided to raise you amongst the humans, and Earth is no place for a creature so thoroughly Limnlike as a genga."

"Why didn't my parents choose to live here?"

"Why," said Mr. Ingle, "your father was human, and Limn had begun to take its toll on his health. It was only natural that he moved back to his own kind. Eloise practically forced him back into Earth. She thought it would save his life. She was wrong, poor dear."

"My parents really are dead, then?" Lottie whispered.

Mr. Ingle looked ashamed of himself, like he had just told a terrible joke. Still, he nodded. "They really are. Didn't you know?"

"I knew," said Lottie. "I just—well, Mr. Ingle, do you ever like to pretend that things aren't quite the way you've been told they are?"

Mr. Ingle shook his head.

After a long silence, Lottie said, "I guess that was very stupid of me."

"No, not stupid," said Mr. Ingle, patting Lottie's arm. "But they are dead. You mustn't deceive yourself about that any longer."

Lottie looked down at her genga, which was roosting on her knee. He breathed deeply, his dark body glinting in the lamplight with every rise and fall of his tiny chest. Lottie measured her own breaths by the genga's. She was working up the courage to ask something.

"How did they die?"

"Aaah," Mr. Ingle sighed. "The Plague took your mother, same as it took all the other Fiskes."

"The Plague?"

Mr. Ingle lowered his eyes, his walnut face producing still more wrinkles. "The Plague struck all of Albion Isle some years before you were born. Our island has long suffered from pestilences, but this was the worst of them all. Many Southerlies died, and Northerlies too. Plants withered and trees rotted. The disease took ahold of the will o' the wisps in a strange manner, changing in ways it did not with sprites; it torments them still. Fiskes were particularly susceptible. No one knows why, though some think it was because their keen had grown so weak. They no longer had their former abilities."

"What abilities?"

"Didn't Moritasgus tell you?" Mr. Ingle shook his head. "Each of them possessed a renowned ability to command. Mab the Great, the very first queen of Albion Isle, was a Fiske. But then—no one knows why—the Fiskes began to lose their abilities. Their keen grew weaker and weaker, until a Fiske king abdicated. He thought it best for the island, but everything went to ruin after that. Up sprung the Northerly and Southerly Courts and all types of mayhem. That was generations ago."

"I don't have any—special abilities," said Lottie.

"Yes, it would seem that human halflings don't have keens," said Mr. Ingle. "Though you're very rare, you know. Your mother herself wanted nothing to do with politics, but she was strong. She had a marvelous heart. Moritasgus and I were very good friends with your mother and her family, growing up. When she grew sick, she entrusted us both with the task of caring for you and your father in Earth. Then your father died of his own illness, and you were taken away. We thought we had lost you. But Moritasgus did not stop searching, and he found you at last in New Kemble. Just before your sixth birthday, I believe it was."

"Yes," Lottie whispered, and found she had begun to cry. "That was just when it was. That was when I found the copper box."

Mr. Ingle looked very frightened to be in a room with a crying girl.

"I think," he said, "you'd better get some rest, don't you? You're leaving first thing in the morning, and it won't be an easy trip if you're avoiding the main roads."

"So," said Lottie, "my mother was a sprite and my father was a human. Is that why Mr. Grissom is after me? Because I'm a halfling? Does the Southerly King not like humans or something?"

Mr. Ingle shook his head. "The king doesn't like *Fiskes*. These are hopeless times for many sprites, and there are wishful stories about a Fiske returning to take the throne."

Lottie's genga exhaled a low, mournful whistle.

"But that's ridiculous! I don't want his stupid throne."

Mr. Ingle leaned forward, his voice suddenly hushed. "Listen closely, Charlotte, for this is important advice: once you arrive at the Southerly Court, the two Wilfer children must make a formal petition to the king to save their father. That is how things are done. You, however, should stay out of sight. Don't show your face to the king. Don't even breathe the name Fiske.

"As for that Fife boy," Mr. Ingle added, "it'd be smarter if he stayed out of this matter entirely. Marked Northerlies like him are neither wanted nor welcome in the Southerly Court."

Lottie's brow creased. "I don't think there's a chance of him staying out of the matter."

Mr. Ingle smiled. "No, I don't think so, either. That boy reeks of a thirst for adventure. Your mother smelled the same."

Lottie liked Mr. Ingle, but all this talk about people's scents was a little unsettling.

"Now," Mr. Ingle said, "time for bed."

There was still so much more that Lottie wanted to know, a press of questions she hadn't even formulated yet. But Eliot came first, and Lottie was not fool enough to think she could walk a day's journey without sleep. She sighed and nodded.

Gingerly, she scooted her palm across her leg, toward her genga. The bird stooped to inspect Lottie's fingers. Then he gave a merry hop back onto her hand.

Lottie looked nervously at Mr. Ingle. "Am I really supposed to just put him in my pocket?"

"He's in no danger," Mr. Ingle said. "Gengas don't breathe like we do. In fact, I imagine he's quite eager to be close to you after so long a separation."

Lottie gave the bird an apologetic look. Then she closed her eyes and, in one swift movement, she tucked him into her coat pocket. She removed her hand. Then she glanced down. Her pocket rustled, and a happy little chirp emerged.

"That's going to take some getting used to," she said.

"You'll catch on soon enough."

Mr. Ingle rose to his feet. He opened the door and ushered Lottie past him into the hallway.

"Thank you, Mr. Ingle," said Lottie. "Thanks for telling me things. Especially, you know, things about *them*."

"Don't thank me for sharing memories," Mr. Ingle tutted, shutting the door to a mere crack. "These days, it's memory that keeps me alive."

"Mr. Ingle?"

"Hm?"

"What are good names for a genga?"

"Your mother named your genga when she named you." Mr. Ingle's wrinkled smile was visible even through the crack in the door. "She named him Trouble."

<hr />

In the hallway, Lottie could hear the voices but not the words of the others, who had all gone into the boys' room and shut the door behind them to have their "deliciously secret" conversation. The murmur was only occasionally broken by sharp yells from Adelaide or Fife, which Lottie assumed were directed at each other.

Lottie creaked down the hall to the only open doorway, the bedroom set aside for her and Adelaide. It was a bare and dusty room, no bigger than Mrs. Yates' garden shed. A tiny bed was shoved in the corner.

Adelaide's frilly jacket was draped on the bedpost, and as Lottie passed it, she saw peeking from one pocket the faintest of red glints. She stopped and looked again. Yes, a red glint. An anxious red glint. It was Mr. Wilfer's medicine. Lottie glanced toward the bedroom door. No one there. She snuck out the vial marked *Otherwise Incurable*.

One ingredient missing. Just one final ingredient to add. That was what Mr. Wilfer had said. And now Mr. Wilfer was gone—had been taken—and no matter what Mr. Ingle said, Lottie knew now that she was partly to blame. Being a Fiske meant something in this world, and while not the nasty things it had meant back at Kemble School, something still unpleasant and *dangerous* here. Had Fiskes like her really ruled this island, ages and ages ago? Lottie closed her eyes and tried to picture her mother's face—the freckled, laughing one from the photograph. She pictured her mother here in this strange world, perfectly at home. She pictured her with dancing eyes as she named a little black bird Trouble. She pictured her mother dying of a horrible plague, embraced in her father's arms. These were not pictures she had ever allowed herself to imagine when her copper box was open. They were nothing like the stories she had made up and told Eliot. These were far more vivid and more terrible altogether.

"There she is!"

Lottie's opened her eyes to find Adelaide, Oliver, and Fife all peering in at her from the doorway. Adelaide looked enraged.

"She's trying to steal it again!" Adelaide said, storming across the room and snatching the vial from Lottie. "I told you two, didn't I?"

"For the love of Oberon," Fife said, "calm down. She was just looking at it, Ada."

"I *was* just looking at it," said Lottie.

"With your eyes shut?" Adelaide snapped. "Don't touch it again. It's Wilfer property, which means that Oliver or I carry it. Not. You."

Lottie glared but said nothing.

"You and Mr. Ingle done with your top-secret talk?" said Fife.

"It's not a secret," said Lottie. "I think you all know everything anyway. You know, about how I'm a halfling?"

"Whoo! Thank Oberon, you've finally figured it out," Fife said, wiping imaginary sweat from his brow. "We thought we were going to have to sit you down and explain where you came from."

"Did Mr. Ingle tell you about the Fiskes?" Oliver asked.

Lottie nodded. "I know why the king wants me. Those things the messenger said at Iris Gate, they were about me, weren't they? I'm the public enemy. You're aiding and abetting *me*."

There was a strange silence in the room, one in which Lottie felt like she was standing outside a conversation and trying to break in. But no one was talking. They were just staring, all staring at each other and not at Lottie. She tried to catch Fife's eye, attempt a smile at Oliver. She had thought, after all, that the three of them were beginning to get along. She wasn't so sure anymore. At last, Fife spoke.

"Glad it was a good chat," he said.

Lottie nodded. "Don't worry. I'm sure that we'll save Mr. Wilfer. All we have to do is make that petition, and Mr. Wilfer is going to be safe, and Eliot's going to be better. It's like I can just feel it now. Maybe," she ventured, "maybe it's the sprite in me, huh?"

"Maybe," Oliver said softly, his eyes turning a deep, thoughtful green.

"Maybe," agreed Fife. "But right now, the sprite in me says it's time to get some sleep."

———

Once, in her English class at Kemble School, Lottie had heard Mr. Kidd say that misery acquainted a man with strange bedfellows. She had never been entirely sure of what that meant, but now, as a scowling Adelaide climbed into a tiny bed with her, Lottie decided that this was precisely what Mr. Kidd had been talking about. When Adelaide's cold toes touched Lottie's feet, she knew that something had to be done, or it was going to be a long, cold-footed night.

"Adelaide . . . ?" Lottie ventured.

Adelaide sniffed. That was promising. Either that, or Adelaide had dust allergies.

"Look, about what happened downstairs. I know you don't like me very much and you don't want me to come along, but I really do want to help you rescue your dad."

Another sniff.

Lottie sighed. "Is this because you think I'm too unrefined and snoopy, or whatever?"

Adelaide shrugged. "Oh, most people are unrefined. Fife, for example, is one of the worst. You see how he treats me. He's always making fun of me, even when he doesn't say a word. It's always been like that, ever since we were little. He and Oliver would go off on adventures in the fens and woods—"

"And they wouldn't invite you?" guessed Lottie.

"No, that's just it! They *did*. I refused to go. Imagine, getting muddy and mixing with will o' the wisps and sometimes even, they said, *Northerlies*. I'm sure those sort are acceptable in their own way, but . . . well! Really! Fife would torment me about it. He called me Prissy Miss Priss, the Superior."

Lottie turned off the bedside lamp to hide her smile, but a tiny giggle still slipped out.

"What?" demanded Adelaide. "*What?*"

"Nothing," said Lottie. It wouldn't be a good idea to tell Adelaide that she thought Fife's title for her fit perfectly.

"Go ahead, take Fife's side," huffed Adelaide. "I can see how he'd appeal to you. I bet your Eliot is just like him."

"Eliot isn't like anyone I know. He's just Eliot. And even if he isn't refined, he knows how to live. That's why I'm not about to let him die."

"Is that so," Adelaide said flatly. "He must be important enough, for you to want to go through all this danger."

"Yes," Lottie said. "Eliot is important enough."

Adelaide sank down into her pillow. To her shock, Lottie saw in the moonlight that there were tears clinging to Adelaide's eyelashes.

"I wish," said Adelaide, "someone cared about me that much."

Lottie tried to think of something to say. This was why social calls with Mrs. Yates' stuffy friends always ended so poorly at Thirsby Square. Lottie could ask a few decent questions like "Where did you buy your atrocious hat?" or "Is your psychotic old cat finally dead?" but she could never think of good answers. Once, when asked most politely by Mrs. Kirkeby what her favorite pastime was, Lottie had replied, "The Renaissance," at which a mortified Mrs. Yates had explained to Lottie that "pastime" and "past time" were two different things. Now what had started out as a simple conversation had turned into something more serious, and Lottie was at a loss as to what to do.

"You don't have to say anything," Adelaide said, guessing Lottie's thoughts. "I already know the problem. No one wants to be my friend. I'm too spoiled and snotty. Then you come along, and the others like you because you're new and exciting. You don't even have to work at it."

"What?" Lottie laughed in disbelief. "Just follow me around back in New Kemble. No one wants me there. I stick out like a sore thumb."

"Really?" Adelaide sounded hopeful.

Lottie nodded. "Eliot is the only friend I've got."

"So," Adelaide said, frowning, "why do you want to go back there?"

Lottie thought about this. "I guess," she said at last, "that even one friend is enough reason."

The girls were silent for a long moment. A gust of cold air rattled through the rotting slats of their window. Lottie's teeth chattered.

"Lottie?" whispered Adelaide. "Maybe I was a little harsh back there on the road."

Lottie squinted at Adelaide's blotchy face in the moonlight.

"I don't know what I'd do if I were in your shoes," Lottie confessed. "I mean, it's been a rotten day for you, to have your father kidnapped and to be kicked out of your own house. So it's okay. I forgive you."

Adelaide stiffened. "That wasn't an apology."

Before Lottie could reply, a sudden, sharp pounding of wood made the girls jump.

"Open up!" shouted a muffled voice from six floors below. "Open in the name of the Southerly Court!"

CHAPTER EIGHT

Wandlebury Wood

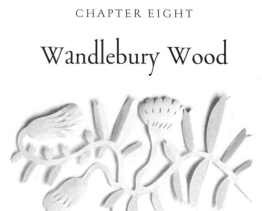

LOTTIE AND ADELAIDE scrambled out of bed and into the hallway. Oliver and Fife were already there, and Mr. Ingle was starting to descend the rickety staircase, which squealed with every step that the innkeeper took. When he reached the first landing, Mr. Ingle looked up and shooed the four of them back.

"Go to my room!" he ordered. "Closet. Trapdoor. Adelaide, I'm giving you permission to eavesdrop."

Lottie hurried with the others to Mr. Ingle's room. A closet door stood ajar in the corner. Fife flung it open wide.

"A trapdoor! What an inn!" he said. "You first, eh, Oliver?"

Oliver crouched inside the empty closet and tugged at something on the floor. There was a thud, and dust swirled across the floor as the trapdoor flew back. A moment later, Oliver had disappeared through the floorboards. Fife and Adelaide followed, leaving Lottie to stare down into the gaping square hole. She wasn't particularly ready to jump into an unknown abyss, especially in a dead house like this one.

"Nothing to be scared of!" Fife called. "It's just a tiny room. Solid floor underfoot."

"Come on!" insisted Adelaide's voice from below. Her pale hand reached up and tugged on Lottie's foot.

"And shut the door after you!" said Fife.

This, Lottie reminded herself, was for Eliot. She and Eliot had climbed in and out of ye ol' porthole in his bedroom ceiling plenty of times; she convinced herself that this was just the same. She grabbed the knotted rope attached to the trapdoor, hoped there wouldn't be cockroaches waiting at the bottom, and jumped down.

She had sealed them up in utter darkness, save for the light of Oliver's eyes, which were glowing yellow like a cat's.

"He wants us to eavesdrop?" said Lottie. "How is anyone supposed to eavesdrop in here?" The only thing that she could hear well was her own unsteady breathing.

"Not just anyone," whispered Oliver. "Adelaide."

"What can you make out so far, Ada?" Fife whispered.

"Shhh!" said Adelaide. "One doesn't just tune through half a dozen flights of wood. Hang on, I'm getting something now. Mr. Ingle's opening the front door."

"What else?" said Oliver. His eyes now glowed a luminescent green.

"He's opening the door," Adelaide said in a tight voice. "It's the Southerly Guard."

"How many?"

"Two, by the sound of it. Yes. There are two of them. Ugh. One of them's got a nasty cold, too. I wish he'd blow his nose already."

Lottie stared into the blackness, in the direction of Adelaide's voice. How could Adelaide have possibly heard all of that? She had to be making it up.

"What are they saying?" Fife asked.

"Shut up!" snapped Adelaide. "Just let me listen!"

Lottie tried unsuccessfully to adjust her eyes to the dark. She still couldn't see a thing. Suddenly, there was a hand on her shoulder.

"Oi, Lottie," Fife whispered, "keeping tense like that leads to high blood pressure and heart complications. Don't stress, hm? No way those Southerly rats will catch us."

Lottie's shoulders relaxed. She hadn't even realized they'd been squeezed up to her ears.

"Th-th-thanks," she whispered, nervous now only at the fact that Fife's hand was still on her shoulder.

"Mm-hm." Fife's hand lifted, and he rustled back into the dark.

Adelaide spoke again. "The Guard says they're searching every house in the city. They're asking Mr. Ingle if he's seen any suspicious characters. Mr. Ingle's saying that he hasn't. Hold on. Wait! He's telling them that he thought he saw four children our age running to the fenland, northward. I think—I think they believe him. Yes! They sound excited now. They're getting out their gengas to alert the rest of the Guard. They're leaving."

Fife heaved a long sigh of relief. "Smart thinking. Though he didn't have to call us *children*."

"No!" cried Adelaide. "Wait, wait! They're coming back. They've got another question. They're asking if he's seen any wisps around."

Fife made a sputtering noise.

"He's saying he hasn't," Adelaide went on. "They're warning against the dangers of wisps, they're reminding him to report suspicious behavior. One of them keeps sniffing. I can't tell if it's Mr. Ingle or not."

"Now they're leaving," Adelaide said after another pause. "Yes. Mr. Ingle's closing the door. He's coming up the stairs. He's running."

"The dangers of wisps?" Fife's voice was low, like a growl. "What liars."

"Why're you so angry, Fife?" whispered Adelaide. "It's not like you've got the Plague or anything."

"What are you all talking about?" asked Lottie. "What are wisps?"

"Mr. Ingle's here," said Adelaide.

The trapdoor flew open, and Mr. Ingle leaned in, puffing uncontrollably.

"Out! Out!" he cried. "You're not safe. They suspect something. I could smell it on them."

Mr. Ingle pulled Adelaide out of the secret room first, followed by Lottie and Fife. Oliver then flung up his arms and struggled to hoist himself out on his own.

"Oh!" said Lottie, bending to reach down. "Need help?"

"No, no, no!" Adelaide shouted, pulling Lottie back. "What're you, crazy? Don't touch his hands!"

Oliver looked up at Lottie with a strange stare, his eyes a saddened gray. She suddenly felt a sting on her left arm. She rubbed it away.

"What makes you think they suspect something?" she asked Mr. Ingle.

"Child, when you've braved as many winters as I, you can smell out distrust. Not only that, but one of those sprites has been trained to smell out wisps."

Mr. Ingle looked pointedly at Fife.

"But Fife is a sprite like us," said Lottie. Then, less certainly, "Isn't he?"

"Not quite," muttered Adelaide.

"Oh, come on, Ada," Fife said. "Just say it. I'm a halfling. That's why Ada hates me," he continued, turning to Lottie. "It's 'cause I don't have a Wilfer family tree as tall as a redwood."

"Children," said Mr. Ingle, "this is not the time to bicker."

"Mr. Ingle's right," said Oliver, who had gotten his footing and pulled himself out of the secret room and was talking in a tone of voice that Lottie had not heard him use before. Instead of poetic and breezy, it was hard, commanding. "There isn't time to argue. If the Guard suspects something, then they'll be back."

"Quiet, everyone!" Adelaide had closed her eyes, her face scrunched in concentration. After a long minute, her eyelids snapped back open. "Mr. Ingle's right. They're still talking out on the street. One of them smelled Fife. They know Mr. Ingle's lied to them. Hang on. They're coming back to search the house! To search the *whole* house."

"You must leave," said Mr. Ingle. "Now."

"Come on," said Adelaide, tugging Lottie out of the room.

Far too much was happening and far too quickly for Lottie to make any sense of it. Back in the girls' bedroom, Lottie laced up Eliot's sneakers and tugged on her periwinkle coat. Adelaide was just about to shove the vial of Otherwise Incurable into her satchel when Lottie caught her wrist.

"It won't be safe like that! Not if we're running and it's bumping around in there. Here." Lottie pulled her green scarf out from her coat pocket. "Wrap it in this. It should keep the glass from shattering."

Adelaide made a face at the scarf, but she grabbed it and did as Lottie had said.

When the girls returned to Mr. Ingle's room, Oliver and Fife were already gone, and Mr. Ingle was leaning over the trapdoor.

"I've given the boys instructions," he said. "This is the old servants' corridor of the inn. Each secret room leads down to another trapdoor, you see, until you reach the back pantry. Then you must run, run, run toward Wandlebury Wood."

Lottie shook her head, bewildered.

"The others will know the way, Charlotte," Mr. Ingle reassured her, placing a hand on her shoulder. "I have given them my best gas lamp for the journey."

A wall-shaking pounding tremored up all six floors of the inn.

"INGLE!" boomed a voice below. "OPEN UP! Open in the name of the Southerly Court!"

"Quickly," said Mr. Ingle. "Through the door."

Adelaide nodded and slipped down into the secret room, hugging her satchel close to her chest.

"What about you, Mr. Ingle?" asked Lottie. "What will they do to you?"

"Don't you worry yourself about that," Mr. Ingle said. "I'll distract them. I've seen worse times than these, and the ol' nose always sniffs me through. More than that, I've got a nephew in high places who's only a genga's flight away. Now listen closely, because there's one last thing I must tell you. These are words to help you should you ever need them on your journey. Remember the words *Vesper Bells*. Can you do that?"

"Vesper Bells," Lottie repeated, nodding. "But when should I say them?"

"When there's nothing left to say," said Mr. Ingle. "When you need them most."

The pounding continued. Something fell and shattered a few floors below.

"Do you have Trouble?" Mr. Ingle asked.

Lottie felt in her pocket. Her knuckles brushed against a small, warm bundle. She nodded.

"I'll take very good care of him."

"Of course you will," said Mr. Ingle. "He's your genga."

"Goodbye, Mr. Ingle," Lottie said.

"Goodbye, Charlotte. And don't worry while you're out there. There's none more suited for danger than a Fiske."

With a nudge, Mr. Ingle sent Lottie down into the secret room and slammed the door shut.

Once, back in Thirsby Square, when Lottie was eight years old, she had decided to run away from home. She had stuffed four oranges, two packages of cheese crackers, and a stockpile of chocolates into her then oversized periwinkle tweed coat and set off in the direction of the bus station. It had been a very emotional parting between her and the green apple tree. She had considered cutting off a branch as a memento, but she finally decided that this would be the equivalent of sawing off one of her own fingers, and therefore a final act of brutality, not love.

Using all of her pocket money, Lottie had meant to catch the 5:25 bus to the harbor and then the 7:30 ferry to Boston, where she would make her living as a street performer until a talent scout discovered her and put her on Broadway. (This was, of course, before Lottie and Eliot had met and concocted their own brilliant plan.)

There was only one flaw in the scheme: Lottie had a horrible sense of direction. She had managed to get lost in the first five minutes of her escape, and Mrs. Yates' cook had found Lottie curled up and sobbing on the steps of an abandoned cannery. Since then, Lottie had not cared for venturing off anywhere without clear direction. She had learned her way to the library, to school, and to the Barmy Badger, but if ever she had to bike somewhere else, she was sure to bring along a map and clear directions. Even then, she usually arrived some ten minutes late and on the verge of a bad spell.

Now, as Lottie bounded after a fast-fleeing Oliver, Fife, and Adelaide through the back garden of Ingle Inn and onto a cobblestone road, that eight-year-old fear crept into her gut.

"Where are we going?" she puffed.

"To the Southerly Court, of course," said Adelaide, grabbing Lottie's arm and dragging her at a dizzying speed. "Now hush. I'm trying to listen to what's going on back there."

Oliver ran ahead of them all, holding aloft Mr. Ingle's best gas lamp to light their way through the dark of midnight. He led them around a corner, down an alley, and past two more bends of cobblestone roads and tall brick houses. Even though it would not have helped, Lottie wished that she could at least make out the names of the streets.

"Anything else?" Oliver called back to Adelaide.

Adelaide shook her head. "Poor Mr. Ingle. It sounds like they're turning the place inside out."

"How can you hear all that?" Lottie asked, breathless.

Adelaide ignored the question. "We're running out of my range, Oliver," she called instead. "Yes, I've lost them. I've lost them completely."

"There!" shouted Fife, pointing ahead to a green break in the brick houses. "There it is, Wandlebury Plaza! It'll lead us straight to the wood."

"Are you sure?" asked Adelaide.

"No, Ada, that was just for kicks," Fife shot back a pinched smile. "Sure, I'm sure."

The plaza was little more than a well-trimmed square of hedges and rosebushes, but a statue of a fierce-faced, winged creature towered above them all, and in the plaza lamplight Lottie could make out the inscribed name KING OBERON I at the statue's feet. He was far more intimidating than even Quincy Francis Eugene Wilfer, but he did not intimidate Lottie for long, because they were already pushing on through the plaza and into a shroud of trees behind it.

"We're going into the wood now," Oliver whispered

back to them, anxious blue eyes aglow. "So just keep close. Everyone all right?"

Lottie nodded and then proceeded to trip over a tree root.

"Hang in there, Lottie Fiske." Fife laughed. "There's a clearing a little ways up."

By "a little ways up," it turned out Fife had meant a good hour's worth of stumbling. No one spoke another word on the journey into the wood, and though Oliver eventually slowed his impossibly fast run to a brisk walk, the pace still wore Lottie down. By her twelfth stumble, she felt mindless, breathless, and chilled down to her toenails. What made it worse was that the others plowed on without tripping or gasping for air or even shivering.

Branch, ditch, plod, plod, shiver, branch, root, *ouch!*, thistle . . . plod, plod. Lottie's thoughts dulled, and her discomfort began mingling with her envy of the others' ease. Adelaide had been right: Lottie *was* slowing them down. Maybe being sprites gave the others an advantage for navigating the dips and branches of the wood. Maybe being half human made Lottie just as inept in this world as she had been back in New Kemble.

Lottie shiveringly yanked her foot out of a puddle of mud that Adelaide had gracefully hopped over and, at last, she cleared her throat. She had to insist on a rest. She just had to! As she opened her blue-lipped mouth, though, Lottie noticed that the trees were thinning out. The moonlight became steadier and steadier overhead until, in a minute's time, they were finally in the clearing that Fife had promised. The grassy space was bordered on all sides by old ash trees, warped and tangled in the same way that Lottie's hair looked on a particularly windy day.

"If we were being followed," Oliver said, "we would know it by now. Mr. Ingle must've been able to ward off the Guard."

"Do you think they hurt him?" Lottie wasn't sure she wanted to hear the answer to her question.

"Not a chance," Fife said, licking his lower lip. "The Southerly Guard couldn't arrest Mr. Ingle if they didn't find us in his house. And they didn't, because he saved our hides, Puck bless him."

Lottie felt a little better, though not entirely reassured. Then they all agreed to stop for the night. Oliver and

Adelaide took it upon themselves to "scout the perimeters," as Adelaide called it, and Lottie and Fife scrounged around for dry branches and brush to start a fire. When they met back up, Adelaide picked out the sturdiest branches that Lottie and Fife had collected and produced thin blankets and twine from her satchel.

"For making tents," she explained.

After assembling the two tents, everyone agreed that they were hungry, since the flower-bulb soup that Mr. Ingle had served them earlier that night hadn't been the most filling dish. They huddled around a small campfire that Oliver had started by using a matchbook from Adelaide's pack.

"Thought of everything, didn't you, Ada?" said Fife.

"Don't call me Ada." Then Adelaide dug into her satchel to produce some bread and sharp cheddar cheese. "*Now* you can thank me for thinking of everything."

Even Lottie had to admit, she was glad that Adelaide had spent those extra minutes filling her satchel in Iris Gate. They would've all been far hungrier and colder otherwise.

"Watch this," Fife said, spearing his piece of cheese with a sharp stick and singeing it in the fire. "It's better toasted."

Adelaide glowered at Fife like he had just pronounced that meat was better eaten raw, and Lottie stifled a laugh into her hunk of bread. Oliver took an oversized bite of his cheese, swallowed, and spoke up.

"Right," he said, dusting bread crumbs off his hands and into the flames. "The next order of business is setting up a night watch. I think we should have a rotation, always someone on guard while the rest of us get some shut-eye."

They all agreed. Oliver offered to take first watch. Lottie jumped at the chance to volunteer second, relieved to be able to contribute something to a group in which she kept feeling outdone. Adelaide was to take the third watch and Fife the last.

"You might have a little trouble waking me," Fife told Adelaide. "I'm a very sound sleeper."

"No worries," Adelaide said sweetly. "I'll just kick your face till you come to."

That settled, Fife, Adelaide, and Lottie retired to their tents, leaving Oliver stationed on a log next to the campfire. Inside their tent, Lottie and Adelaide nestled into the extra blankets that Adelaide had packed. The blankets may have been dusty and moth-eaten, but they were warm, and Lottie was asleep in moments. Her last thought was of Eliot's green sneakers, still on her feet.

Lottie was home again. Or, rather, she was at the Barmy Badger. She and Eliot had climbed out of ye ol' porthole and were sitting up on the rooftop facing the back garden, their heels propped in the leaf-clogged gutters. Eliot was eating a green apple, a treat that Lottie had brought over from Thirsby Square. When he was finished, Eliot tossed the apple core off the roof, where it landed in the thick underbrush below.

"Careful," Lottie warned him. "You might end up with an apple tree in your own backyard!"

Eliot laughed. "Maybe then I'll get my own magic box and birthday gifts."

Lottie giggled. Eliot looked better, much healthier than he had the last time she'd seen him. He even looked a little—younger.

Then Lottie realized that she was dreaming, and not just dreaming, but *remembering*. It was a memory of last September, when she and Eliot had spent a whole Saturday eating themselves sick with apples atop his roof. It had been damp and windy that day, and the next Monday Eliot had missed school because of a cold he'd caught. He'd missed Tuesday, too, and Wednesday, and then the whole week, and it was then that Lottie had thought for the first time that Eliot might be *very sick*—permanently sick, *broken*.

"Eliot," she said now, though it was her memory-dream and not really her saying it, "just think. A few more years and we'll be out of this place, in Boston, together."

"Taking the world by storm!" said Eliot, fist-bumping the air.

"Lottie and Eliot."

"Eliot and Lottie."

"Unstoppable!" she cried.

"Incurable," said Eliot.

Lottie froze.

No, that word was not part of the memory. Not at all.

"What did you say?" Lottie asked quietly.

When Eliot turned to face her, the healthy gleam in his eyes had gone. He was no longer the Eliot from one year ago, but the Eliot from that last night in the Barmy Badger, when she'd stormed out on him without bothering to apologize.

"Incurable," Eliot repeated. "Only two, three weeks to live."

Lottie woke cold and rolled over to discover that Adelaide had stolen every spare scrap of blanket. She could not remember her dream, but whatever it had been had left Lottie with an achy, empty feeling, and the desire to move around. She poked her head out of the tent. The small campfire was dwindling. Oliver was hunched over it, facing the wood. A single bronze-colored curl was wrapped around his thumb, and he was twirling it slowly. Lottie checked her wristwatch and gasped. Oliver started at the sound. He smiled guiltily when he saw Lottie and dropped his hand from his hair. His eyes were a cautious shade of green.

"You let me sleep through half of my watch!" she accused.

"You need the sleep more than I do," Oliver said, shrugging back toward the wood. "You're still getting used to a new world."

Lottie drew near the fire.

"Maybe I was tired," she admitted, rubbing at her still drooping eyelids, "but heroes need their sleep, too, you know."

Lottie had heard that line in a war movie once and thought it clever to use now.

Oliver poked the fire with the branch in his hand. "I'm not a hero," he said, looking uncomfortable.

Perhaps not quite so clever as she imagined.

"Well," Lottie said, "what else do you call a mysterious boy who goes around quoting poetry and then taking charge like you did back there at Ingle Inn? That's heroic enough."

"Wilfers always take charge," said Oliver. "And poetry? Poetry's what makes it worth it."

"Makes what worth it?"

"Life."

"Oh." Lottie rubbed her chilled hands together. "Well, if you are going to take over my post, can I at least join?"

Oliver tensed. "If you'd like," he said.

Lottie sat down, and Oliver shrank away to the opposite side of the log. Lottie frowned. Did Oliver not want to sit next to her? Did he really not like her that much? Lottie ducked to sniff the underarm of her coat. She had been wearing the same clothes for a while now, and she was a little smelly. Lottie blushed and found that, unlike when she was around Eliot, with whom she'd traipsed through mud and stinky things since she was a kid, she actually minded if Oliver thought she stank.

"Oliver," she said, eying the distance between them, "if I asked you a question, would you answer it? I mean, really answer it, not just quote poetry."

"As I ponder'd in silence," said Oliver, "returning upon my poems, considering, lingering long, a Phantom arose before me, with distrustful aspect."

Lottie blinked. "Did you just call me a phantom?"

A grin crooked up Oliver's face. His eyes turned violet. "Lottie Fiske," he said. "I think we're beginning to understand each other."

Lottie laughed, but as she rolled her eyes, she found that tears were unexpectedly coming out of them. Something, *something* about Oliver had tugged her memory to Eliot—their card games and stargazing under ye ol' porthole, Lottie posing for painted portraits and her and Eliot's exchange of sweet-so-sours.

Oh, yes. She remembered: "You and I," Eliot had said one day, as they took turns peering out of his telescope through the open porthole, "we understand each other, Lottie Fiske."

Lottie's throat stung as her dream washed back over her. Had Eliot grown more ill in the past day? The tears came faster, and Lottie stopped them with her sleeve.

"Lottie?" said Oliver, looking flustered. "I'm sorry! I didn't mean to be difficult. I just—I find it hard to speak to people sometimes. It's easier for me to say what I feel using poems. But you can ask me anything. Please, just ask."

Lottie patted the tears away hurriedly, letting out an embarrassing hiccup. *Terrific*, she thought, *now I'm smelling bad* and *blubbering*.

At last, she found her voice.

"Fife showed me his mark earlier. The mark of the Northerly Court?"

Oliver looked at Lottie with that sly expression from the night before, when they'd first met. "Is it true you don't have one?" he asked.

"What, a mark?" said Lottie. She tugged her wrist out of her coat sleeve to show Oliver. "No, of course not."

"Then it is true," said Oliver, leaning over to get a good look. "You haven't got a mark, and you're a Fiske to boot."

Lottie leaned in closer at the mention of the name Fiske. As she did, Oliver backed farther away, inching down the log.

I must smell terrible, Lottie thought miserably.

She put her hands in her pockets, and her fingers closed around Trouble's warm and downy body. She pulled him out. Trouble gave a terrific rustle of his feathers and a grateful tweet. He fluttered out of Lottie's hand and perched on her shoulder.

"His name is Trouble," Lottie told Oliver, and she couldn't help but feel a little proud at the introduction. "Mr. Ingle had been keeping him safe for me."

"He's beautiful," Oliver whispered.

He reached out a finger to stroke Trouble's head, but Trouble gave an offended squawk and nipped at Oliver's hand with his tiny beak.

Oliver quickly tugged his hand away. "I guess there's a reason he's called Trouble."

Lottie suppressed a smile, then took Trouble up in cupped hands and fixed him with a disapproving look. "Trouble," she said, "that's not nice."

Trouble just rustled his jet-black wings and gave a careless chirp. Lottie smiled and then carefully tucked him back into her pocket. It was still such a strange sensation, and Lottie half felt like she was doing something wrong.

"I've never seen a warbler genga before," Oliver said lowly. "Wilfers are served by finches."

"So, what, there's a different type of bird for each family?"

Oliver nodded. "And every family member's genga is a different—"

"Color!" finished Lottie. "I remember now. Adelaide has a purple finch. It helped us down the apple tree in Thirsby Square. She called it— Lila, right?"

Oliver nodded. "Mine's called Keats. Father named him after his favorite human poet."

Lottie bit her lip, then scooted in more confidentially. Oliver had reached the end of the log by now and had nowhere left to scoot. His eyes shifted to an apprehensive golden shade.

"Do you know how to use yours?" he asked her.

Lottie nodded. Then she paused. Then she shook her head. "But I'm going to learn."

"You'll learn fast," Oliver said. "It's not that hard. Gengas are very intuitive to their owners, you know. All of us are born with one. No one really knows how it happens, but we need gengas. They're what connect us to the magic in Limn; they help us to sense it and use it. They help us to travel by tree. Only gengas can tell us which branch of an apple tree is a silver bough—that's the bough we have to pull to make an apple tree work. And, well, they're just nice to have around. I always feel much happier when my genga is flying."

Lottie remembered the white finch back in Thirsby Square. She nodded. She thought she understood what Oliver meant.

"Gengas can do other things, too," said Oliver. "Some are extremely talented. But you've got time to figure out what yours can and can't do."

Lottie glanced down at the little lump in her pocket. Oh, the time she could spend just imagining what Trouble might be able to do!

"So . . . gengas are what make sprites special?"

"Well," said Oliver, "that and their keens, of course."

"Keens?"

The word was familiar. Lottie remembered Mr. Ingle using it when he had talked about her parents.

"Yeah," said Oliver. "You know the five senses?"

"Of course."

"Well, of our five senses, each sprite's got one sense stronger than all the rest. I guess you'd call it a sort of—sharpness. It's a sense that's keener than usual."

"Is that why Adelaide can hear things from far away?" Lottie asked in sudden understanding. "She's got a sharpness of hearing?"

Oliver nodded. "Though the keen is different for everyone. Some sprites with a hearing keen can only hear into the next room. Some can hear across oceans, if they're trained properly. Others can even hear certain types of thoughts."

"And that's why Mr. Ingle talked about smells so much, isn't it? He can smell things that others can't, like how suspicious the Southerly Guard were!" Lottie was growing more and more excited. Like the proper flip of a lever, Oliver's explanation had started a whir of gears in Lottie's head. "That's why Fife—! Oh. What is Fife's keen, exactly?"

"Fife can—um, *taste*."

"Taste?" echoed Lottie. She frowned. "Taste what?"

"Words," said Oliver. "Though you're better off asking him about it. He's got this particular way of describing it. Something having to do with soup. He calls it 'flavoring.'

But Fife doesn't like people talking about his keen behind his back."

"Oh." Lottie hadn't yet lost her excitement. "You can tell me about your keen, though. It's why your eyes change color, isn't it?"

Oliver's eyes turned a cloudy gray. "That's part of it, yes."

Lottie nodded expectantly, eagerly. "So, what? Can you see special colors? See from very far away? Can you see through things, like X-ray vision?"

"No," said Oliver. "I mean, there are sprites who can do those things, but my keen doesn't have anything to do with sight."

"Then what is it?"

"Touch. My tutor calls it involuntary pigmentary transference."

Oliver's voice had been growing lower, grittier, and more sullen the longer they talked. He was not looking at Lottie anymore, and the firelight cast deep shadows on his face.

"What's involuntary pigmentary transference?"

Lottie felt dizzy, as though she were suspended at the edge of a precipice, about to be pushed.

Oliver's eyes finally met hers. "Have you really not figured it out?"

Oliver nodded toward her left arm. Lottie clasped it instinctively. She pulled back the sleeve of her periwinkle coat, and the firelight lit a fading handprint. Another finger had disappeared from the handprint. The imprint of only three fingers remained, and even those had lightened from black to gray. Oliver leaned in to get a better look at the mark. His face was drawn tight about the eyes and mouth.

"What?" Lottie asked.

"Nothing." He straightened up and scooted away, regaining his cautious distance from her. "It's—it's nothing."

Lottie, in turn, found herself looking over Oliver's wounded arm, bandaged up from wrist to elbow.

It came together with startling force: the white finch, the falling tree, the hurt boy at the Flying Squirrel. Lottie understood.

"Your genga is white, isn't it?"

Oliver did not need to nod.

"It was your genga I saw in my apple tree all those mornings," she said softly. "The white finch. It was *your* genga that I saw in Skelderidge Park, after the accident with the falling tree."

"After Father got your last letter, he asked me to do him a favor," Oliver said. "He wanted to help your friend, but he didn't know if you'd be ready to visit our world yet. He also wanted to know if you were safe. So I sent Keats to Thirsby Square all those months ago, and he reported back to Iris Gate every night."

"Reported?"

"I told you," said Oliver. "Gengas can do lots of interesting things. Keats would report to me, and then I'd report to Father."

"What did you report?" Lottie asked, her chest thrumming.

"That you were up to coming here," Oliver said. "That you seemed pretty terrific as far as humans go."

Their eyes met, and Lottie felt like laughing. At least he hadn't said that she was smelly.

"As far as humans go?" she repeated.

"Well, I'd never met a human before," Oliver said defensively.

"And that night at Skelderidge Park," said Lottie, "you were the one who rescued me from the tree."

"A rumor got loose in Limn a few weeks ago," said Oliver, "that there was a Fiske still living in Earth. The king heard the rumors and wanted you captured. So he gave orders to my father and Grissom."

"The king's right- and left-hand sprites."

Oliver nodded. "Of course, Father already knew all about you. He'd been keeping you safe and hidden for years, ever since your parents passed away. Well, Grissom got nosy. He found out who you were and where you were living, and he also found out that Father was trying to keep you from the king. Father knew Grissom didn't trust him and that he was monitoring all his movements. That's why, on the night Grissom tried to kidnap you, Father sent me and Adelaide into your world, to rescue you."

"And you did," Lottie whispered. "Adelaide rescued me from Grissom, and you're the one who rescued me from that tree."

"I'm the one who gave you that," Oliver corrected, pointing to her arm.

"Involuntary pigmentary transference," Lottie whispered. "That means—that means that you turn things colors without meaning to."

"Skin," Oliver said. "I turn skin colors. Your skin, anyone's skin. Most sprites can choose whether or not to use their keen. Not me. I can't shut it off. When I touch someone, or they touch my hands, I hurt them. I hurt them terribly, and I leave a mark. The stains last for months and months. And my eyes? They'll always change, whether I want them to or not. I can't have a single feeling without it showing up in my eyes."

Lottie stared at the fading mark on her arm. Her stain didn't seem to be lasting for months and months. At the rate it was disappearing, it might be gone in a few days. Perhaps Oliver was being too hard on himself.

"I don't understand," she said. "Why can't you control it?"

"I'm messed up," Oliver said matter-of-factly. "I'm a fluke. Tutor says it's a pigmentary imbalance in my body. There's not a why to it, that's just how it is."

"Well," said Lottie, trying to be helpful, "why can't you wear a special sort of gloves, so that you don't go around turning people different colors?"

Oliver shook his head. "It's not that easy. The color bleeds straight through, from skin to skin. There are potions and trainings and diets that don't work, either. My father's a healer, Lottie. Don't you think he's tried everything to make me better?"

"But that's not fair!" Lottie said. "Aren't these keens supposed to be a good thing? Why would you get one as awful as that?"

Oliver opened his mouth, and he looked very much like he was about to quote another poem. Then he seemed to change his mind.

"I don't know," he said.

Nothing more. Lottie stared at Oliver and wondered if being so honest was peculiar to sprites, or just peculiar to Oliver. A gust blew through the wood, carrying along a batch of breeze-borne leaves. One caught in Lottie's hair, but she paid no mind to it.

"I think," she said at last, "that it's very brave of you."

"Do you?" Oliver asked. "Is it brave to just exist when something is wrong with you?"

"Existing can be brave enough some days, don't you think?"

Their gazes met, and Oliver gave Lottie the smallest of smiles.

"That," he said, "is the most decent thing anyone's ever said to me."

Lottie no longer felt so self-conscious about being smelly. "Glad to be of service," she said.

That was when Lottie heard it: a scampering sound from behind the circle of ash trees. Oliver had heard it, too. He sprang to his feet with Lottie, and they both stood, quiet, listening. Ten seconds, then twenty, then thirty passed. Finally, Lottie spoke up.

"I don't think there's anything to worry—"

Her words were interrupted by a shrill scream. As Lottie fell to the ground, something sharp pierced her wrist, and the shrieks grew louder and shriller. Only as the ground began to slide beneath her back did Lottie realize that the shrieking was her own.

CHAPTER NINE

The Barghest

LOTTIE FISKE HAD NOT been a spectacular child growing up. She had never won an essay contest or a spelling bee, and Mrs. Yates had never put her artwork on the refrigerator. In one thing, however, Lottie was most singularly distinguished: she didn't make a fuss when she got hurt. When she scraped her knee or fell off the monkey bars or had a bad spell or even broke her collarbone, the most Lottie offered were a few sniffs and a tear or two. Once, she had fallen down an entire flight of stairs at Kemble School, courtesy of the hand of Pen Bloomfield, and just to spite

Pen, Lottie had gotten up and limped off without so much as a yelp.

Lottie thought that because Mrs. Yates was such an emotionless person herself, her guardian secretly liked this one quality—if only one—in Lottie. Once, Lottie had overheard Mrs. Yates say to a boarder, "Mind like a sieve, that child, but she has a good head on her shoulders when it comes to scrapes." Those words had been as precious as chocolate to Lottie, and she had made it a point ever afterward to have just as good a head on her shoulders as she could muster, even when one of those shoulders got dislocated.

So now, even though Mrs. Yates was miles, even worlds away, Lottie promptly stopped her screaming, shut her mouth, and craned her neck to see what had caused her to fall over in the first place.

It was a dog. Or a wolf. Or a lion. Lottie could not quite make out which. It was a slick, black thing with a gray mane running down its back and with silver pinpricks for eyes—those pinprick eyes from the mulberry bushes at Iris Gate. The owner of those eyes had been real after all, and now its teeth were dragging Lottie toward the wood by her right wrist. Once Lottie had made sense of all of this, she acted quickly. She wrenched her free hand toward the creature's muzzle and made a desperate swat at its nose. The animal unclamped Lottie's wrist just long enough to give an annoyed snap at her swatting hand. Teeth sunk into skin. There was a sudden spray of blood that wet Lottie's cheeks and turned her stomach. Then the animal reclaimed its grip on her wrist and continued to drag Lottie toward the wood.

That's when the bad spell began. Lottie closed her eyes and clenched her teeth. She felt her chest crumple like a sheet of scrap paper being wadded into a ball. She tried to breathe in measured gasps, just as she had been taught by the doctor as a little girl, but each time she breathed in, she could only smell the fierce metallic scent of her own blood. She heard Adelaide shouting and she saw Oliver's feet chasing after her, but the closer Oliver's feet got, the faster the animal dragged Lottie and the more pain that shot through her wrist. At last, the mess in her chest began to fade, and Lottie found her voice again. She yelled the first, idiotic thing that came to mind.

"STOP!"

In the crack of a second, the animal stopped, heaving rasping breaths. The crumpled paper inside Lottie began to smooth itself out. She blinked, amazed. Was it possible? Had the animal actually *obeyed* her?

"Let go of me!" she sputtered.

Immediately, the animal unclenched its teeth, sending a new shooting pain through Lottie's wrist. The creature stooped over her, panting as though it would still like nothing better than to sink its fangs back into her.

"G-go!" she said, forcing herself up on her elbows.

The animal made a small, whining noise and dashed off. Its tail smacked Lottie's cheek as it fled into the darkness of the wood. Lottie watched the animal's retreat, and though she was still trembling from her bad spell and could see blood oozing from her hand, she had never before felt so strangely *powerful*. She looked up to see Oliver staring after the creature in mint-eyed astonishment.

"H-how—?" he stammered. "How did you do that?"

Fife and Adelaide pushed past him, offering Lottie hands that Oliver could not, and Lottie leaned on their shoulders as they dragged her back to the campfire. Adelaide lowered Lottie to the ground, propping her against the log by the fire.

Fife knelt by her side. "Still with us?"

Lottie produced a strangled noise in the affirmative.

"That was incredible," Fife said. "You're, like, my new hero! No wait, heroine?"

"Fife," snapped Adelaide, "she's losing blood."

"Right," said Fife, and he riffled in his shirt pocket to produce a kingfisher the color of daffodils.

Fife lowered his lips to the bird's tiny head.

"Medical supplies, Spool, please and thanks."

The genga shivered at Fife's command. Lottie rubbed at her eyes with her bloodied hand, but she was not seeing things: something coming out of the bird's mouth—something too unnaturally large to have fit inside a kingfisher, let alone a kingfisher's beak. It was a silver canister covered in yellow film. Fife caught the canister in one hand.

"Good girl," he said, and after a kiss to the bird's head, Fife tucked her back into his pocket.

"My medical canister," Fife explained calmly to Lottie, swiping away at the canister's filmy covering and unscrewing its lid. "It's a vital tool for anyone aspiring to be a healer's apprentice."

"What's Oliver doing?" Adelaide whispered.

Oliver was still on the very edge of the clearing. He was hunched over and scooping something off the ground.

Lottie glanced over. "He's found some—ow!"

"Sorry," Fife said, turning over Lottie's bloody hand. "Just assessing the damage. It looks like he bit you pretty badly here. There's an awful lot of blood for such a small wound. It must be deep."

"FIFE. JUST FIX HER."

"Okay! *Okay,* Ada. Sheesh."

Fife rummaged through the canister and produced a bottle and a small metal compact. With unnatural quickness, he untucked his white cloth shirt, ripped a sloppy square of fabric from its hem, and bunched it in his hand. Tipping the bottle, he dabbed its contents onto the cloth. Lottie braced herself for the sting of rubbing alcohol as Fife brought the cloth to her skin, but, surprisingly, she felt nothing more than cool dampness.

"That's good stuff," she mumbled.

Fife smiled warily and continued dabbing. "It's Piskie Juice," he told her. "Exceptionally effective and utterly painless."

"Fife's not a trained healer," whispered Adelaide, who was watching Fife's work intently. "He just thinks he knows what he's doing."

"Encouraging words, Ada, as always," Fife said, pulling a needle and thread from the metal compact. Lottie's eyes widened. She thought it best to look away.

"This is going to hurt," apologized Fife, "but if it makes you feel any better, I learned how to sew from the best."

Lottie nodded, her gaze still averted.

"Lucky he didn't snap off a finger, eh, Lottie?" Fife went on. "Personally, I prefer you with all of your digits."

Lottie glanced up at Fife's nervous face and felt a surge of gratitude. She understood: he was trying to distract her from the pain. Though the stitching took longer than Lottie thought she had stomach for, and though each prick in her hand bit just as strongly as the one before it, the damage was finally sewn up. Next, Fife turned his attention to the wrist by which the creature had dragged Lottie.

"Not so bad, this one. I would've thought it'd be worse, the way he was hauling you. But it's only badly chafed right here."

He rubbed his thumb across her reddened wrist. Lottie jerked it back.

"It still hurts," she informed him.

"Right," Fife said. "I'll just dab some more Piskie Juice and wrap it up, too, for good measure. To prevent infection."

"For Titania's sake, Fife," groaned Adelaide. "Stop talking like a professional."

Fife ignored the remark and kept right on dabbing.

At last, Lottie's wrist had been securely wrapped up in yet more fabric from Fife's shirt so that, by the end of the process, Fife looked the part of a street urchin who had just come out of a fistfight, clothes torn and bloodstained.

Oliver returned from the edge of the clearing, his eyes a dark, troubled gray. He dropped something at Adelaide's feet. Adelaide picked the object up, cried out, and threw it to Fife as though it had burned her. All three shared a look of horror.

"Looks like we've got new company," said Fife.

"What do you mean?" asked Lottie.

Fife placed the object in Lottie's bandaged palm. It was a rusted bronze tag, and on it was etched, in black, the shape of a diamond. Lottie recognized the symbol from Fife's arm.

"Seems the Northerlies know about you, too," Oliver said.

"So, what are we going to do?" Lottie asked.

"Clear out of here as fast as possible," said Fife, and Adelaide actually nodded in agreement. "I dunno why the Northerlies are after you, but believe me, you don't want to run into them out here in the wood."

"This one must've been a scout," said Oliver, "which means there are bound to be more where it came from. If that's true, we're going to need protection for the rest of our trip. We've still got a good day and night's walk left to the Southerly Court, and I don't think we'll be making it unwatched."

There was a pregnant silence that made Lottie look up. Oliver and Adelaide were staring at Fife. He shrank back, scratching his messy mane of black hair.

"Oh, no," he said, shaking his head. "No, no, no. You couldn't drag me back there by wild harpies!"

"Fife—"

"NO!"

"You know it's the safest way."

"It's under quarantine."

"What a stupid excuse," said Adelaide. "Ollie and I are inoculated, and halflings are immune to the Plague. You know that."

"Think of Lottie, Fife," said Oliver, but he was smiling. He looked like he already knew he would win this argument.

Fife lolled his head toward Lottie. "It's a bad business, this trying to be a good sprite."

"Fife—" began Adelaide.

"Yes, I know!" he interrupted. "Fine. Fine! But I'm telling you, I don't know how much they'll be willing to help. And you"—he pointed fiercely at Oliver—"owe me one. Two, more like. Don't think I've forgotten that I practically saved your life at the Flying Squirrel."

"It's my fault," said Lottie. "I sent that thing back into the wood. It would've been better to kill it."

"It's never better to kill," said Oliver.

"Anyway," said Fife, "a Barghest doesn't die."

Barghest. So that was what the creature had been. It seemed even fiercer now that it had a name.

Packing up went far quicker than unpacking. Adelaide shoved blankets and twine back into her satchel in a slipshod jumble that made the bag bulge at the latches. When Adelaide heaved the satchel onto her shoulder with a grunt, Lottie realized how heavy a load it must be. Fife had noticed the same thing.

"Here," Fife said, tugging on the bag. "Let me help."

"I'd like to see you try," challenged Adelaide, jerking the bag free from his hands. "I'm every bit as strong as you, Fife Dulcet."

"I didn't say you weren't! I just—"

"I'm fine," said Adelaide, though she was bent with the satchel's weight. "Shouldn't you be worrying about navigating us out of here? You're the one who knows where we're going now, genius."

Fife snorted. "Fine, Prissy Miss Priss, the Superior," he muttered, brushing past Adelaide and Lottie and pointing into the trees. "Light, please, Ollie."

Oliver clicked on Mr. Ingle's lamp. He glanced back at the girls with a grim smile, his eyes a soft peach color. Then he joined up with Fife. Lottie gulped. She wasn't quite ready to go wood-conquering again. Adelaide was stooped beside her, marching determined steps with the satchel she had so stubbornly kept. Lottie rolled her eyes. She had a good mind to let Adelaide keep at it, but that resolve only made it so far as the edge of the clearing.

"Oh, honestly," she sighed, tugging at Adelaide's satchel. "Let me have a turn."

"You're injured," said Adelaide, yanking the satchel back. "I don't want your help. Didn't you hear what I just told Fife?"

"Yes," said Lottie, "but that's because it was Fife."

Adelaide looked shocked.

"I guess it is just because it was Fife," she slowly admitted.

Then, to Lottie's surprise, Adelaide began to giggle. Lottie laughed a little in return.

"What's so funny?" Fife called back.

"We're running from a Barghest, the Southerly Guard, and who knows what else through a cold, dreary wood in the middle of the night!" Adelaide called back. "What's funny about that?"

"Exactly!" Fife sounded satisfied.

"Let me carry it?" Lottie offered again, this time more kindly. "Please?"

Adelaide hesitated a moment more, then nodded. She handed the satchel over to Lottie's keeping.

"That's—surprisingly refined of you."

Lottie smiled. "Yeah, well, maybe you're rubbing off on me."

"Possible. Now hurry up, or that buffoon of a boy will leave us behind."

To Lottie's horror, they moved through the wood at an even faster pace with Fife in the lead. At the outset, she tripped every other step and jumped at the sound of rustling leaves, remembering all too well the Barghest's pinprick eyes and fierce jaws. They pressed on and on and on, and at last Lottie began to master the art of maneuvering underbrush with fewer stumbles and scrapes.

Hours passed. The leaves began to grow less dense and the dark less thick, and the slats of the growing morning light finally ate up enough shadow for Oliver to turn off his lamp. Without the need to keep near the light, Lottie slowed her pace behind the boys, close enough to see them but far enough to regain some strength.

Lottie heard a faint chirping sound. She frowned and looked down at her coat pocket. *Trouble.*

She tucked her hand inside and removed the bundle of black feathers. Trouble peered up at Lottie and then gave a violent shake of his feathers that Lottie couldn't help feel was *indignant*. Then he gave another chirp, louder than the rest, his eyes fixed on Lottie.

"I'm sorry," Lottie said. "I haven't forgotten about you."

Trouble made a low, rumbling sound. He seemed to be assessing her apology.

"He's rather ill-behaved, isn't he?"

Lottie looked up to find Adelaide walking in stride with her.

"No, he isn't," she said defensively, cupping her fingers around the bird's head as though to shield him from Adelaide's words. "He was just lonely and—and concerned. He'd been in my pocket too long."

Adelaide snorted. "Gengas are *meant* to travel in pockets. Lila hasn't been complaining. But then, Lila was properly trained."

Trouble turned his head toward Adelaide and squawked. Lottie smirked.

"Maybe," she said, "Trouble is just more adventurous."

"Hm. I suppose. If you want to call it that."

Lottie gave Trouble an approving smile and stroked back his soft feathers. Trouble pressed his head against the crook of Lottie's finger with a happy tweet. Then he fluttered out of Lottie's hand and swooped upward, flapping his wings in a blithe, lazy way as the girls walked on.

"Adelaide?" Lottie said. "Have you heard anything?"

"You have two ears," said Adelaide. "Aren't you using them?"

"I meant," puffed Lottie, crossing over a narrow trough of rotting leaves, "your *keen*."

She was secretly very pleased with herself for the use of her new vocabulary.

Adelaide trotted in silence for a moment longer. Then she shook her head. "No sound of the Southerly Guard. And animals, yes, but not so much as a breath from that Barghest."

Lottie nodded. "Okay. Thanks."

Then she couldn't help it. She had to ask.

"Have you always been able to hear like that?"

Adelaide slowed her pace a fraction so that Lottie could better keep up with her.

"Since I started sharpening, yes," she said.

"What's sharpening?"

"You know," said Adelaide, "sharpening your keen? Learning how to control it, sharpening what it can do. I started a little early, but Father said I was ready at five."

"You mean a keen is like a—sword?" said Lottie.

Adelaide frowned. "I don't know. A keen just *is*. Everyone talks about it that way. You start sharpening your keen at six and you keep at it until you're sixteen. Dedalus, our tutor, says that by my sixteenth I'll be able to hear the goings-on of all of New Albion, if I want." She paused. "Of course, Oliver wasn't like that. He started using his keen right away, but that's not common. And he's not a freak, if that's what you're thinking. Just because he can't touch other people—"

"I didn't say he was a freak!" said Lottie. "I think it's great."

"Great, huh?" Adelaide sniffed. "Is it great for the shiest sprite in all Albion Isle to have his every emotion showing in his eyes?"

"He isn't *that* shy."

"Yes, he is," retorted Adelaide. "When we were growing up, he barely said a word. He read, though. Father gave him books of poetry. Human poetry. He said that it would help Ollie to express himself. And now you see what that's gone and done. Ollie hardly spoke a word that wasn't a quotation until he met—"

Adelaide's face twisted up like a wrenched washcloth.

"Fife," Lottie guessed. "He was worse before he met Fife, wasn't he?"

Adelaide nodded stiffly. "But that still doesn't mean that Fife is good for him. Southerlies aren't supposed to be friends with people like that."

"It must be exciting," Lottie said, skirting around the subject of Fife, "to be able to hear all the things you do."

"You might think that," Adelaide said, "but you'd be surprised at how little you'd like to hear when people are behind closed doors, or when your back's turned."

Lottie had not thought of it that way. She would not at all have liked to hear what Pen and the other girls at Kemble School said behind her back.

"That must be—uncomfortable."

Adelaide sighed loudly. "I'd like to walk alone now, if it's all the same to you."

"Oh. Okay."

Lottie plodded ahead on her own. Trouble swooped down to perch on her shoulder and gave a tired tweet. Lottie curled him up in her hand and tucked him safely back into her pocket. Then she hugged the periwinkle tweed coat closer and buried her nose in its oversized collar.

"I'm coming, Eliot," she whispered into it. "I'm going to find Mr. Wilfer. We're going to finish the Otherwise Incurable. I promise."

"Who are you talking to, Lottie?"

Lottie jolted her head out of the coat. Fife was hovering by her side, looking very much amused.

"Um! No one."

"That was quite a show back there," Fife said, pushing back a branch for her to pass under, "giving that Barghest orders. I've never seen anything like it."

"You mean they don't normally act that way?"

"Barghest, take orders? Not a chance. The Barghest are the beastliest things on Albion Isle. They've been allies with the Northerly Court for time out of mind. You run into one of them, it's always bad news. They can catch and kill anyone who displeases the Northerly Court. But what happened back there, it looked like that Barghest wasn't even trying to hurt you."

"Not trying to hurt me?" Lottie flapped her bandaged hands. "What does this look like?"

"A lot better than the usual, which is dead," said Fife. "You're still alive. He didn't even use his venom on you."

"Venom?"

"It's lethal," Fife said. "Flips your intestines inside out and turns your blood thick, like puree. Just a drop in your veins is enough to do the trick, and in the end, all that's left of you are your nose hairs."

Lottie squinted in disbelief. "It can't be *that* bad."

"Yeah, it is," said Fife, "so just count your blessings. By the way, how're your hands feeling? I can apply some more Piskie Juice next stop."

"Should you?" Lottie frowned. "They feel fine."

Fife frowned back. "They shouldn't. Bites like that can take weeks to heal. Not to freak you out or anything, but your hands will smart for a few more days at least."

"Not to freak *you* out," said Lottie, "but they're fine. Really. I'm not even trying to be tough."

Adelaide made a squeaking noise from behind them. Lottie turned in time to see her hands flung up in a shushing gesture.

"I hear something," she whispered. "Something's coming this way. Coming after us!"

No one said another word. They ran.

Lottie's newfound footing came in handy. She leapt over knotted vines and skirted past tangles of bramble, feet pounding as fast as her heart.

"They're getting closer," Adelaide panted. "They're surrounding us!"

Suddenly, Fife whipped around in front of them. Lottie tripped into Adelaide as they all came skidding to a halt.

"Why are you stopping?" Adelaide shrieked. "Fife, why are you stopping?!"

Fife was not just stopped; he was smirking, as though their run through the wood had been nothing but a race that he had won.

"It's okay," he said. "You can all calm down. We're here."

Lottie looked around. They were standing in a grove dense with yew trees. That is, the trees looked like yews, but of the most peculiar sort. Their branches did not sprawl out veinlike, as Lottie would expect any normal tree to do. Instead, they curled inward upon themselves in splintery spirals. Their bark and their leaves were pure white.

"We're here," Fife repeated, "in Wisp Territory. Honestly, Ada, don't you know a wisp when you hear one?"

Adelaide turned raspberry red. "Of course I don't. I've never been cavorting around with wisps!"

"I don't see anything," said Lottie. The wood looked just as empty now as it had been before they had run.

"They don't reveal themselves unless provoked," said Oliver, "or without a proper plea."

"No fear there," said Fife. "I've got us covered."

Fife closed his eyes and held his arms out, palms upward. Then, just as he was opening his mouth, he seemed to remember something. His eyes fluttered back open.

"Lottie," he said quietly, "I don't think it's a good idea for you to mention to anyone here that you're a Fiske."

Lottie nodded. She hadn't been planning on it. Fife nodded back, then closed his eyes again and resumed his reverent posture.

"We lost, weary travelers," Fife began in a flat voice like the one Lottie used to recite Latin verses at Kemble School, "implore the aid of the lights of the forest. In the name of the revered Lyre and Silvia Dulcet, patrons of this arbor, do we seek sanctuary. Hear us, oh will o' the wisps. Et cetera, et cetera, blah, blergh, blooey."

Fife drew his arms back in and opened his eyes. The yew trees swayed slowly, almost purposefully. One white branch swayed toward Lottie's face. She shrank back, waving away a leaf that tickled her nose. Then, to Lottie's amazement, the branch spoke.

"Lost?" asked a voice as low as a cello's.

Lottie stumbled backward, eyes darting this way and that to find from what part of the branch the voice had come. Then she saw that the branch of the yew had not merely been swaying in the wind; it had been *uncurling itself.*

More silvery branches craned and stretched themselves out, all with a tremendous creaking sound. Then lights, small at first as Lottie's fist, but soon pulsing to the size of crystal balls, appeared in the ghostly trees. They looked like lightbulbs, strung out above the wood like fresh dew would string along a spiderweb. Then the lights grew nearer, and Lottie saw that they really shone from large wooden, swinging globes and that the globes swung in the hands of people—people who had come floating out of the trees.

Though Lottie wasn't sure if she could properly call them "people." Their skin was a sickly white and so tissue-thin that Lottie could see the bulge of colorless veins weaving and webbing through their limbs. On each of their heads rested a thick sprawl of soft black hair that floated gently in the air, as though fanned out in water.

But the eyes! The eyes were strangest. In the face of each of those dozen-some lantern bearers stared glassy green eyes that reminded Lottie of things she most wanted to forget. At a glimpse into one pair of eyes, she remembered the dread of her first nightmarish sleep without a night-light. The gaze of another reminded her of the disgust she felt at discovering dead spiders in the back of the crawl space at Thirsby Square. Another set of eyes, much closer to Lottie, conjured the memory of her first day at Kemble School, when she'd tried to sit with Pen Bloomfield's girls at lunch and been laughed away.

Lottie shook off the creeping feeling from the back of her head in time to realize that the voice she had heard earlier had not come from a tree after all, but from one of the hovering lantern bearers. Now it spoke again.

"Lost?"

Six voices echoed the query. "Lost?" they asked in unison.

The lantern bearers descended until their feet hung just above the stony ground. The sound of splintering wood started again. This time, the yew branches curled inward, not outward, to hide the gaping holes from which the lantern bearers had emerged.

Then came a sound that Lottie had not expected: laughter. Sudden and sharp, it drew a tingling down her arms as the sound swelled louder and louder, so loud that she raised her hands to her ears. Adelaide looked just as petrified as Lottie felt. Oliver was shifting nervously from foot to foot. Only Fife seemed at ease. In fact, he looked irritated, like he had just heard the punch line of a worn-out joke. Then, just as suddenly as it had begun, the wisps' laughing stopped.

"Oh, look," said one of the lantern bearers. "The love child has returned."

Fife lifted his chin, green eyes hard with something that looked like pride. Lottie was fairly certain that Fife had just been insulted.

"I'm here to see her, Cynbel," said Fife, directing his words to the brightest of the globes.

"What do you say to that, wisps?" said the will o' the wisp called Cynbel, his voice cool and emotionless. "Is he wanted? Would she want to see him?"

The creature closest to Lottie, the one who had spoken first, drifted over to Fife. "It depends on what he's here for," said the glacial voice. "Well, halfling? What are you here for?"

Fife batted the wisp away with an angry swat. He turned his attention back to Cynbel.

"We need safe conduct through this wood on our way to the Southerly Court. We're being tracked by the Barghest."

"What?" cried one of the wisps. "The Barghest have not been in this wood since before the Plague."

"Well, they're back," Fife said through gritted teeth. "We're also being hunted by the Southerly Guard. My mother, Seamstress of the wisps, swore an oath that she'd honor any request I presented when I returned to this wood. Well, I've returned, and I'm presenting a request."

"That is true enough," said Cynbel. "Though we decide if you get that chance."

At that moment, the first full rays of dawn peeked through the leaves, revealing clearly the faces of the wisps. Lottie felt her cheeks grow hot. They were each of them uncomfortably handsome . . . and strangely familiar. Their skin was paler, black hair longer, jaws sharper, but Lottie could find, in the oddest nooks of their noses and cheekbones and cool smiles, traces of Fife. Without warning, the lead wisp shifted his gaze from Fife to Lottie. Her hot cheeks grew hotter.

"Who are your guests?" he asked.

"That's of no concern to you." Fife stepped in front of Lottie. "Now, stop dawdling and take me to my mother. She wouldn't be pleased to know how long you've already withheld the hospitality of your court to her only son."

"You realize, of course," said Cynbel, "that your mother never need know that you and your friends ever visited. Did you ever think on that, halfling? My fellow guards and I earn our keep by making stragglers like you disappear."

Then the will o' the wisps let out a collective laugh that, like the one before it, made Lottie feel as if someone had rammed a knitting needle down her ear. At last, Cynbel's mouth sealed up into a simper.

"Only a jest, sweet thing," he said, patting Fife on the head like he might a puppy. "No need to look so wild in the face. We will take you to your precious mommy. Only follow our lights."

Cynbel drifted back toward his six ghostly companions, and they all raised their swinging globes above their heads.

"Into the wood!" Cynbel cried.

The band of will o' the wisps led them onward.

CHAPTER TEN

Under Quarantine

MORNING LIGHT did no good in this part of the wood. The farther onward that the wisps led Lottie and the others, the thicker the leaves crowded above, swallowing dawn and shading their route through the white yew wood. The wisps' lantern light shone on dozens upon dozens more yew trees that lined the path. Each tree was as strange as the next, branches curled in ghost-white whorls. Their trunks were scaly and twisted, and their needle-leaves shot spine-like from the smaller branches. Occasionally, a mournful creak echoed through the forest, and a new branch would begin to uncoil. Lottie didn't wait to see what would emerge from the trees. Seven will o' the wisps were quite enough to deal with at once.

Lottie began to notice wooden signs that hung from the yews and swung in the cold breeze. CARPENWISP read one sign. GLAZIERWISP read another, and from its smaller branches, in place of needly leaves, shards of blue and green glass hung like Christmas ornaments. At the roots of a yew marked SMITHWISP lay an abandoned anvil and fire pit. In fact, now that Lottie looked closer, she realized that each of the dozen shops that she passed was abandoned. There was no movement within or without them, and the paint peeled and flaked from the signs as though long unattended. Soon the shop signs disappeared altogether, and the white yews grew even thicker and more twisted along the path.

Birds did not chirp here. Nothing stirred or darted from brush to bush. A stink that Lottie had first thought had come from a burst toadstool by the path did not go away after she had passed by it. Instead, the stench grew stronger, so strong that her eyes stung and her tongue swelled with a heavy, salty taste.

"What is this place?" she whispered to Fife.

He looked sullenly back at her. "It's where I come from."

"One impulse," Oliver murmured, "from a vernal wood may teach you more of man, of moral evil and of good, than all the sages can."

"That's rot, Ollie," said Fife.

"No, this *smell* is," said Adelaide, whose words sounded thin through her daintily pinched nose.

Up ahead, a bronze archway stretched over the path. It was thick, sturdy, and ugly. It seemed so out of place in the wood that Lottie almost laughed, but the urge caught in her throat when she came close enough to read the words inscribed on the archway:

YOU ARE NOW ENTERING A TERRITORY DEEMED
CONDEMNED AND QUARANTINED.

BY ORDER OF HIS SUPREMACY, KING OF THE SOUTHERLY COURT, ALL WISPS EXHIBITING SYMPTOMS OF THE PLAGUE ARE HEREBY RESTRICTED TO THE PERIMETERS OF THE WISP TERRITORY. ANY WISP, INFECTED OR OTHERWISE, TO SET FOOT IN THE SOUTHERLY COURT OR ANY DISTRICT UNDER SOUTHERLY DOMINION WILL BE DULY APPREHENDED AND PUNISHED.

"If it's under quarantine," Lottie whispered, "then doesn't that mean we could get sick?"

"Of course not," said Adelaide. "Ollie and I are properly inoculated against wisp strains every year. And you and Fife are immune to the Plague. All halflings are."

"I didn't know that."

"Now you do." Adelaide grabbed Lottie's hand and jerked her past the quarantine notice. "Just don't mention the Plague here, and whatever you do, don't look around."

Lottie, however, could not help but look. With an increase in that putrid smell came an increase in noise: ragged coughing, muffled moans, and shrieks that hurt Lottie's ears even more than the wisps' laughing had. The sounds came from the air, from the trees, from deep in the wood. Lottie saw lanky figures huddled into yew roots. Their green eyes had hollows around them, their black hair was flat around their faces, and their skin had gone oily and sallow. A few of them raised their spindly arms toward Lottie in a silent plea that she could not understand. Braver ones called down from the trees.

"Southerly scum!" one shouted, causing Adelaide to jump and nearly yank Lottie's shoulder clear out of its socket.

"Scum!" repeated several other voices, hoarse and discordant.

"Down with the Southerly houses!" cawed one.

"Down with all Southerlies!"

"Down with the Southerly King, the Great Enslaver!"

"The Mighty Coward!"

Adelaide buried her head into the crook of Lottie's neck.

"Oh dear, oh dear, oh dear," she whimpered. "They're just too awful. Do you hear them? How can they say such dreadful things?"

Lottie winced. Adelaide's fingernails were biting into her bandaged wrist.

"What do they mean?" Lottie asked Oliver.

Oliver shook his head. "Can I see another's woe, and not be in sorrow too? Can I see another's grief, and not seek for kind relief?"

Lottie groaned. "Oh, would you stop quoting!"

She realized only too late that the words had come out as a shout. The shout echoed, and the cries of the plagued wisps stopped. The lantern bearers turned around, all eyes fixed on Lottie as though they expected an apology. Lottie stared up at them defiantly. She wasn't about to apologize. But as she stared harder into Cynbel's eyes, Lottie remembered with sudden vividness the time she'd had to explain to an enraged Mrs. Yates that she had smashed her prized potted gardenia with a soccer ball. It was a paralyzing memory that forced Lottie, at last, to lower her gaze.

"Fine," she whispered. "I'm sorry. I didn't mean to shout."

"Very good," said Cynbel. "Not another peep from any of you."

They trudged on. Lottie ventured a look at Oliver. Here was the boy who had saved her from certain death in Skelderidge Park, and Lottie had yelled at him for quoting what, under other circumstances, would've been a pretty bit of poetry. What had gotten into her? The same thing, she supposed, that had gotten into her two nights ago at the Barmy Badger.

"I'm sorry," she repeated, this time for only Oliver to hear. "Really."

Oliver just nodded.

"Please, oh please, show mercy on a child!" cried a strangled voice from above.

A wisp in the branches clutched a pale baby to her chest. The child coughed and cried and coughed again. A hollow-eyed boy, no older than Lottie, stared down at her from another branch. She unwillingly thought of Eliot.

Adelaide tugged Lottie on. "I told you not to look, remember? Their eyes can trigger memories. Good memories or terrible ones. They use their eyes to manipulate you. The Plague is all very sad, of course it is, but there's nothing we can do about it."

As they pressed on, the yews began to thin again, and the path grew broader. The shouts from the trees eventually died down into an uneasy quiet. In time, Lottie saw no more stares from the branches or hands stretched up from the ground. In fact, the sickly looking wisps had dwindled away altogether, and, to Lottie's great relief, so had the putrid smell.

"Where've they all gone?" Lottie asked.

"They have been cleared out," announced Cynbel. "None of the plagued are allowed into royal territory."

Lottie looked around. This *was* different territory. The yews were taller here. Underfoot, grass had replaced the stone path. The grass, like the yews, was pure white, and it reached as high as Lottie's knees. The wood remained frighteningly silent. Birds still did not chirp, and all Lottie could hear was the creak of the wisps' lanterns and the swish of grass against her legs.

When their guides finally floated to a stop, it was at the threshold of a great pergola. Columns stretched ahead in two long rows, and above, beams crisscrossed in a thick latticework, so tightly woven that only the smallest chinks of sunlight shone through to the floor below. All of it, the entire pergola, was made of clear, shining glass.

Lottie gaped at the sight. She took a step toward it.

"Watch out!" cried Oliver.

But it was too late. Lottie's leg was thigh-deep in warm water. She was standing in a narrow river. Its current tugged Lottie's feet over the slippery stones below, and she flailed her arms, trying to regain her balance.

Then she was lifted up, floating. Fife's arms were around her middle.

"This is no time to take a dip, Lottie Fiske," he scolded, lowering her to solid ground.

Lottie reddened tremendously. She even forgot to tell Fife thank you.

It was as though the river had appeared from nowhere. It was silent and slow, and so clear that Lottie could see straight through to its white stone riverbed.

"It's the River Lissome," Adelaide whispered. "It looks so different here than it does back home."

"That," said Fife, "is 'cause it hasn't been tapped and tampered with by Southerly authorities."

"What's the River Lissome?" Lottie asked, shaking out her soggy sneaker.

"It's the river that runs all through Albion Isle," said Oliver. "It starts in the Northerly Wolds and leads straight to the Southerly Court."

"Oh!" Lottie's eyes lit with understanding. "I think you mean Kemble River."

"Is that what the humans call it, then?" said Fife. "How fantastically original."

"That's how we get a lot of our energy in New Kemble," Lottie said. "We've dammed most of the river up."

Fife made a face like he'd just eaten a pouch full of jacks. "Suit yourselves."

The will o' the wisps had paid no mind to their guests' conversation. Half of them had disappeared altogether into the dim wood. Another two had floated into the great glass pergola itself. Only Cynbel remained beside them. He wore a bored expression and made no effort to add a wise word or two about the nature of the River Lissome. The two wisps who had gone inside the glass pergola now reappeared. Each whispered something into either ear of Cynbel, and then they too floated off into the wood.

"Well," Fife said, "what did they say?"

"The Seamstress has already retired to bed," said Cynbel. "You and your company will have to wait for an audience when she awakes this dusk."

Fife made a honking noise. "Can't you just wake her up?" he demanded. "Titania's sake, I'm her son!"

Cynbel folded his arms severely. "And she is our Seamstress. No subject of hers would dare disrupt her dreaming."

Fife's expression softened. He licked his lips. "Please, Cynbel?"

"Put your tongue away, son of Silvia," said Cynbel. "Your keen has no power over me. Do you think that the Tailor and the Seamstress would appoint a captain of the wisps who was susceptible to silly sprite tricks?"

"It was worth a try," Fife muttered. "And for the record, hot stuff, I'm not a sprite."

"Oh?" Cynbel pointed to Fife's wrist. "How, then, do you explain that abomination?"

Fife tugged his shirtsleeve over his black diamond tattoo. "I—I—" he faltered into silence.

"Do not presume," said Cynbel, "to count yourself amongst the honorable wisps or to question their practices. You're lucky, halfling, that the Tailor has traveled to the northern territories this autumntide, or such an audience with your mother would be forbidden."

"He can't tell her what to do," Fife said, voice low. "Mother promised me that—"

With no warning but the swipe of his arm, Cynbel grabbed Fife by the shoulder and hoisted him a full five feet in the air.

"That is enough of your presumption, halfling!" he shouted. "You will not question the power of the Tailor in these woods. You will approach your mother when she awakens, and no sooner. In the meantime, you will receive the hospitality that wisps show all guests of Her Seamstress—lodging, sustenance, and protection."

Cynbel tossed Fife to the ground as if he were no more than a piece of litter. Fife picked himself up, glowering at Cynbel and rubbing his shoulder.

"I have rights here, too," he muttered.

"Halflings," said Cynbel, "have no rights. You should be groveling at our feet in gratitude for the kindness we are showing you, and that is not for your sake; it is for the sake of our Seamstress."

Cynbel threw back his floating black hair and motioned to the right of the River Lissome, away from the towering glass pergola. "Now follow me."

Cynbel's glowing globe led them onto a broad dirt pathway. The dirt, like the trees and grass here, was white; it coated Lottie's wet green sneakers like powdered sugar.

"Marvelous," Adelaide grumbled. "Just marvelous. We were supposed to reach the Southerly Court today. That's a whole day lost, just because your mother chooses to turn in early. Are you sure there's no other way—?"

"There's no other way," snapped Fife. "If you want the trip to be short, you can go find the Southerly Guard. And if you want it to be really short, you go can find the

Barghest. The Seamstress is the only one who can grant us safe passage through the wood. We'll just have to wait."

"But it's past dawn," said Lottie. "Why is your mother sleeping, anyway?"

"Wisps are nocturnal," said Oliver. "They sleep during the day and craft at night."

That did make a certain sense, Lottie supposed. After all, in so dense of a wood, it did not make a difference whether it was properly night or day.

"Craft?" she echoed. "What sort of crafting do they do?"

"They practice trades," said Fife. "You know, carpentry, weaving, welding, glazing—that sort of thing. Every wisp family specializes in a certain trade. Then they ship their stuff out on the River Lissome. It's how they make their living."

Lottie now understood the meaning of those signs that hung from the yew trees. Carpenwisps carved wood and the Smithwisps fashioned metal. But did they do so with an abandoned anvil?

"Those trees looked deserted, though," she said.

"They are," said Fife, "because the wisps are dying."

Lottie felt ill. "I'm sorry, Fife," she whispered. "I didn't know that things were like this."

"Oh, stop it, please," groaned Fife. "If you apologize, I'll have to stop secretly hating you for making me go through with this."

"I wish we'd never come," Adelaide said. "To be humiliated and taunted by those awful wisps, to see all those terrible things. And for what? We would've been better off running from the Barghest. We would've—"

"Shut up, would you?!" shouted Fife. "All of you, just SHUT UP!"

The other three stopped in their tracks, stunned.

Cynbel, clearly irritated by the slow going, turned back. "I will wait for neither stragglers nor bickerers."

"We're coming, you white-veined ninny," Adelaide snapped, and she pushed past Fife in a brisk, stiff march after Cynbel.

Oliver's eyes had turned a deep, troubled black. He started to say something, but Fife stopped him short.

"I think I've done quite enough by bringing you all here, all right? Never in my sane life would I come back home. I did it for her"—he pointed accusatorially at Lottie—"not for my own emotional health. So I'd thank you all very much to keep your noses out of family affairs and let me decide how I'll deal with Her Grand Seamstress. Got it?"

There was a horrible silence, and then Oliver motioned Fife aside. He said something too low for Lottie to pick up. Whatever it was slackened the tight lines in Fife's face. He did not look quite so angry, but Lottie was still scared to say anything more. What if that terrible look on Fife's face was meant for her alone? Lottie did not want to know. She turned and ran on ahead.

"I think Fife hates me," she said once she had caught up with Adelaide.

Adelaide sniffed, and Lottie noticed that her cheeks were blotchy, like she'd just had a cry.

"Fife doesn't hate you," Adelaide sighed. "He's just plain angry. He always gets like this about his family."

Cynbel stopped overhead. They were standing on the edge of a canopied meadow where long sugar-white grass bent under the weight of a breeze. Here it was not so dark. Drooping swathes of thin, silvery fabric hung across the break in the trees, filtering the meadow's sunlight into a dappled haze. Below the chiffon arches, strands of globed lights crisscrossed on thin strings and cast teetering shadows. In the middle of the meadow stood three gnarled yews, their branches uncurled.

"All that you will need," said Cynbel, "has been provided within the trees, courtesy of the Wisp Court. Be at
your leisure, rest, and take victuals and libations. I will call
again just before dusk, to take you before Her Seamstress."

He gave one dismissive nod, then drifted off, leaving
Lottie, Adelaide, Fife, and Oliver alone.

"Be at our leisure," growled Fife. "Our leisure, my
foot."

He pushed past Lottie and Adelaide, still muttering to
himself as he stalked away. He hopped onto the uncurled
branch of one of the yews and floated his way up to the
gaping hole in its trunk.

"Well, go on," Fife called over his shoulder. "You
heard him. Be at your *leisure*."

With that, Fife slipped into the hole and out of
sight. The yew shuddered, and the branch that Fife had
climbed now curled in on itself until it was in the shape of
a perfectly whorled snail's shell.

"We shouldn't have come," Oliver said in a small voice.

"Nonsense, Ollie," said Adelaide. "You shouldn't
feel bad. Fife is unrefined, and his behavior just now was
accordingly unrefined. That's all there is to it."

"No." Oliver shook his head. "We should never have brought Fife back here. *That's* all there is to it."

Oliver climbed up the branch of the second yew tree until he too was swallowed into the tree trunk and the branch had creaked back into a tight roll, sealing him inside.

"Well," sighed Adelaide, "nothing to do but go on and wait until dusk. I've never stayed in a wisp yew, obviously, but I've heard they're surprisingly luxurious."

"Luxurious" was hardly the first word that came to Lottie's mind. Apple trees had been one thing. Yews looked much more dangerous. There was something fundamental within Lottie that told her it was not a good idea to go sliding into tree trunks.

Adelaide grabbed Lottie's hand. "Oh, come on," she said. "It can't be that bad. We'll go together."

The two of them inched their way up the last uncurled yew branch. A cool draft was blowing from the hole in the trunk, and it smelled unexpectedly nice, like caramel and nutmeg. Lottie peered inside, but she could not see so much as an inch beyond her eyelashes.

"How far down do you think it goes?" Lottie asked, just as her foot lost its treading.

Lottie lurched for one horrible moment, then felt weightless for two more, and then she collided with something solid but soft. Adelaide was screaming above her like a maniac.

"LOTTIE FISKE, CAN YOU HEAR ME?"

"I can hear you, Adelaide. I can *see* you. I'm right here."

"WHERE?!"

Lottie reached out of the trunk hole, which wasn't any higher than her chin. She caught ahold of Adelaide's shoe, and Adelaide shrieked again.

"It's just me, you loon," said Lottie, poking her head out. "Come on, I think it's safe in here."

After just a little more persuading, Adelaide finally dropped into the trunk. A splintering sound followed, and the girls watched as the branch they had climbed curled in toward them and sealed them up in darkness.

"Stupid wisps," said Adelaide. "They didn't even think of lighting."

The moment the words had left Adelaide's mouth, the tree was flooded with light. A chandelier made of willow reeds creaked above them. Its twelve candles had lit at the same time, all of their own accord.

Adelaide, it turned out, had been right: as far as tree trunks went, this was the height of luxury. They were standing on a massive ottoman made of fine purple silk that filled the width of the hollowed-out trunk. On one side of the circular room was a pile of downy pillows. A wooden ledge jutted out from the opposite wall, and on it rested a platter piled with fruits and nuts, a large bronze pitcher, a jar of sugar cubes, and two thimble-shaped tumblers.

The berries on the platter were so bright that Lottie squeezed one to make sure it wasn't fake. Its tight skin broke between her fingers and juice splattered out. She gave her thumb a cautious lick, then proceeded to eat twenty more.

Adelaide, meanwhile, had gone from criticizing the wisps on the lack of light to criticizing them for its very existence ("a complete fire hazard, twelve open flames inside a tree!"). Eventually, she calmed down and identified the bitter-smelling liquid in the brass pitcher as Wisp Wine. Lottie took one sip of the liquid and promptly spit the tongue-burning stuff back into her cup. She decided that she did not like wine, no matter what Adelaide muttered under her breath about Lottie being "thoroughly unsophisticated." After all, Lottie noted, Adelaide did not so much as touch the pitcher.

After taking a taste of all the fruits and nuts, the girls were more than full, and they settled down into the mound of plush pillows with nothing to do but wait for dusk.

"So Fife's really half wisp?" Lottie asked Adelaide. She was still worried about Fife's outburst.

Adelaide nodded. "So testy about it, too. Though if I had to call a rotting place like this my home, I guess I'd feel the same way."

"What about his father?"

"No one knows who that was," Adelaide said in a hushed tone. "All anyone knows is that he was some Northerly, since Fife has the mark on his wrist to prove it. They say the whole thing was a nasty business. Wisps have ancient laws against halflings in these parts. The Tailor, the Seamstress' older brother? He was outraged. He banished Fife from the wood when he was old enough to float. Not that I think Fife would've wanted to stay. Who would?"

Those were terrible truths to utter, but there was a sparkle in Adelaide's eyes as she spoke, as though she almost enjoyed this revelation of secrets. This was a scandalous matter, and Lottie knew from life at Kemble School that the more scandalous a matter was, the more thrilling it was to let it slip from the lips.

"So Fife is a halfling," said Lottie, "like me."

"I don't know why you want to find stuff in common with Fife." Adelaide rolled her eyes and nibbled on a hazelnut.

Lottie could tell that Adelaide wasn't in the mood to talk about things concerning Fife.

"So," Lottie said instead, "why is everyone here sick?"

"It's the Plague," said Adelaide, who looked delightfully terrified to be saying so many scandalous things in one go. "Plagues have been on the Isle since—well, since the beginning of Limn, I guess. But there's never been an outbreak so bad as this."

"The wisps back there were shouting things about the Southerly King," said Lottie.

Adelaide nodded. "But what can he do? He's not the king of the wisps. It isn't his fault that wisps haven't got the medical resources that the Southerly Court has got. Southerlies are very advanced. We hardly ever get sick."

"Does that mean you have a cure for the Plague?"

"Oh, of course," said Adelaide. "Every Southerly is inoculated against the Plague now, standard-issue. But the ingredients are rare. We don't have enough to hand out to everyone. So the wisps barter for what they can, and the important wisps get the inoculations. Not that keep-ing their rulers alive is doing the rest of the wisps much good. My tutor says that wisps stopped trading with the Southerlies out of protest, but it hasn't done any good. The king's not giving in, and the wisps are just getting poorer and sicker."

"Then what's going to happen to them?" Lottie asked, though she was afraid she already knew the answer.

"They'll go extinct. Nearly a quarter dead as it is. I guess by the time Ollie and I are grown, there won't be any more wisps left on the Isle."

Adelaide rattled off this information like she would a boring newspaper headline, topping it with a long yawn. She sank deeper into the pillows and looked just seconds away from sleep.

"That's horrible," said Lottie.

"I guess it is," Adelaide said with a noncommittal shrug. "But you have to understand, Southerlies and wisps despise each other. They did long before the Plague ever struck."

"It must make things extra hard for Fife to have a sprite for a father, then."

"I don't know," said Adelaide. "He never talks about that. I don't think he cares about the wisps at all. Not much reason to, at the rate they're going."

"So, Southerlies hate Northerlies, and wisps hate Southerlies. Does anyone get along in your world?"

Adelaide yawned. "Do they in yours?"

While Lottie was thinking this over, Adelaide began to produce delicate, high-pitched snores.

Lottie wasn't tired, and she decided that she wasn't going to spend the rest of the day cooped up in a yew tree, however luxurious it was. She needed fresh air, and she needed fresh thoughts.

Escaping the tree turned out to be easier than Lottie had first thought. She hadn't needed a secret password or an incantation or a magical wave of her hands, though she tried out each of these methods. Only after an hour of tiring attempts did Lottie actually try touching the branch that sealed off the tree hole and, like magic (which Lottie guessed it was), the branch moved at once, uncurling from Lottie in a loud crackle. She glanced back to see if she'd woken Adelaide, but the thin-limbed girl was still sprawled out on the pillows, her snores deeper and daintier than ever.

Clumsily, Lottie crawled down the tree. Then she set out at a fast trot toward the edge of the meadow and settled into the long, white grass. It felt heavenly, after so much running and tripping in the forest, to simply sit out-of-doors. Even though dew was soaking through her clothes, Lottie preferred this to the silken luxury of the yew tree.

Lottie sank onto her back and spread her hands out in the downy white stalks of grass. A shiver traveled from her fingers to her chin. It was cold here, so close to the ground, as though Lottie were lying on packed ice. Every time a fresh breeze shuddered into the meadow, Lottie could hear—if she concentrated hard enough—the creak of branches. That smell of nutmeg that had been inside the yew tree still teased its way in and out of Lottie's nose. When she lay like this, with her eyes closed and her legs numb, it was hard to think that there were will o' the wisps dying of the Plague just paces away. Or that an evil king had kidnapped Mr. Wilfer. Or that Lottie was a whole world apart from Eliot. All was blank and cold and quiet, and in that blankness Lottie fell fast asleep.

She was back in the Barmy Badger, in Eliot's room. Eliot sat propped in bed with a sketchpad on his lap. He was pale, and beads of sweat hung around the rims of his glasses. As Lottie drew nearer, Eliot looked up.

"Lottie!" he cried.

On his sketchpad was a charcoal-drawn girl who looked remarkably like Lottie herself, and under the picture were the words MISSING PERSON.

"Lottie," said Eliot, "I've been worried sick!"

Warm relief washed over Lottie. Eliot was still alive. She reached out her arms to hug him but found that she could not. She had no hands with which to touch him. She had no skin, no substance at all.

"I'm coming home, Eliot, just as soon as I can," she told him. "I'm going to make you better."

But Eliot shook his head. "What's that? I can't hear you."

As he spoke, the edges of his room began to curl back into darkness, like a piece of paper withering in a fire.

"Are you all right?" Lottie asked frantically.

Eliot reached out a hand. "I can't hear you!" he said again, his own voice fading.

Then Lottie was no longer in Eliot's room, but wandering through a row of dark, looming mulberry bushes. Leaves rustled and owls hooted. The mulberry grove was deserted; there was not another person in sight. Lottie began to run.

Two pinprick eyes appeared in front of her. The Barghest emerged out of the darkness, snarling and champing its teeth like it was laughing at her. Its voice was a wretched noise that sounded like the creature was choking on broken glass.

"The Heir of Fiske," growled the Barghest, sauntering closer to a frozen Lottie. "The Heir of Fiske." Its eyes went greedy, and it leapt toward her, mouth gaping.

Lottie was screaming, screaming as she never had before in twelve years of frights and nightmares. Her eyes shot open. She was wrapped in damp grass, her hair matted to her neck in a coating of sweat.

"Lottie? Lottie!"

Fife was running toward her, his hair wild and flopping. Adelaide and Oliver were trailing close behind.

"Queen Mab!" Fife swore, sliding to his knees and grabbing Lottie's hands. "You had us scared out of our wits! When Adelaide told us you'd snuck out—and then, all that awful yelling . . ."

Lottie stared at the warm, pulsing hands that Fife had clamped around hers, and rather than feel embarrassed, she was simply relieved. Fife did not seem to hate her after all.

"Just—just a nightmare," she said.

Oliver nodded, his eyes a pale, uneasy green. "We had them, too."

"It goes with the territory," Fife muttered. "Literally."

"Mine started out so nice," said Adelaide. "We were back in Iris Gate, and Father had these very well-respected ladies over from the Southerly Court to tell me all about the latest hairstyles. Then"—she shuddered—"they all started to rot. Just rot with the Plague. I could see straight through their rib cages, down to their spleens."

"So you all woke up screaming, too?"

The three looked uneasily at Lottie.

"Not exactly," said Fife, licking his lips. "Not that you're a coward or anything! I should've warned you; nightmares are common around here."

"What was the dream about, Lottie?" asked Adelaide.

"Nothing," Lottie said hastily. "It was nothing. I'm fine. Promise. I didn't mean to make anyone worry."

"Too late for that," said Fife. "But it's as good a time as any for us to be awake. It's nearly dusk."

Lottie looked around. The meadow was darker now than it had been when she'd fallen asleep, but it was impossible to tell where the sun hung in the sky—if it was still hanging at all.

"How do you know?" she asked.

"Wisps always know what time it is."

He stuck his tongue out teasingly at her, and Lottie could not help but smile.

"Come on," said Fife, helping Lottie to her feet. "Let's leave this sorry place behind."

CHAPTER ELEVEN

The Seamstress of the Wisps

FIFE LED THEM down the path back to the glass pergola, holding aloft Mr. Ingle's trusty lantern. Lottie had not realized how much brighter Cynbel's lantern had been— or perhaps just how very dark it was in this part of the wood. Whatever the reason, even with lantern light, Lottie could barely see well enough to place one foot in front of the other.

Then the strange white dirt began to lighten beneath her feet, reflecting a warm glow that came from the glass pergola, just ahead. A minute later, the glow had grown so bright that there was no need for Mr. Ingle's lantern at all. A minute more, and they had crossed a thin glass bridge that crossed the River Lissome and led up to the wide steps of the pergola. A chill seeped up from the glass steps, right through the rubber soles of Lottie's sneakers. Lottie shivered. She grabbed her elbows and bit her lip to keep her teeth from knocking into each other.

"Why is it s-s-so cold?" chattered Adelaide.

Oliver touched one of the threshold's columns. "It's enchanted," he said.

"Didn't you know that?" said Fife, who plowed past them, decidedly not intrigued by their discovery. "The Seamstress likes her home kept cold. I'm sure it must've come up once or twice in our conversations about home."

"You never talk about home," said Adelaide.

Fife raised an eyebrow. "Ah. There you have it. That might be why you didn't know."

Inside the vast pergola, columns lined up before Lottie for what seemed like an eternity, and through the very middle of the glass floor flowed the River Lissome itself, cutting the walkway into two clean, even paths. She saw now that in the open spaces between the columns, steps led down and out of the pergola on both its sides into miniature courtyards, each hedged by a fence of willow reeds. Beyond those fences, the wood of white yews grew as thick as ever. One of the courtyards contained a five-tiered glass fountain that gushed and splattered silvery water. Another, a little farther on, was lined with the most marvelously carved wooden benches that Lottie had ever seen. Oliver had stopped in front of a courtyard decked by swords. The weapons were fixed along the fence's willow reeds as though they had grown as naturally from their perches as blossoming flowers. They were strange swords, pronged at their ends like snake tongues, and their hilts were nearly as long as their blades.

"Wisp blades," Oliver murmured. "I bet these haven't been touched since the Liberation."

"They're beautiful," Lottie said.

"That's because the wisps made them," said Oliver. "They say that the blacksmiths here devote an entire year to the welding of just one sword."

"What's the Liberation?" Lottie asked, but Oliver had walked on.

Then came a most unexpected sound that Lottie had not heard since she left Thirsby Square. It was something sweet and limber, like warm taffy. It wasn't quite giggling or singing or humming, but it sounded like each and all of those. It was everywhere, filling the glass pergola with a coziness that Lottie had not thought could exist in this wood. It was *music*.

A coracle was floating down the slow-moving River Lissome, and inside it sat two wisps. They held a long, clear instrument that spiraled at one end and flattened at the other. One wisp moved his long fingers over openings on the flattened end, while the other blew long gulps of air into the spiraling funnel. The sight was entrancing, like watching the weaving of a tapestry, and the notes slipped into Lottie's tendons and marrow, so deep inside that her very body sang with the melody. It was a mournful song, yet somehow clever, too—like a court jester singing a dirge.

One of the musicians looked Lottie's way. This wisp's eyes did not remind her of something bad. Instead, she remembered a night in Thirsby Square when she had snuck a Danish pastry up to her bedroom and eaten it under her bed in sheer delight. She heard, too, in her memory's ear, the notes of a song that a visiting orchestra had played in Kemble Town Hall. The name of the song, she remembered, had been "Gymnopédie No. 1," and it had filled Lottie with inexplicable happiness. Lottie felt a rush of that happiness once again. She took a step closer toward the music . . .

. . . and her foot sank into the River Lissome for the second time that day.

"Easy, there," said Fife. He was at her side, and he laughed as Lottie hung on to his arm and pulled her foot out of the water. "Have you got a death wish, or what?"

Lottie rubbed at her eyes. "The music was just so nice."

"Those guys are on their way to wake up the Seamstress," said Fife. "Nice alarm clock, if you ask me. Foot all right?"

Lottie nodded. "The water's warm. I didn't expect that."

"The Lissome gets warmer the farther south it flows. They say that the Northerlies use it as a road, to ice-skate here and there. It's chilly up in New Albion. And down in the Southerly Court, the palace taps it for their hot baths."

"If the river goes straight to the Southerly Court," said Lottie, "then doesn't that mean we could follow it there?"

Fife nodded. "That's what we're going to do. If Her Seamstress ever decides to wake up, that is. Now c'mon, let's dry up that foot of yours."

He led Lottie into one of the courtyards. This one was not like the others. It was entirely enclosed in glass. At its center stood a great bronze basin, and from that basin shone a blinding white flame. This was, Lottie realized, the source of the light that filled the whole pergola.

"Behold, the Great Lantern!" said Fife. "Don't look straight at it, or you'll burn your eyes out of their sockets."

Fife grabbed one of the dozens of empty globes that hung along the courtyard wall and that looked just like the ones Cynbel and his lantern bearers carried. He held the globe up to the flames licking from the bottom of the basin, and the center of the globe caught alight.

"There," he said, holding the globe near Lottie's soaked foot. "This sort of fire will have you dried up in no time."

Just as Fife had promised, Lottie's foot did dry, all in the space of seconds. Fife blew out the flame from the globe and hung it back on its peg.

"What sort of fire *is* it?" Lottie asked.

"It's the fire that keeps the wisps alive," said Fife. "Or at least, it keeps them free. The Great Lantern's been lit for as long as anyone can remember. A long time ago, the Southerly Guard floated their boats up the Lissome, stole the lantern, and took it back to the Southerly Court. From then on, the Southerlies had the power to enslave the wisps. They forced them to craft for free—all the swords and carpentry and clothes and pottery. It was like that for, I dunno, about three hundred years? Then this guy named Dulcet came along. He was sick of slaving away for the Southerlies, so he built up a resistance, and he made an alliance with some Northerlies. Together they stole back the Great Lantern, called it the Liberation. That was a hundred years back, and the flame's been kept in this courtyard ever since, under enchantment. No one but the Dulcets have access to it."

"But we're here," Lottie pointed out.

Fife smirked. "Dulcets and their *guests*."

Lottie stared. "You mean, that Dulcet guy was your great-grandfather?"

"Great-*great*-grandfather, if we're going in for the specifics," said Fife. "There he is, right there."

Fife nodded Lottie to the back of the courtyard, behind the Great Lantern, where a bust was carved into the glass wall. Its features were hard and handsome. Lottie could see Fife's own face in them, and for some reason, that frightened her.

"He's sort of a hero," Fife said with a shrug. "Ever since he won back the lantern, a Dulcet's always been on the throne. Mom and my uncle were twins, so they've joint-ruled the place since before I was born."

Lottie touched the icy cheek of the wisp named Dulcet. "That makes you royalty, then, doesn't it? You're an heir to the throne!"

"Halflings aren't heirs," Fife said. "Halflings aren't anything around here. Anyway, I'm nothing like them. Dulcets are great sewers." He pointed to Lottie's stitched wrist. "That's the only sort of sewing I enjoy."

"Well," said Lottie, "you're good at it."

Fife smiled without feeling.

The musicians on the Lissome had begun a new song, and unlike the one before it, this one was lively.

"They're playing the Sempiternal," said Fife, and Lottie was sure that he had looked wistful for the briefest of moments.

She followed Fife out of the courtyard of the Great Lantern, and together they watched as the musician-laden coracle drifted farther away from them, under an icy archway at the end of the pergola and toward (Lottie presumed) the Seamstress' bedchamber. Even now that she could no longer see its source, Lottie could still hear the music. Oliver and Adelaide could, too; they were dancing to it along the River Lissome's bank.

Adelaide was twirling, her cheeks pink with laughter. Even Oliver grinned as he clapped his hands in a sweeping circle.

"Doesn't he have to be careful?" Lottie asked Fife. She felt instinctively at her arm, just where she knew there to be the fading mark of a handprint.

"Careful not to touch Ada, you mean?" said Fife. "Sure. But that's the beauty of the Sempiternal. In this dance, the hands are forbidden."

"What keeps the dancers together, then?" Lottie said, staring transfixed as Adelaide and Oliver spun around each other, their hands lifted above their heads as though to catch falling snow.

"The elbows sometimes," said Fife. "But most of all, the music."

He ran up to the dancing pair with an indignant shout. "Hey! Leaving out me and Lottie, are you?" He motioned to Lottie. "Go on, Ollie. Teach her."

Lottie suddenly felt hot and shy all over. No human boy had ever asked her to dance before, let alone a sprite or a wisp.

"I'm not a good dancer," Lottie said, by way of an excuse.

"Oh come *on*," said Fife. "Everyone in all of Limn knows how to dance the Sempiternal. Sprites *and* wisps . . . probably even the rabbits."

Oliver, to Lottie's great surprise, had extended his arm to her. "Take my elbow," he offered, his eyes an earnest blue, "and I'll teach you."

"I—"

"Just do it," Adelaide commanded. "It's a refined dance, and Oberon knows you could use some refinement."

It was Oliver's smile, not Adelaide's or Fife's words, that convinced Lottie. Carefully, she latched her fingers around the crook of Oliver's elbow. He pulled her toward the riverbank.

"Ollie's an excellent teacher!" Fife cried triumphantly. From her periphery, Lottie saw Adelaide whack Fife upside the head. Lottie giggled, and Oliver smiled.

"So, what do I do?" she whispered to him.

At the moment, she was only swaying from side to side, her hand still lodged against Oliver's elbow.

"Father always told me," said Oliver, "that the key to the Sempiternal is to imagine that you're a bird. Not a genga, just an ordinary bird—one that's been trapped inside a cage and hung over the edge of the steepest cliff in the Northerly Wolds. You've been trapped there, hanging all day."

Lottie winced. "That sounds painful."

"Yes," Oliver said. "But then your cage is cut free. You fall and fall, and just before your cage crashes on the rocks below, your cage door rattles open in time for you to fly free. The Sempiternal is that split of a moment, when the door hinges pop and you *know* that you'll survive. You may be falling, but you can *fly,* and because of that you've got the most terrific feeling of freedom. That's what the Sempiternal is about. You've got to think of it like that."

Lottie nodded. "Okay."

"Now," said Oliver, "we link elbows."

They did so. Lottie's fingers were quivering. She clenched them into a fist.

"Then we spin around, five times in a row," said Oliver.

They did so, slowly, so that Lottie's mind wasn't reeling too badly with dizziness when it was all done.

"Then," said Oliver, "we release the elbows. You spin—just twirl in a circle. Yes, like that. And I clap. Then we spin around each other, twice, our hands raised.

"Then," he said, slipping his elbow back into hers, "we do it all over again."

So they danced the Sempiternal again to the now faint music of the wisps. Oliver's blue eyes shone, and he gave an encouraging smile when Lottie tripped over herself on one of the spins. When they had danced it through, they began a third time.

"Oliver," Lottie said, once she felt she could talk and move at the same time. "When we first met, you were afraid to so much as sit next to me."

Lottie lost sight of Oliver's eyes as they twirled past each other. When they came back into focus, they were a pale orange.

"Yes," said Oliver.

"So, why are you dancing with me now?"

"Dancing is . . . different," Oliver said softly. "I don't know how to explain it. It's like poetry, but for your limbs. I feel comfortable dancing. I feel comfortable dancing with *you*."

Lottie didn't know why she had gone warm in the face. "It's hard, though. Poetry, too."

Oliver nodded. "They're not supposed to be easy, just worth it. Keens, too, you know. Sharpening your keen can be very uncomfortable, until you find the balance of it. Balance—that's the beauty of the Sempiternal. There is a magic made by melody. A spell of rest, and quiet breath, and cool heart, that sinks through fading colors deep."

Lottie smiled. Then she tripped again. But this time, rather than catch herself, she kept falling forward, her arm unthreading from Oliver's and her feet tripping over each other until Lottie hit something hard and spice-scented. She looked up in a panic and found herself staring into the eyes of Cynbel the wisp. She'd run straight into his hovering knees.

"Oops," she said, breathless.

Cynbel paid Lottie no mind. He was looking beyond her, at Fife. "I thought I told you, halfling, that I would take you to your mother's presence in due time."

"Yeeeah," Fife said, squinting. "I vaguely remember that. What can I say? We got bored."

Cynbel grunted. "If you weren't her son, I swear to Stingy Jack himself, I'd run you through with—"

"Calm down, Cynbel, or you're gonna ground yourself," said Fife. "Is my mom awake, or what?"

"Yes," said Cynbel. "She is."

"Then what are you waiting for, ignis fatuus?" he said. "Lead on!"

Cynbel hesitated, as though he were still half considering running Fife through with one of those strange, pronged wisp swords. Finally, he seemed to give that idea up, and with another grunt he led them on.

They passed several more courtyards and then, abruptly, the pergola ended. Beyond the last of the columns loomed the largest and whitest weeping willow that Lottie had ever seen. An awning of gauzy netting stretched beneath the tree's drooping branches, and there amongst them hovered the cross-legged figure of a woman. She was as tall, pale, and dark-headed as the other wisps, but her hair had been cropped short about the ears and laced with a shoot of baby's breath. In the woman's lap rested a ball of white thread. In her hand, which seemed to have stopped mid stitch, was a threaded glass needle.

Cynbel raised his glowing globe before the lady and gave a deep bow, which Lottie thought looked a little ridiculous when done in a hover.

"May I introduce Her Grace," said Cynbel, extending his arm toward the woman, "Silvia Dulcet, Seamstress of the wisps."

In New Kemble, Lottie had once gone with Eliot to see a film at an old, run-down cinema that had since closed. The film had been silent, from the twenties, and the only sound in the entire auditorium had come from the live organist, Mr. Jeliby (whom Lottie and Eliot both liked for giving them free oranges to eat during the feature). On the screen, there had been a short man with a square mustache and a short lady with a bob cut, rouged-up cheeks, wide eyes, and a puckered mouth. For every extraordinary thing that happened in the film (which was always the man's fault), the little woman would widen her wide eyes, pucker her puckered mouth, and lift her hands up to her cheeks.

She made no sound, of course, but Lottie could distinctly hear the woman's scream in her mind. It was an insincere, overly dramatic scream, to match the woman's face.

"What a fake!" Lottie and Eliot had agreed when they left the cinema. "What an absolute fake!" Actors were paid to fake things, Lottie had acknowledged, but they certainly did not need to remind the audience of it every other second. Of course, that film had been made in the 1920s, and no one acted like that anymore.

No one, Lottie had thought, until she was introduced to Silvia Dulcet, Seamstress of the wisps.

At her introduction, the lady inclined her head downward toward the four of them. Immediately, Silvia's wide eyes went wider and her puckered mouth puckered further. Then, since this was real life and not a silent movie, a sound really did emit from the woman, and it was just as fake a thing as Lottie had ever heard.

"My son!" Silvia cried. She tossed aside her needle and thread and swooped down to bundle Fife into an embrace.

Silvia proceeded to shower Fife in kisses and breathless, enthusiastic questions that she gave him no chance to answer. By the look on Fife's face, Lottie wasn't sure if, given the chance, he *would* have answered. He remained stiff in his mother's arms and, when finally released, did nothing more than redden and lower his head.

"Would you just look at her?" Adelaide whispered, leaning toward Lottie in hushed awe. "They say that even the ladies of the Southerly Court take their fashion cues from Silvia Dulcet."

Lottie, who had been preoccupied with the fake pucker of Silvia's lips, had not yet given consideration to her gown. But Adelaide was right: Silvia really was prettily dressed. Thick, silver-colored silk spilled off the Seamstress' shoulders. A belt of braided flower stems hung loose across her narrow waist, and long, glassy stones slipped like tears down the gown's floating train. Lottie would never have dared to wear something so grand even to a Kemble School dance, but it suited the Seamstress extraordinarily well.

When she was done with Fife, Silvia became aware of his companions and asked, mouth pleasantly puckered, to be introduced. Fife sulkily obeyed. Silvia beamed at Oliver and Adelaide as Fife introduced them. Oliver looked curious and Adelaide positively terrified to make the Seamstress' acquaintance.

Then Fife motioned to Lottie, and Silvia's expression changed. A frown disfigured her pretty lips. When Lottie dipped into a curtsy, following Adelaide's example before her, she saw Silvia put her finger to her nose, as if she had just been given a difficult math problem to solve.

"So," said Silvia, "all of those absurd rumors are true. A Fiske child does exist."

Adelaide gave a small cry. Oliver, too, looked startled. Fife just slapped his hand over his face. So much for keeping her identity a secret.

Silvia glided closer to Lottie, her head tilted. She reached out a thin, spindly-fingered hand toward Lottie's cheek and stroked it. Her touch felt like a trickle of cold rain.

"How do you know about me?" Lottie asked.

Silvia lifted Lottie's chin with her thumb.

"Why," she said in a soft, lazy drawl, "one can see it in your face. Such a striking resemblance. So much of her in you."

"You knew my mom?" Lottie asked with some difficulty.

Silvia smiled. "I was acquainted with the House of Fiske in my time. Normally, I care very little for such things that intrigue common sprites and"—she wrinkled her carefully upturned nose—"*humans*. Still, I do keep up with the times. It is my privilege. It is my duty."

"Your duty as the queen of the wisps?" said Lottie, braver now that Silvia's hand had left her skin.

If Lottie had known that her question would cause Silvia to laugh—that painful sound!—she would not have asked. Even the laugh, even *that* was fake. It rang out hollow and deliberate, as though the "ha-ha-ha!"s themselves were conscious of being heard.

"*Seamstress* of the wisps," she corrected Lottie with an indulgent smile. "You realize, don't you, how very important it is to address a wisp by her proper title? It would be a horror, you know, to misaddress a sculpting Gambol as a glassblower or a welding Aspen as a weaver."

"Dulcets sew," Fife said helpfully. "That's their craft."

"Oh," said Lottie. "Sorry, Your Seamstress."

"Mm," Silvia said. "Granted, in the old days, before the embargo, my job was more extensive than simply sewing." She sent a sweeping gesture toward the River Lissome. "I would inspect each of our coracles on their way to the Southerly Court. It was hard work, but the ruler of the wisps must ensure the quality of exported goods!

"And now—now all that is left for me and my brother to do is to inspect coracles piled with the dead. Now, my trade is little more than a mortician—sewing up the coffins of the plagued and sending them to their graves. It is a very thankless task."

"Mother," said Fife, sounding tired, "Lottie doesn't want to hear about your troubles. She's got enough of her own. We all do."

Silvia's eyes widened into two awful bulges.

"What Fife is saying, Your—erm—Seamstress," said Lottie, curtsying again for good measure, "is that we're trying to get to the Southerly Court."

"And we're having difficulties," added Fife.

"Yes, yes," Silvia sighed, waving her hand. "Of course you are. You're mere babes. Babes in the wood, with Southerly fiends and Northerly dogs chasing after you. Tragic."

At this, Silvia produced a teary hiccup and blotted the edge of her eyes with her silk-cuffed wrist.

"You do know," she said, "that the king would very much like to get ahold of your pretty friend here? A Fiske in the Southerly Court—that doesn't sound wise."

Lottie hesitated. Slowly, she said, "We know it won't be easy, but we have a plan. The others know—"

"So," interrupted Silvia, who looked monumentally bored, "you've come to me to seek safe passage through the rest of the wood, is that it?"

"Just until we reach the edge of the Southerly Court," said Fife. "If you remember, you promised you would—"

"Yes, yes," said Silvia, rolling her eyes. "I swore I'd honor any request of my son, should he return to my bower. And you have asked so little of me, Fife. Visited so little. How could I not oblige you and your darling friends with this little favor?"

Fife looked worn. "That's really nice of you, Mother."

"Yes, it is, isn't it?" said Silvia. "Very well, then. You shall have what you've requested, sweet son of mine."

The sweet son of Silvia looked like he'd just been rapped on the head with a saucepan. He stared at Silvia stupidly, as though she'd begun talking in Greek and he couldn't make sense of what he'd just heard.

"Uh, Fife?" squeaked Adelaide, poking him in the elbow.

Fife shook his head. "You're joking," he said at last.

"Joking? Fife, darling, I do not joke. Why, you act as though I wouldn't want to help you." Silvia looked hurt—phenomenally hurt. "All I ask in return for my generosity is that you grant me a little tête-à-tête with your little friend here."

The Seamstress smiled encouragingly, and it took Lottie a few dumb moments to realize that Silvia was talking about her.

"That's very kind of you to offer, Your Seamstress," said Lottie, "but we really should be getting to the Southerly Court. We've already lost a day, and we're in a hurry."

"She's not offering," Fife said darkly. His fingers were clenched so tightly into his palms that Lottie was afraid that the nails would draw blood.

Silvia's smile broke open to reveal teeth. "No, I am not offering. I am demanding."

Adelaide gave a consternated cry.

"Oh, darling girl," Silvia said, shaking her head at Adelaide, "don't disfigure your face in that nasty way. It's exceedingly unbecoming. I really can't comprehend all these glum looks. It's not as though I'm requiring something painful from you. There are merely some things I need to discuss with the Fiske girl."

"Is that all you want?" said Fife. "To talk to Lottie?"

"It is the price you must pay for safe passage," said Silvia. "Unless you'd rather risk it alone back in that dangerous wood?"

"I'm your son," Fife whispered.

"Yes," said Silvia, her smile disappearing. "Had you not been my son, Fife, love, I would not have even entertained your request."

"Fife," Lottie said, stepping forward. "It's all right. I'll have the talk with the Seamstress. It's just a talk, after all."

Silvia turned from her son to Lottie. "There!" she said. "Your friend knows what's good for her. A brief, private audience, and then we'll all be on our way."

Silvia took Lottie's hand in hers, and Lottie's sneakers left the ground. She was floating like Silvia, though not nearly so gracefully. She had to flap her hands to keep from tumbling into a back somersault.

"Fife," said Silvia, "I'm sure you can entertain your guests in our absence. The Fiske child and I will be on the roof."

"The roof?" Lottie flapped more frantically, this time propelling herself into a front flip.

Silvia floated higher. She pulled Lottie past the highest branch of the willow tree and upward still, until they alighted on the tightly woven glass beams atop the pergola.

At her feet, Lottie could see the three small blurs that were Oliver, Adelaide, and Fife. Here, above the trees, a slivered moon spilled down its silvery beams.

The rooftop edges were curled and chiseled into grand arabesques, and crawling white moss hung over them in cascading clumps. Down the middle of each glass beam ran thick lines of potted white soil filled with stakes of birch wood, and about the stakes hung clusters of pale, tufted flowers.

"This is where the Halcyons, our gardeners, come to harvest their flowers," said Silvia. "Care for some? They're perfectly edible."

The Seamstress held out a cluster of the flowers between her pale pinky and thumb.

"No thanks." Lottie may not have made much of a dent into Spenser's *Faerie Queen,* but she'd read enough of the Brothers Grimm to know that taking food from a strange woman was not advisable.

"Let us walk," Silvia said.

Even up here, with only Lottie for company, Silvia strolled with measured, self-aware steps. Her chin was tipped carefully upward, as though she suspected that at any moment men with cameras might jump out from behind the flowers and take her photograph. Lottie just tried to keep up with Silvia's long-legged steps.

"What do you think of our territory here, Miss Fiske?" Silvia began.

"It's pretty," Lottie said truthfully. "I've never seen grass like yours. Or trees. Where I come from, branches stay in one place." She reconsidered this. "Generally speaking,"

"Do you consider it a tragedy, then, that my people are dying?"

"Yes . . . ?" Lottie wondered if this was a trick question.

Silvia tilted her chin higher, expectantly, so Lottie went on.

"I think it's horrible. My best friend is very sick, you see, and that hurts me so much some days that I can hardly breathe to think about it. If Eliot is only one person, then to live here where so many people are suffering—that's got to be unbearable."

Silvia strode to a stop. "So you will help us?"

Lottie blinked at the Seamstress. "Beg your pardon?"

"This is no time for false modesty, child!" Silvia cried in a most melodramatic pitch. "You are a *Fiske*. You are the only Fiske left alive, and you've come to our world at a very dark time, just like so many islanders have hoped you would. So are the rumors true, or not? Do you have the keen of the ancient Fiskes, or not? Can you command?"

Lottie thought of what Mr. Ingle had told her back at Ingle Inn. The Fiskes' powers, he said, had faded away over centuries and centuries. How could Silvia expect *her*, a halfling, to be able to do anything?

Lottie backed up a pace. "I don't have a keen. I'm only a halfling."

Silvia puckered her lips, considering this information. Then she grabbed Lottie's right hand and yanked back her coat sleeve.

"Impossible. You aren't even marked." Frowning, she looked up. "Give me an order."

"What?"

"You heard me. Command me to do something."

Lottie swallowed. "Um. Turn in a circle?"

Silvia remained still. "Another."

"Clap your hands."

Silvia did not clap her hands. She was staring at Lottie with a stunned, glassy expression.

"I can't command anyone," said Lottie, feeling more confident now that, for the first time, Silvia looked *un*confident. "If that's what you're talking about. I can't rule like those old Fiskes used to do. I'm just Lottie."

Silvia dropped Lottie's wrist. She closed her eyes, and she breathed in once—slow, long, and deep. She opened her eyes again. They looked wet in the moonlight.

"Yes," Silvia said. "You're only a halfling. I had thought—my son, you know, has the abilities of a sprite. I thought it would be the same with you. Sprites have always said that the Fiske keen would return and that they would rule the Isle again. But then, sprites are exceedingly stupid. All they have is a legend."

"I told you," said Lottie. "It doesn't matter if I'm a Fiske. I'm not good for anything."

"No," said Silvia, "you're not. King Starkling will continue to rule, and my people will continue to die. All the same, I had to ask."

Silvia was no longer puckering her mouth. Her eyes were not wide, but only drooped and dull. For some time now, Lottie realized, the Seamstress of the wisps had been nothing but sincere.

Silvia's mouth quivered in a thin, bleak line. "Well, life is full of these little disappointments. My brother warned me that my hopes were foolish. He himself is in the northern territories to seek out a new cure, but I know that he will return empty-handed."

"I'm sorry," whispered Lottie.

Like the crack of a struck match, Silvia's smile notched back in place. Whatever sliver of sincerity the great lady had just revealed was now gone. Lottie could see that even before Silvia spoke.

"There's nothing more that our little interview can afford me," she said, "and I trust you won't mention its purpose to anyone else. It's time that you and your friends were on your way."

CHAPTER TWELVE

Sweetwater

"MY SEAMSTRESS," said Cynbel, once Silvia had floated Lottie back down to the pergola floor, "three new corpses have arrived, in need of your needle's attention."

Silvia dismissed the captain with a wave of her hand; her fingers, Lottie noticed, were trembling.

"So," Fife asked, "are you finally going to let us go?"

Silvia twittered out a laugh, and the sound corkscrewed pain deep into Lottie's ears.

"Let you go? Cobwebs and peaseblossoms, child; by the way you talk, you would think that I was holding you all captive here!"

"Well," said Fife, "weren't you?"

Silvia smilingly ignored her son. "Cynbel was instructed to give you all provisions for the journey."

In answer, Adelaide raised up her satchel. A few nuts and berries came skittering from the satchel pockets, which were packed to overflowing.

"Very good," said Silvia. "Now kindly follow me."

Silvia led them down the steps of the pergola, past the white weeping willow, along the River Lissome, and into the wood itself. There were no more yews in this part of the wood, only tall birches clumped together and lining the River Lissome. Above the water and the wood hung white, netted strings. They began at the river's edge and sprawled out and up into the darkness, forming a canopy over the forest, as wide across as the river and as thin as gossamer.

"You know the way to the Southerly Court from here?" asked Silvia.

"Follow the River Lissome," said Fife. "Take it southward until the webs run aground again."

Silvia nodded. "You know the risks of the webbings, my son, but do your little friends?"

"What are webbings?" said Lottie, and even as she asked the question she realized that those netted strings stretched before her were not strings at all. They spanned out just as a spider's web would, in patch after patch of interwoven circles.

"They were Dulcet the Great's idea," Oliver said excitedly, "when the Southerlies invaded the wood during the Liberation. Using the webbings, Northerly allies could look out and attack from above, same as the wisps. They say that Dulcet spent thirteen nights straight sewing the webs all by hand. In fact, there's a fragment of a poem that tells about how his needle—"

"Ollie," Fife said. "Not the time, mate."

"I did promise that I would give you safe passage," said Silvia. "Walking aloft on the webbings, you'll be clear out of any danger of the Barghest or Southerly Guard, right up until you reach the borders of the Southerly Court."

"But how do we walk on *webs*?" asked Lottie.

"They're enchanted, fretful child," said Silvia, turning up her snub nose. "You'll be perfectly safe on them. The only thing that could possibly undo that enchantment would be for you to follow a swamp flame off your path, and I trust that none of your band would be foolish enough to do that. Now! Kisses all around, and be on your way. What a sweet sadness parting can be!"

"Oh, positively saccharine," muttered Fife.

Silvia observed her son for a half moment. She stooped, ran one spindly finger down the swoop of his nose, then drew him into her arms and pressed a kiss into his hair. When Silvia backed away, hand raised in farewell, Lottie thought she saw a solitary tear glint on one of her long lashes. Of course, it could have just been Lottie's imagination, or the shadow play of the moon and the swaying birch branches.

"You *do* know what sort of danger you're placing yourself in?" Silvia said, turning to Lottie. "If the king got his hands on you, I fear you'd come to a nasty end."

"I—I'll be careful," said Lottie.

"Goodbye, Your Seamstress," said Oliver. "Thank you for your kindness."

Oliver bowed, Adelaide curtsied, and Lottie forgot what she was supposed to do and ended up making an awkward curtsy-flop-trip. Fife did nothing but turn on Mr. Ingle's lantern, hold it high, and float off, up the steady incline of the webbings over the river.

"Well," he said, "are we heading south or what? We're burning moonlight."

Oliver and Adelaide, like Lottie, remained still. They were all eyeing the webbings with distrust.

"Oh, c'mon," said Fife. "You heard her: it's completely safe."

"That's easy for you to say!" said Adelaide. "You're *floating.*"

"Well, I can't help that. You want me to hold your hand or something?"

Adelaide's eyes burned. "*No.*"

Still, she did not move. Oliver's eyes had turned a grainy brown, like cinnamon. He was uttering something under his breath—poetry, Lottie guessed.

Lottie made the mistake of looking up through a wide gap in the silken webs, which climbed foot after foot into the air, high above the dark wood. It was a long way to fall. Lottie shifted her sneakers back from the riverbank. Eliot's sneakers. *Eliot.* He couldn't get any better if she didn't move forward.

Lottie stepped out. She placed one sneaker on the web, then the other. It was that easy. Just as Silvia had promised, the web held. Lottie did not even need to balance herself.

She stood upright with perfect ease, as though she were merely taking a stroll in Skelderidge Park back home.

"Told you," Fife said. "Now come on, the rest of you. Are we going to the Southerly Court or not?"

Lottie turned back to tell Silvia something. What, exactly, Lottie wasn't sure of, even as she turned. Perhaps a "thank you" for the enchantment and the safe conduct, or an apology for not being able to do anything for the Seamstress' plagued people, or maybe just a simple goodbye. But Lottie did not end up saying a thing. The Seamstress of the wisps was gone.

❦

The strands hummed with wind as the quartet walked along the webbings, over the River Lissome. Fife swooped ahead to lead the way, the light of the lantern bobbing and darting along with him. He kept well ahead of the others, his expression creased in lines that Lottie now knew meant that Fife was in no mood to talk.

Lottie had thought that walking on webs would be a slow, arduous process of watching her every step, edging along gaps in the threading and constantly balancing and rebalancing. Instead, Lottie felt the enchantment of the webbings working on her feet; her shoes shifted and slid of their own accord, a shoot of web always firmly under her steps as she followed the webbings up a sloping incline, from just above the river water to high up in the trees. The only real difficulty turned out to be that Lottie tended to forget she was quite so high up, and each time she accidentally looked down, a sickening swash of vertigo swam up her throat.

Lottie tried to distract her thoughts, but they kept circling back to the memory of how Silvia Dulcet had looked at her, back at the glass pergola. How could someone as important as the Seamstress of the wisps really think Lottie could be a ruler? That she could take the place of a king? Lottie, of course, knew that was a ridiculous idea. She had enough trouble making good grades at Kemble School, and Mrs. Yates had told Lottie that she wasn't even responsible enough to own a hamster. There wasn't a chance she could run a whole island full of sprites and will o' the wisps and quarrels and plagues. That might be true, but the rumor was still out there, and the king still wanted her dead because of it. Lottie thought she might just agree with the Seamstress of the wisps. How stupid these sprites really could be.

They traveled along the webbings for full hours, mostly in silence. Lottie walked alone, just behind Fife's guiding light. She glanced back once and saw an ashen-faced Adelaide holding Oliver's elbow.

"It's going to be all right," Oliver whispered, and he placed a careful kiss on his sister's temple.

Adelaide, Lottie noticed, was having trouble breathing. She inhaled in short, raspy retches.

"What if we're too late?" Adelaide wheezed at last. "We've wasted so much time. King Starkling could have already held his trial. Father could already be—"

"No," said Oliver, his eyes a determined indigo. "We'll get there in time."

The webbings had begun to dip so that now the four were no longer walking above the trees on either side of the river but alongside them. Here, birches mingled with thickly twisted pines. The grass grew green, short, and jagged, and then it disappeared completely under a siege of watery ground.

Now black reeds edged the bank of the River Lissome, and gnarled, moss-covered conifers emerged from its waters. The river was slowly broadening, turning into swamp. The webbings, which until now had stretched as wide as the river, stretched wider still to accommodate the breadth of the darkening waters. It was a quiet swamp; there were no buzzing bugs or bellowing bullfrogs. It did not smell putrid here, as it had back in the quarantined Wisp Territory. In fact, it smelled pleasant—so pleasant that Lottie thought she ought to stop walking altogether, close her eyes, and breathe the air in. Not for too long . . .

"None of that," said Fife, shaking Lottie's arm. "That's what they'd like you to do."

"Who?"

"Them."

Fife pointed ahead, and for a moment Lottie saw nothing but dark, rippling water. Then a green flame trembled into focus. Then another, over there! And another! There were dozens flitting this way and that, all along the edge of the swamp.

Adelaide breathed harder. "Where are we? Are those— are those flames? Fife Dulcet, where *are* we?"

"Sweetwater."

"WHAT?"

"Look, I didn't tell you we'd be passing through before because I knew you'd freak out."

"Well, of course I'm freaking out!" shouted Adelaide. "Sweetwater is the most dangerous place in all of Wisp Territory! Even the wisps are afraid of it!"

"Yeah, well, the wisps are a bunch of spineless dolts," Fife said. "Don't be such a priss, Ada. We've got to go through the swamp. It's the only way to the Southerly Court."

"I don't want to," whispered Adelaide.

"Then go home."

"Stop it, Fife," Oliver said, his voice unusually hard. "Don't take it out on her."

Fife licked his lips and crossed his arms. Oliver turned to Adelaide.

"Fife knows this territory better than the rest of us," he said. "If going through Sweetwater is the only way, then we'll just have to. That's my vote. What do you think, Lottie?"

"How is Lottie supposed to know?" Adelaide cried before Lottie so much as opened her mouth. "She doesn't know all the horrible stories about the swamp. She doesn't know the danger!"

"There isn't any danger," said Fife, "if you pass through the right way."

"Oh, and I suppose that being half wisp makes you a qualified guide?" Adelaide grabbed Lottie's hand. "Don't let him take us there. That's where all of the *bad* wisps go."

Lottie flustered under the stares of the others. "Is it really that bad?" she asked. "It's just a swamp, isn't it?"

"Well, no," admitted Fife. "The swamp's filled with oblivion. You know, *pure oblivion,* not from concentrate."

"It'd help," said Lottie, "if I knew what oblivion was."

"It's dangerous stuff," said Fife. "Gets to your brain, turns you batty."

"HA!" Adelaide pointed at Fife in triumph. "You just admitted it. It *is* dangerous!"

"Like this entire trip of ours has been a walk in the park," said Fife, rolling his eyes. "Anyway, I'm not suggesting we take a skinny-dip in the swamp. We walk the safe route. We're fine if we stick to the center of the webbings, away from the banks."

Lottie considered all of this for a long minute.

"I vote yes," she decided.

Adelaide's face contorted, gaping and livid.

"I'm *sorry,*" Lottie told her, "but it sounds like Fife knows what he's talking about. What's important now is getting to Mr. Wilfer as soon as possible, isn't it?"

"Don't bring my father into this!" said Adelaide. "Fine, go on, then. Right down to Sweetwater, to our pretty deaths, just so Fife can show off!"

"I'm not showing—"

"Quiet, all of you!"

It was the first time that Lottie had ever heard Oliver shout. The forest fell silent.

"We voted," said Oliver. "Three to one. That's how we decided this, and that's what we're going to do. Agreed?"

"Agreed," said Fife.

Lottie looked warily over at Adelaide. "Agreed," she said.

"Have it your way," mumbled Adelaide. "But don't blame me when you're choking in oblivion, half dead, your body stripped from your soul. No, no! On our merry way!"

Fife had stopped paying attention to Adelaide and instead pulled Spool from his pocket. He ducked his lips against the yellow kingfisher's back and whispered a single, indiscernible word. The genga fluttered from Fife's hand and straight into the swampy blackness beyond.

"I'm sending Spool ahead of us, in case we run into trouble," said Fife.

"Good idea," said Oliver, reaching into his own pocket.

Keats emerged, a blinding flurry of white feathers, and swooped toward the swamp, following Spool into the darkness. A flash of lavender followed him, trilling a shrill song—Adelaide's genga, Lila.

Lottie drew Trouble out of her pocket. He looked particularly small and still in her hand, and Lottie realized that he was sleeping. She poked lightly at his back.

"Um, Trouble?"

Trouble opened one eye. He gave a short, unhappy tweet.

"Come on, Trouble," Lottie whispered. "Don't you want to go with the others?"

Trouble closed his eye. He ducked his head and went right on sleeping.

"Are you *ignoring* me?"

She looked up and saw that Adelaide was suppressing laughter.

"It's okay," said Oliver. "You're still learning."

"What am I doing wrong?" she demanded.

"Nothing," said Oliver. "Trouble just seems to be—um—"

"Badly behaved," said Adelaide. She sounded smug.

Lottie felt her cheeks go red. She slipped Trouble back into her pocket.

"Now listen up, ladies and gent," said Fife, "'cause this is important: the key to getting through the swamp is to keep your mind focused, steady, and tuned to one thing. It doesn't matter what. Could be a phrase, or an image—but just one thing. Simple. If your mind starts to muddle up, just remember that one thing and keep walking straight. That's how you get through the swamp."

"Have you done this before, Fife?" asked Lottie.

"Uh." Fife licked his lower lip. "No."

"We're going to die," Adelaide said.

"We are *not* going to die!" Fife snapped. "Just keep your mind focused. The deeper we go into the swamp, the more of those flames there'll be. They can't touch you as long as you walk straight. They're not allowed past the swamp banks."

"I heard they suck your soul out of the soles of your feet," Adelaide whispered.

"That's just Southerly garbage," said Fife.

"But what *are* the flames?" Lottie asked.

There was such a long silence that Lottie thought Fife might not have heard her.

"They're wisps," he finally said.

"What?"

"They're bad wisps. Criminals. When wisps are found guilty for crimes, they're disembodied down to their flames and sent to the swamp to live."

"You mean," Lottie said, trying to keep her stomach in its proper place, "we're walking through a jail?"

"More or less," said Fife. "See, the prisoners want their old bodies back, but since they can't get those, they'll settle for anyone's; that's the only way they can ever escape the swamp. They stay on the edges of Sweetwater, where the oblivion's strongest. If you wander that way, the oblivion water will drive you so stark raving mad that whichever wisp is quickest can steal your body and rekindle it for its own. That's the only way prisoners get their freedom around here."

"What a brutish penitentiary system," whispered Adelaide.

"We don't all believe in dungeons and fifthing like the Southerlies do," Fife said coolly. "Now, let's get this over with."

Under Fife's lamplight, the webs shone bright, thin and translucent as lightbulb filament. They hung so close to the earth now that if Lottie had bent, her hands could have skimmed the swampy waters. Not that Lottie would do something as thoughtless as that. She was trying, instead, to come up with a *one thing* to focus on. The image flashed, once only but vivid, across her mind. She thought of Eliot's ceiling, of the deep blue sky and yellow stars that he had painted, and the way in which they swirled about ye ol' porthole. Yes, that is what she would concentrate on: Eliot's painting. She would think of the rough grain of Eliot's ceiling and the smell of fresh paint, and not on the sleepy, sugary scent misting up from below.

"It'll be all right," said Oliver, turning back with reassuring blue eyes. "We are called, we must go. Laid low, very low, in the dark we must lie."

"Ollie, please, not poetry," sniffled Adelaide. "Not now. It's tough enough to walk a straight line."

Adelaide really was having trouble walking. She wobbled at every step, her oversized satchel vise-gripped in her arms. Her breaths had become little more than unsteady coughs and heaves.

"Just think about your one thing!" Fife called back.

Suddenly, Adelaide stopped walking altogether.

"I can't do this," she choked. "I can't do it anymore."

"Yes, you can," said Lottie, inching to Adelaide's side. "Fife says we just have to—"

"Fife doesn't know what he's talking about!"

"Here," said Lottie, an idea lighting on her, "why don't you let me carry the satchel?"

"W-would you?" Adelaide stopped mid step. "I think that might help. Yes, I think that'd help."

Carefully, Adelaide lumped the bulging bag into Lottie's arms, while Oliver and Fife went on ahead, oblivious to the exchange.

"That's better," Adelaide told Lottie. "Much better. Thanks."

"Sure," said Lottie, "Now, let's get to the end of the swamp, huh?"

Only, Adelaide was not listening. Adelaide was not even standing where she had been just a split second before. She was running, *running* across the webbings—not forward, but outward, toward the edge of the swamp.

"Fife!" Lottie cried. "Oliver!"

But the boys must have been too far ahead, or some eerie magic over the swamp was too thick, because they did not turn at her call. So Lottie ran after Adelaide.

"Adelaide!" Lottie leapt across the web, from string to string. "Adelaide, come back!"

To Lottie's surprise, Adelaide stopped running. She turned back, her face tear-streaked in the moonlight.

"I can't do it anymore," Adelaide whispered. "Don't you see? We're never going to get to the other side."

"Yes, we are," Lottie said gently, even though she felt a jittery lurch inside. "You're just not thinking of your one thing."

Lottie realized as she said it that *she* wasn't thinking of her one thing, either.

"You know what my one thing is?" Adelaide said. "Father. All I can think of is getting Father safe, and all I can think of is how we never, ever will!"

Lottie stretched out a hand toward Adelaide. "We *will*. We're going to save your father, and we're going to save Eliot, too."

Adelaide slapped away Lottie's hand. She was staring at her suspiciously. "Why did you offer to take my satchel?"

"Wh-what? What do you mean? I took it because you were tired, because—"

Adelaide gasped. "You took it because the Otherwise Incurable's inside, didn't you? *Didn't you?*"

"Of course not!"

"YOU DID!" Adelaide was hysterical. "Give it back! Give me the satchel back!"

"I don't think that's a good idea," Lottie said, stepping back. For the first time, her balance on the webbings wavered. "Something's wrong with you, Adelaide. I—I think the oblivion is getting to you."

"Give it!" Adelaide shrieked.

"Fine!" said Lottie. She tossed the satchel to Adelaide, but it wasn't a very good throw. Her limbs felt strangely heavy. "There. You can have it."

Adelaide caught the satchel. Immediately, she rummaged through it. "Where is it?" she demanded. "What did you do with the medicine? Where is it? Wait! Here. *Here* it is."

Lottie gave an unwanted yawn. She tried to take another step, but her knee buckled and she fell, her shoulders catching in a thick curve of web. A scent began to wrap around Lottie, thick and musty. She wiped at her blurring eyes. Flashes of green flame bobbed into the border of her vision. *Wisps.* She had fallen to the edge of the webbings.

Lottie shivered and felt a numbing sensation rushing up her neck. She tried to move her arms, but found that they were plastered down to the web in a cold and sticky hold. Beneath her, dark water churned and rippled. Green flames hovered closer.

Lottie tried to wrench herself free. She took big gulps of breath but only ended up sucking in more of that dizzying, musty-sweet scent. The green flames came closer still, pulsing nearer and nearer to where Lottie lay trapped.

"Stay back," Lottie whispered. "Stay away."

The flames did not listen. They loomed closer. Lottie's eyelids were itchy and her nose stopped up. Then her feet began to grow cold and heavy. Something wet was creeping up her legs. Lottie felt herself slipping out of the bindings of the web and into the the river. It was warm, so warm, and she was tired, so tired. The sweet smell grew stronger.

The last thing that she remembered was the sound of her own name.

CHAPTER THIRTEEN

Route and Crag

"LOTTIE!"

Lottie's eyes snapped open. She coughed a warm,
sweet liquid from her throat.

"She's all right," said a shrill voice. "Fife, get over here!"

Lottie heard herself say, "Riddle larks and crackers?"

She tensed, staring up at Adelaide's face in alarm.
What she had meant to say was "Where are Fife and
Oliver?"

She did not have to wonder for long. The boys came
into view, one behind each of Adelaide's shoulders.

"All hail the conquering heroine!" cried Fife.

Lottie moaned and shifted, and for a moment she panicked. She was still caught in a web, just as she had been before she had passed out. But there were no green flames here, no heady scents. The air smelled blank and crisp.

"The oblivion's just addled her brain," Fife said, pressing a hand to Lottie's forehead. "It'll wear off in a little while. If we hadn't lost the satchel back there, we could've given her some food to help soak it out of her system."

They had lost the satchel? Lottie sputtered out some of the remaining sweet taste from her mouth.

"Where's the Otherwise Incurable?" she tried to ask, which came out instead as "Whippersnapper on the fourth, why can't you, please?"

Fife snickered. Adelaide slapped him on the shoulder.

"This is your fault, you idiot," she said. "I told you we shouldn't have gone through the swamp."

"We voted on it," Oliver reminded Adelaide.

"And we're alive aren't we?" said Fife. "No thanks to you, Miss Priss. It was *my* genga that chirped us to safety. If anyone's to blame, it's you. You didn't focus on your one thing. You ran off like a scared little—"

"I wasn't scared! I was—I was confused." Adelaide held up the scarf-wrapped vial of Otherwise Incurable in her hand. Lottie sighed in relief. Eliot's medicine was safe.

"We all were," said Fife, "but at least Lottie had the decency to be brave."

"I thought she was trying to steal it," Adelaide whispered.

"Oberon," groaned Fife. "You're so paranoid. Lottie's not a thief."

I'm right here, Lottie thought miserably. It seemed that just because she couldn't speak properly, no one thought she could hear, either.

Except for Oliver. He sat by Lottie's side with an intent look in his green eyes. Lottie half smiled at him. He half smiled back, glanced at the bickering Fife and Adelaide, and rolled his eyes. He shrugged as though to say, "What can you do?"

She pushed herself up to a sitting position and looked around. They were under the cover of pine trees, and beneath them the swamp water had cleared and narrowed back into the placid River Lissome.

"We're out of the Sweetwater," she said. "We're safe."

And this time, to Lottie's great relief, those were exactly the words that came out of her mouth.

Fife and Adelaide stopped, mid bicker, and stared at her.

"Yes," said Oliver. "We're past the swamp. The safe part, I'm not so sure about."

Oliver's teeth chattered a bit. His bandaged arm was exposed, and Lottie could see gooseflesh puckering up his elbow.

"Where's your jacket?" she said.

"We used it to dry you off," said Oliver. "Those flames had dragged you halfway into the water by the time we pulled you out."

"Oh." Lottie looked down at her chilled legs and soggy sneakers.

"Close shave, that," said Fife, sticking his tongue out at her. "You very nearly got sucked up. Just think! If we had gotten to you a moment later, some wisp murderer could be inhabiting your body this very second. Wouldn't that be the *weirdest* thing? Creepy, too. No one would expect some nice-looking girl to be a bloodthirsty murderer."

Lottie, who had been close to tears, now couldn't stop a smile from surfacing. The idea of one of those green flames possessing her body was a horrible one, but somehow Fife made it sound funny. And he had called her nice-looking.

"How did we get away from them?" she asked.

"It was all Ollie, really," said Fife. "After we pulled you out of the swamp, the oblivion started to get to us, and bad. You'd passed out, I couldn't think straight, and Adelaide was having a breakdown. But Ollie? He was the hero. I don't think the oblivion even broke his concentration. You see, that's what comes from being a poetry-quoting machine: phenomenal powers of focus."

"You're exaggerating," Oliver said, eyes pink. "I just kept reciting my favorite couplet, that's all."

"Whatever," Fife said. "Ollie could hear the gengas chirping from the other side of the swamp. So he rounded us all up and led us in the right direction till we were clear of the oblivion and the flames altogether. Now is that one for the books, or what?"

"Definitely one for the books," said Lottie, shooting Oliver a smile. "I'd say it's poem-worthy."

Oliver's cheeks went red. He lowered Mr. Ingle's lantern to hide his face in the shadows.

Adelaide had been strangely quiet all this time, and when Lottie looked her way, she quickly turned, eyes downcast.

"It's okay, you know," Lottie told her. "I'm not mad at you for running away. We were all confused back there."

Adelaide shrugged and said nothing.

"Right!" said Fife, clapping his hands. "It's over, and everyone's safe. That's what's important." He turned apologetically to Lottie. "I know you've had a scare, but do you think you could keep walking?"

They were losing time, Lottie realized. She did not know how long she had been unconscious, and part of her was afraid to ask. She nodded groggily and tried to shift her knees up.

She had to think of Eliot. She had to picture his ceiling, covered in fresh-painted stars and swirls. She had to think of the days they spent on the roof of the Barmy Badger.

You and I, we understand each other, Lottie Fiske.

"We've got to—to save Eliot," Lottie struggled to say, "and Mr. Wilfer. Got to—got to keep going."

"All of the above," Fife encouraged.

He offered Lottie the support of his shoulder, which she took with a wobbly smile.

The oblivion may have worn off Lottie's tongue, but a fuzziness still hung over her mind and she occasionally got the strange urge to shout "Badminton!" The webbings were as stable underfoot as before, and they sprawled under the shelter of pine, over the babbling river.

Fife stayed back with Lottie, steadying her muddy-minded stumbles until she walked with greater surety. In the lamplight, Lottie saw that Fife had a long, ugly weal running down his cheek.

"Did you get that from trying to save me?" she asked.

"What, this beauty?" Fife ran his finger along the red mark. "I consider it an improvement, don't you?"

"I'm glad you came after us," Lottie said quietly.

"Yeah," said Fife. "You had me and Ollie pretty freaked out when we found you. And Ada? You should've seen her when we pulled you out of the oblivion. She couldn't make up her mind about whether you were a rotten thief or her savior. She called you both."

"She did?"

"Look," said Fife. "I know that Adelaide doesn't act like it, but she was really torn up about what happened back there. She wouldn't leave your side until you woke up. I think she's just too embarrassed to admit she was wrong."

Lottie looked ahead at Adelaide's proud, swiftly striding figure.

"I think she has a hard time apologizing," Lottie said.

"She's *never* apologized to me," Fife said cheerfully.

"Fife," Lottie said, "how did you and Oliver get to be friends anyway? It's kind of hard to imagine how you made friends with any of the Wilfers."

"You mean, I seem a little too *unrefined* for their lot?" Fife snorted. "Sheesh, Lottie, that hurts."

"You know what I mean."

"I know what you mean." Fife sighed. "Well, you saw what it's like in Wisp Territory. I hated growing up there. The Tailor despised me, of course, and so did all the other wisps. I'd go out of Wisp Territory every day, into the fens and Southerly grounds. One day, I found Oliver wandering around the wood like a Mad Hatter, book of poetry in hand, quoting to the trees."

Lottie smiled. "You helped him shake a lot of that, didn't you?"

"Yeah," said Fife, "I guess. But he helped me out, too. We started exploring together. Oliver was fascinated by wisps, and I wanted to know everything there was to know about sprites. Then he introduced me to Mr. Wilfer and Adelaide. We would've made it a trio, but Adelaide, well—"

"She told me," said Lottie. "Exploring isn't a refined activity."

"Decidedly unrefined," agreed Fife. "Anyway, when I was born, the Tailor ordered my mother to banish me from the wood. She bargained with him to let me stay until I turned ten—that's when wisps learn how to float. So on my tenth birthday, I left. Mother promised protection if I ever returned and blah, blah, blah. But I was ready to go."

"And you're going to be Mr. Wilfer's apprentice, right?"

"Mmm-hmm," Fife nodded. "But he thinks I'm not ready yet. Wants me to wait a few more years. He says that I don't understand the 'great weight' of the healing profession, et cetera, et cetera."

Lottie guessed she could understand that. After all, Mr. Wilfer's profession had gotten him imprisoned by the Southerly King.

"I think you'd make a good doctor," Lottie said. "You always seem to know the right thing to say to make a person feel better."

An impish smile notched up Fife's cheek. "I should hope so. That is my keen, after all."

"What? Oliver said your keen had to do with taste. Tasting words, something like that."

"It does," said Fife. "How do you think I know the right words to say? I taste them first."

Lottie stared.

"Think of it this way," Fife said calmly. "Everything that you and I say is just one big, soupy concoction in the air. Depending on how you feel, the soup tastes different. If you're having a bad day, it's bitter. You've run into your worst enemy, it's sour. You've fallen in love, it's sweet! All those emotions leak out in your words. Dramatic examples, but you get the picture."

"Um."

Fife waved his hands impatiently. "It's not that I can taste the words themselves, really. More like the *moods* behind the words."

"So," said Lottie, "you could taste if I was angry, even if I said that I wasn't?"

"Mm-hm," said Fife. "The moment you say a thing, I'll taste exactly how you feel. Which, if you think of it, would be a lame excuse for a keen by itself. But here's the better bit, the bit that I'm still sharpening. I call it *flavoring*. Say I taste someone's words, and they're bitter, or off—bad somehow. Well, all I've got to do is add my own words, and the mood changes—presto!—just like that. It's like adding sugar to cake batter or spices to a soup. I can figure out what added ingredients would switch things up."

"You mean, you can change anyone's mood just by saying the right words?"

"Close enough. It's still a wishy-washy business. Sometimes I mess up, choose the wrong word, end up throwing off the mood altogether. But I've still got three more years to sharpen it, so I'm not too worried."

"Wait. *Wait!*" Lottie stopped in her tracks. "Does that mean you've been changing everyone's moods this whole time?"

"Does it?" Fife arched a brow.

"How do I know that you haven't been flavoring *my* soup, or whatever?" Lottie demanded. "That you haven't been saying just the right things to change *my* mood?"

"You *don't* know, do you?" Fife said, that impish smile still on his face. "That's the fun of it!"

Lottie had begun to feel queasy, and she was certain this had nothing to do with the aftereffects of the oblivion.

"It's not fun," she said. "You can't just go mixing up words and changing people's feelings. How am I supposed to know if I really like you or if it's just you adding sugar and spices?"

"Why? Do you *really* like me, Lottie Fiske?" Fife's eyes were shining with amused curiosity.

"You're making fun of me."

"No," said Fife. "I just knew you'd get all weird when I told you. No one likes having their emotions read. That's why Ollie makes such a good friend, you know. He's used to *everyone* reading his emotions. It's nothing new to him."

"Well, I don't like it, so—so stop, please."

"I can only do that if you stop talking," Fife pointed out.

So Lottie did just that; she stopped talking, folded her arms, and walked on. It wasn't that she didn't trust Fife. Or was it? If only he could just say things straight, with no blurs along the edges. But Fife *was* a blur: a wisp and a sprite, but neither entirely, bursting with enthusiasm and also with anger. She was in a strange place, Lottie reminded herself, and in strange company, with girls who could hear through six stories and boys who could taste her words.

The night wore on, the hours drumming out one by one. As the nip of deep night snagged at Lottie's skin, she began to understand what a tragedy it had been to lose the satchel back in the Sweetwater swamp. Her feet and back begged for the comfort of a blanket, and her stomach groaned for food—even simple bread and cheese.

No one had spoken a word for a good two hours into the morning when the wood began to change. It was growing lighter, and the webbings were dipping lower. In the dimness, Lottie thought she saw the flash of a bird's wings just overhead. Then, unmistakably, she heard a low chirp. It wasn't until a yellow kingfisher had alighted on Lottie's shoulder that she realized what was happening: the others had released their gengas and were letting them fly free.

Spool chirped once more in Lottie's ear and then swooped off to fly a merry circle, like a dance, with white-feathered Keats. Adelaide's lavender finch, Lila, kept close to her owner, flying at a respectable height and gliding with grace.

Lottie brushed her fingers against the small, warm bundle of feathers in her pocket. Carefully, she tugged out Trouble and held him aloft in her cupped hands.

"Well?" she said. "Are you going to ignore me again?"

Trouble tilted his head at Lottie. He tweeted once. Then, in a great jump, he swooped up above Lottie, flapping his wings in what Lottie knew, though she couldn't say *how* she knew, was a very satisfied way.

They walked on like this for an hour more. Trouble bobbed ahead of Lottie, joining in the merry circle-dance with Spool and Keats and then fluttering back to Lottie, as though afraid she might run off if he strayed too far. The others said nothing, but Lottie caught a glint in Oliver's blue eyes and a smile on Fife's and then Adelaide's lips. Lottie had begun to forget just how hungry she was. She felt warmer, too, though she wasn't sure if that was due to the rising sun or Trouble's happy tweets.

The webs drooped lower still, and soon, stones and grass—brown grass, not wisp white—peeked through the gaps in the webs, then intermingled, and then Lottie was not walking on webs but on hard ground. There were no more webs, just a stony path that flanked the River Lissome.

"That's that," Fife said. "The webs have all run aground, which means we're out of Wisp Territory. And *that* means the Southerly Court can't be far off. Half a day at most."

Fife gave a low whistle and raised his forefinger in the air. Spool fluttered to a perch there, and Fife tucked him back into his pocket. Oliver and Adelaide, too, collected their gengas and put them away. Lottie squinted up at Trouble, who was still flying in low, wide circles above their heads.

"Here, Trouble!" she said, cupping her hands up in the air.

Trouble twittered but made no attempt to descend.

"Trouble," Lottie hissed. "Come *here*."

Trouble released a low, whiny note, but after a few more swooping circles, he alighted in Lottie's hands. As she placed him back into her pocket, she noticed the others watching her. Fife had covered his mouth.

"What?" she demanded. "What's funny?"

"Nothing," said Fife, though his voice was full of stifled laughter.

They moved on.

Lottie had not realized just how accustomed her feet had grown to walking along the webbings until now. The rough path felt foreign and unwelcome against her feet. A breeze blew the collar of Lottie's tweed coat up against her face and sent her into a round of sneezes.

Then a strange thing happened: her sneezes echoed. She looked up.

Oliver and Adelaide had stopped walking. Fife floated down to ground level. A great stone doorway arched overhead, and that doorway led into a greater, round stone building—or what had once *been* a building. Lottie squinted up at high stone walls, now crumbling on all sides. The roof of the ancient place had long since disappeared, but some sturdy columns still remained, and thick vines curled out of crevices and underfoot. Its inhabitants may have abandoned this place long ago, but the wood itself had not. Branches of taller trees swayed above, in place of a roof; still others reached their leafy hands through wide chinks in the walls.

"They're ruins," said Lottie.

"*Southerly* ruins," said Fife. "Look! The mark of the Southerly Court, it's everywhere."

Fife pointed to a weathered stone column, where a painted white circle peeked through the ivy. There was another circle like it on the next column over, and on the next, and the next, and through the center of the columned circle the River Lissome flowed on as steadily as ever.

"They were not prepared," Oliver murmured, running his hand down a column, "for silence so sudden and so soon. The day was too hot, too bright, too still, too ever, the dead remains too nothing."

"I don't like this place," Adelaide announced, shivering. "Come on, let's keep walking."

The boys nodded, as did Lottie, but when she took her next step, her foot caught against a thick vine. Lottie grabbed at the closest thing she could find—*another* vine, wound about a column—and just managed to catch her fall.

"Whoa, you okay?" Fife floated to her side, and the others looked on with wide eyes.

"Fine," said Lottie, but Fife had made a face and was pointing at the column behind her.

"Hang on," he said. "Look, just there."

There was a deep notch in the column's stone, carved in the distinguishable shape of the letter G.

"I think something's written here," said Fife, bending back the foliage.

Lottie stepped back to afford everyone a view of the single world cut in stone:

HINGECATCH

"Sweet Oberon," whispered Fife.

Oliver's eyes had shifted to an alarmed yellow color.

"What?" said Lottie. "What's Hingecatch?"

"An old Southerly lookout," Oliver said. "There are poems about it. Dozens of poems."

"It's where the tide of battle turned during the Great Schism," Fife added, "back when the Northerlies and the Southerlies first split up. The Northerly army nearly got to the Southerly Court walls—only, back then it was just the Sprite Court. Yeah, and then the Southerlies slaughtered 'em all, right where we're standing."

"I *don't* like this place," Adelaide whispered.

"But," Oliver said, "the poems also say that the Northerlies took their revenge on the Southerlies. Their blood fed the ground, and the ground produced Northerly vines. And the vines grew and overtook Hingecatch until all the Southerlies were forced to leave."

"But the vines didn't stop there!" Fife said excitedly. "They grew and grew and overtook the whole edge of Hingecatch Forest. They grew right up until they reached the walls of the Southerly Court itself. They say that the Southerly Guard still has to pour enchanted acid down the walls twice a day to keep the vines from creeping in. That's why the walls look bleached."

"What do you know about the walls, Fife?" asked Adelaide. "*You've* never even seen the Southerly Court."

Fife shrugged. "Guess I'm lucky, then, since—"

Fife didn't get the chance to finish that thought, because, quite suddenly, he'd been grabbed by the ankles and hoisted upside down.

Lottie would have reached out a hand or jumped in shock or perhaps said something helpful, like "Fife, you're upside down," but all she ended up doing was shrieking, because the same vines that had snagged Fife's ankles were now snagging hers and the others', lifting all four of them upside down into the air. The vines were strong and, it seemed to Lottie, everywhere at once. They were winding up her calves, now binding her legs together, now crawling up her back and stomach, now cinching around her wrists, now curling their leaves behind Lottie's ears.

We're all going to die, Lottie thought as she forced her eyes shut against a thick shoot winding around her face. *We're going to die, and of all things, we're going to be squeezed to death by* vines.

Then she heard a sound like the shrillest note of a flute, and the vines stopped squeezing.

"What's this?" said a voice just under where Lottie's head hung in midair. "More visitors, is it? Come on, then, Roote, and have a look."

The vines began to move again, but this time Lottie felt them sliding in reverse, loosening up around her face, her chest, and her arms. The last of their strong tendrils fell from Lottie's wrists, and her arms dropped past her head, limp and dangling. Slowly, Lottie's eyes opened to the sight of her hair spilling beneath her. Her vision adjusted, and she saw Adelaide, Fife, and Oliver hanging across from her in bundles of vines, bound like she was.

Two sprites stood under them, one dressed in black, the other in brown. They were older, both lean and gaunt-faced, and each of their short beards matched their leather clothes. The sprite in black held a long, black knife.

"Trespassing, are we?" he grunted, approaching the closest of the group, which happened to be Adelaide. "We'll 'ave you know that this is Northerly ground."

"Tell them, Roote!" said the sprite in brown. "Slice them down to size!"

"That I will, Crag."

Adelaide was trembling so violently that the vines holding her shook. The sprite called Roote caught one of Adelaide's dangling arms and yanked up her right sleeve to reveal the bright white circle tattooed on her skin.

"What a shame. Such a pretty girl to be a Southerly."

"Don't talk to her like that!" shouted Oliver, wriggling unsuccessfully against his bonds. His eyes shone red.

Adelaide bunched her lips, then spat on Roote's face. "I'm *proud* to be a Southerly," she said, though her voice quivered.

In one deft movement, Roote had wiped the spit from his cheek and held the flat of his knife blade against Adelaide's wrist. "Oh, are you?" he growled. "And what if I were to carve that mark right off your wrist? How proud would our pretty little Southerly be then?"

Adelaide gave a sob. Lottie was trying to remember something, but blood was throbbing painfully in her head and it grew harder and harder to think the longer she hung by her feet.

"Ey, Roote, look 'ere. This one's one of us!"

The sprite named Crag was holding Fife's arm aloft, waving it like a flag to show off its black diamond tattoo.

Roote turned back to Adelaide. "Fascinating," he said. "And what, pray tell, would a Northerly and Southerly be doing together?"

Adelaide was too busy crying to answer.

"You can either tell me what you're doing here," Roote ordered, pressing the blade of his knife closer to Adelaide's skin, "or you can *scream* it with a little help."

Lottie beat her to it. "Vesper Bells!" she shrieked.

Roote's attention snapped away from Adelaide to Lottie. He lowered the knife from Adelaide's arm, eyes wide in bewilderment.

"Wh-what did you just say?" he stammered.

But the vines were moving again. They slithered upward from Lottie's waist, uncurling from her bound legs. Then, like cradling hands, they contorted under her, turning her right side up and settling her back down on the ground. The same thing was happening to the others, and the sprite named Crag was hopping about in a circle like an excited child.

"Titania's sake!" he cried. "They're moving, the vines are, just at the name of Vesper Bells! Look, Roote, *look!*"

Roote was looking. He was looking Lottie right in the eye. She gulped and looked straight back.

"Where did a little girl like you hear about Vesper Bells?" he asked. He was still holding his knife at the ready, as though a wrong answer might be Lottie's last.

"Mr. Ingle taught me," she told him. "He said to use 'Vesper Bells' when there wasn't anything left to say."

Roote made a horking sound.

"Ingle?" he said. "Wensley Ingle? *The* Wensley Ingle?"

"I've never heard him called that," said Lottie, "but if he's the same old man who owns Ingle Inn in New Albion, then yes."

Roote looked uncertain for a moment. Then, without warning, a wide grin spread over his face. He sheathed his knife.

"Well, why didn't you tell us that in the first place?" he bellowed, motioning over at Crag. "You hear that, Crag? They're friends of Wensley Ingle."

"*The* Wensley Ingle?" snuffled Crag, staring at Lottie and then the others with starry eyes. "Been years since I've 'eard tell of that stray dog. A Northerly by 'eart, through and through. Don't know why 'e ever moved south by *choice.*"

"Good sprite, Wensley Ingle," said Roote. "Got a nephew in high places, they say."

"Been years, really," Crag was still muttering to himself, "since I've 'eard tell of Vesper Bells. Not since the Rebellion. Not since folk still believed in an Heir of Fiske."

Lottie started, and tripped over a circlet of vine still wound around her foot.

"Steady on," said Roote. "Don't mind the vines. Feisty, they are. Minds of their own."

"The vines," said Lottie, getting her footing again, "have minds?"

"Well, now, don't know about minds," said Crag. "But loyalties, yes. Loyal, through and through, to the Northerly Court."

"Aren't they teaching you Southerly tots anything in school nowadays?" Roote asked in an appalled voice.

"Ollie and I don't go to school," piped up Adelaide, who had recovered remarkably quickly from her sobbing and now looked as prim as ever. "We have a *tutor*. And of course we know about Hingecatch. The Battle of Hingecatch was the most decisive Southerly victory in recorded history."

Only now did Roote seem to remember that there were other people in their company aside from Lottie. He turned to Adelaide with a rueful look.

"No hard feelings, eh, tot?" Roote said. "Rebels like Crag and I don't know who to trust these days. Can't be too careful. Wasn't like I was *really* going to nick your pretty arm."

Lottie wasn't so sure of this, and Adelaide didn't look like she was, either. Oliver stepped in front of his sister and faced Roote down.

"I don't care," he said. "Threaten her again, I'll take you down with my bare hands."

"And me too," piped up Fife. "Though out of the two of us, I'd say Oliver's wrestling would be more—colorful."

"Thanks," Adelaide muttered, "but I could take him down myself."

"Yeah," said Fife, "with your spit. Fierce."

Adelaide aimed a smack at Fife's arm, and this time, rather than float out of the way, Fife just took the blow with a tiny smirk.

"Calm down, boys," said Roote. "What a noble little band you are. No more threats. In fact, how about we make it up to you, hm?"

With that, Roote lifted his hands like a conductor would before an orchestra, and the vines moved once more. Rather than attack anyone this time, they shifted and shaped, and Lottie recognized after a few moments what shapes they were forming: six chairs, made entirely of vines, arranged in a circle like the columns surrounding them.

"Crag and I can't offer much hospitality," said Roote. "Haven't got much more than the clothes on our backs and these old ruins for a house. But what a Northerly's got, a Northerly shares."

They took their seats, Lottie cautiously at first. Her vine-made chair was surprisingly sturdy, and aside from the occasional itch of a leaf against the insides of her knees, it was a comfortable reprieve from all the walking they had done that night.

Crag turned his attention to a dirty sack on his lap; from it, he pulled out the carcasses of three small animals that Lottie did not recognize.

"We've just had ourselves a hunting," Roote explained.

"Fine night of it, too," said Crag. "Roote 'as the best sights for spotting creatures in these woodlands."

"You're welcome to split if you'd like," said Roote, dangling one of the carcasses.

"No thank you." Adelaide sniffed. "I don't eat meat."

"Ah, that's right, innit?" said Crag, chuckling. "You Southerlies don't know what you're missing."

Crag took one of the carcasses and bit into it raw, fur and all. Lottie, Oliver, and Adelaide gave a collective "Ugh!" Fife didn't look surprised.

"So, where is your little band headed, if you don't mind my asking?" said Roote. "One sees strange things in this wood, but nothing so extraordinary as Southerlies and Northerlies traveling together."

Lottie glanced nervously at the others. Even if these sprites did know good Mr. Ingle, was it a wise idea to tell them their plans?

"We're going to the Southerly Court," Adelaide said in a proud, unnaturally high voice. "We've got business there."

Roote shared a look with Crag and the two burst into snorting laughter, Crag dribbling little bits of raw meat down his brown hide vest.

"Got business there?" Roote sputtered between guffaws. "What sort of business have you children got in the Southerly Court?"

"Hey, we're not children!" Fife said. "I'll have you know that I'm a bona fide teenager. My thirteenth was way back at the start of the summer."

"And we've made it this far, haven't we?" said Lottie. "We've gotten past burning fences and the Southerly Guard and Sweetwater and—even a Barghest!"

The sprites stopped laughing. Crag wiped his bloodied mouth with the back of his hand. "A Barghest?"

Lottie nodded earnestly. "He even bit me," she said, showing off her bandaged hands as evidence.

"And aren't you dead, then?" Crag whispered wonderingly.

"Does it look like I'm dead?"

Crag looked suspicious, but finally seemed to decide that Lottie was not, in fact, deceased. He turned to Roote. "What d'you think it means?"

Roote shook his head. "Hard to say. There hasn't been much word from Rebel Gem these days, not since he posted us here to play lookout."

"Rebel Gem?" repeated Lottie.

"Our leader," Roote said solemnly. "The only leader the Northerlies have left. He's the Master of the Barghest. He decides when they come and where they go, whom they trail and whom they kill."

"Right," said Fife, "well, if you see this Rebel Gem on your next social outing, mind telling him to call the Barghest off? It'd make the going smoother."

"Like we'd ever see Rebel Gem," said Crag, chewing on the carcass again, his teeth crimson with blood. "Not 'ardly a soul sees Rebel Gem. Not like 'e's the Southerly King. Lives in 'iding, Rebel Gem, just the same as all us spies. Only things we do these days is keep our noses in our own meat sacks."

"There have been rumors, though," said Roote. "Rumors rumbling though these forests about the Heir of Fiske. But that's impossible."

"Heir of Fiske, my tooth," grunted Crag. "Younger Northerlies, they're as optimistic as schoolchildren, thinking that some new ruler's gonna pop out of the earth itself like a stinkweed. 'Course there aren't gonna be any more Heirs of Fiske. Those younger ones don't remember the Plague like we do. All those Fiskes are dead."

"But," said Adelaide, "Lottie's a—OW!"

Fife had given Adelaide's shin a good kick and shook his head once, decisively.

"I *mean*," Adelaide picked up again, "Lottie's already heard all this, haven't you, Lottie dear?"

Lottie nodded.

"Impossible, like I said," concluded Roote. "Though there are some fine ballads about the Fiskes. Best in the

Northerly repertoire in my opinion. Crag here knows them by heart."

Crag blushed and waved Roote off. "Nothing worth shouting 'bout," he muttered, though he was already pulling out a small wooden flute from his vest, "just some tales the Old Sprite taught me. Though if you'd *really* like to 'ear some . . ."

Without waiting for a response, Crag raised the flute to his lips and began to play. The melody was sad and discordant, like rain on a birthday or sun on a graveyard.

"He sure can play," Fife murmured to Lottie and the others. "I think it's one of the better keens, an ear for music."

"Bid the strain be wild and deep," Oliver said, chin propped on his knees, eyes closed, "nor let thy notes of joy be first."

Only Adelaide remained unmoved. "I still think the one in black was going to cut my arm off."

"But he didn't," Lottie said.

"No," said Adelaide. She added in a hush that Lottie barely heard, "Thanks to you."

Lottie looked up, startled. It was the first time that Adelaide had spoken to her since Sweetwater.

Adelaide went on in a small voice. "I don't admit I'm wrong, you know, because to be wrong is the height of unsophistication. But I think being ungrateful is even worse."

"Oh?" Lottie felt that what Adelaide was telling her just now was something fragile. She didn't dare say anything else for fear of shattering it.

Adelaide let out a sigh. "It's been terribly unrefined of me to not thank you for what you did in the swamp. If you hadn't come after me, I'd be the one who fell in the oblivion. So—thank you."

Lottie ventured only two more words. "You're welcome."

"Thanks," said Adelaide, who seemed very ready to now put an end to the conversation. "I—I'm glad we've settled that."

Crag had finished his flute solo, and a taut pause fell on the ruins. After wiping his hand across his mouth, Crag puckered again and blew a single note from the flute. Then he cleared his throat and began to sing at the same pitch. His voice was hoarse and shallow, but solemn, too, and something in the timbre of it made Lottie's blood warm. But the words, more than anything, kept her fixated:

"Good Queen Mab, in spritely grace,
Was seated on her throne.
Downtrodden sprites from every place
Sought out her aid alone.
Thieves returned their pilfered goods,
The sad produced a smile.
They traveled back into the woods,
And kindness replaced guile.
Dark years passed, and Vik the Fiske
Took up the royal crown
His keen was weak, his throne at risk,
He gathered no renown.
Then one night he fled the court.
No Fiske would rule again!
And chaos poured from every port,
As sprites slayed and were slain."

The last word of the song hung in the air until a breeze slinked through the ruins, shivered up the vines, and dragged the note away.

"That," said Fife, "was the most depressing thing I've ever heard."

"There aren't many chipper ditties up north," said Roote.

"I wonder why that is," said Fife. "It's such a warm and fuzzy place up there in the caves and wilders."

"Speaking of which," said Oliver, "if you two are Northerlies, what are you doing this far south?"

"Eh," said Crag, "there's always been Northerly lookouts at 'ingecatch, ever since the vines drove the Southerlies out. It's 'ard work, so new sprites volunteer each year."

"Lookouts for what?" said Lottie.

"For the Southerly Court, of course," said Roote. "To monitor the movements of the Southerly King and his Guard, should they ever choose to invade our northern lands. You don't think we'd wait until they were snapping at our gates, do you?"

"No," said Lottie. "I guess you can't be too careful."

"You can't," agreed Crag. "Especially not with that King Starkling squatted on the throne. 'e's been the worst of them all."

"Which is why if I were you, little mites," said Roote, "I wouldn't be going anywhere near there."

"And yet we are," said Fife, who had disentangled himself from his vine chair and now stood at the ready. "Aren't we, everyone? Wouldn't you say it's time to go?"

Lottie looked to the sun. It hung almost straight overhead through the open roof of the ruins. Nearly noon. Lottie had been too lost in Crag's ballad to realize that Fife was right: it was past time to go.

CHAPTER FOURTEEN

Discovery

"WHATEVER BUSINESS you have with the Southerly Court," Roote told the quartet as they readied to leave, "it isn't worth the journey. Why not forget the whole thing, hm?"

Crag handed Fife a small bundle of food wrapped in dirty cheesecloth that smelled of raw meat. "What they've got, Northerlies share," he said.

"If you see old Wensley Ingle again," Roote said by way of final words, "remember Roote and Crag to him."

As the sun reached its highest point in the sky, they left the ruins and set out into Hingecatch Forest. It was difficult work, navigating the vines underfoot, but Roote and Crag had directed them to a narrow pathway where the vines were less dense than usual. Lottie only tripped twice before she remastered the art of walking.

The chance to rest seemed to have done a world of good for everyone, and Fife went on for half an hour about how all chairs should be made from vines and how selfish it was of Northerlies to keep the secret to perfect seating all to themselves.

"But the vines are Northerly," Oliver said, "so it's not like they'd bend to the will of Southerlies or wisps."

Fife asked Oliver to stop being so practical and let him rail a little while longer against the injustice of what he was now calling the Northerly Vine Monopoly.

They tromped on until they passed under trees dangling down purple fruits that Fife identified as edible. Oliver opened the cheesecloth bundle that Crag had given them and that contained, true to its smell, the carcass of a small animal that no one was willing to eat. Crag had also packed up some mushrooms and chestnuts, however, and when Fife and Oliver had carefully wiped them free of the carcass's blood, they added them to their stock of picked fruit for a makeshift meal. It was enough to settle the growl in Lottie's stomach, but she missed more than ever the filling bread and cheese that they had lost to the swamp.

When they set out again, Fife and Adelaide took the lead, arguing about the Battle of Hingecatch and whether the victory of the Southerlies had been due entirely to sheer tactical skill and bravery (argued Adelaide) or to the conniving betrayal of Southerly politicians (argued Fife). Lottie and Oliver walked behind them, and for a while the two of them shared a quiet giggle whenever Adelaide called Fife "unrefined," which was, on their timed average, every one and a half minutes. After a while longer, though, the arguing was just unpleasant, and Lottie winced every time Adelaide's voice broke into an extra-shrill octave.

"Are you all right?" Oliver asked.

"Oh, I'm fine," said Lottie. "It's just that Adelaide knows how to hit a high note, doesn't she?"

"No," said Oliver, "I mean, are you *all right*. You went through a lot back there. First the Barghest, then Sweetwater, and then the Northerlies. If I were you, I'd be ready to go home."

"I do want to go home," Lottie admitted, "but not because it's home. I mean, I don't want to go back to Mrs. Yates or Thirsby Square. I really just want to go back because it's the place where Eliot is."

They came to a long rut of mud, and Lottie jumped over it with an ease that she hadn't possessed two days ago, when they had first set out in Wandlebury Wood.

"I think," said Oliver, "that you'd make a good poet."

"*What?*" Lottie laughed. "Some of that oblivion must've gotten to *your* brain, Ollie."

Lottie turned a swift red. She had never called Oliver by that nickname before; it had just slipped out. Oliver, however, didn't seem to notice.

"I'm serious," he said. "Separation and longing, that's the stuff I like best about human poetry. Sighing the lack of many a thing one's sought, moaning the expense of many a vanished sight, and so on and so forth."

"What about Southerly poetry?"

"Southerly poetry isn't about things like that," said Oliver. "It's not allowed to be personal. It's only for recording big, important things, like history. But your human poetry, it's about life. It's the terrific and the terrible all mashed into one big mess. The things more important than the important things."

"The things that make life worth it," said Lottie, recalling what Oliver had said by the campfire.

Oliver smiled, his eyes shifting to a gentle blue. "You remembered."

"I think you and Eliot would get along," said Lottie. "He's an artist, too. But me? I don't think I've really got that sort of art in me."

"Sure, you have," said Oliver.

"You think I'm refined, then?" Lottie grinned. "Thanks."

"I think you're Lottie," Oliver said with a shrug. After a silent minute he added, "And you can call me Ollie, you know. I don't mind. It's what all of my friends call me."

Lottie swallowed hard. His friends? Did Oliver think of her as his friend? She hadn't thought of herself as Oliver's friend, really, or Fife's or Adelaide's; there hadn't been time to. Now that she thought on it, though, Lottie felt good, more than good, about the idea.

"Thanks," she said, smiling.

The forest grew sparser. As the sun sunk overhead into late afternoon, its rays shone between chinks of foliage. The plum-tinted light was just turning into a gloomier shade when Oliver motioned them to a stop.

"Look through the trees," he said.

They crowded around where Oliver had stopped and peered through the branches of a birch tree into a wide expanse of green grass. They had come to the forest's edge. On the distant horizon loomed the outline of something thick and white.

"The walls of the Southerly Court," said Fife. "Told you. Don't they look just like bleached bones?"

"They look smaller than I remember them," said Adelaide. "Last time Father brought us here, Ollie and I were little. We didn't stay for long. Father said the court wasn't a good place for children."

"He said," murmured Oliver, "that the court wasn't a good place for *anyone*."

Fife had begun to add his own two cents about the Southerly Court when a harsh, brassy blast swallowed his words up. The sound grew louder, low and insistent. It was the sound of horns, and of something more, like a dozen harps whose full sets of strings had all been plucked at once. The noise was unforgiving and final. Then, just as soon as it had started, it stopped.

"What *was* that?" asked Fife.

Adelaide was bent over, hands clenched to her ears. "Is it over?" she shouted.

The others nodded. Adelaide straightened back up, eyes watering, and for the first time Lottie considered the fact that if a sound was painful to her own normal sense of hearing, it must have been doubly so to Adelaide's.

"It's the changing of the Southerly Guard," said Oliver, his eyes dimming. "It means that we're too late."

"What do you mean, too late?" said Lottie.

"He means it's too late to enter the court tonight," Adelaide sighed. "Isn't that right?"

"The gates close at dusk and open at dawn," Oliver said with a nod. "We've just missed them."

"So now we've got to wait until morning?" Lottie said.

"There's nothing else to do," Fife said glumly.

"It isn't right," said Adelaide. "Father is so close."

But, as Fife had already pointed out, there was nothing else that they could do, and night was coming on fast. They backtracked deeper into the wood, where the trees were thicker and provided better shelter, and made camp for the night. Oliver began a fire with brittle pinecones.

"If we're so close to court," said Lottie, "won't the Southerly Guard be able to see the campfire smoke?"

"Travelers camp outside the court every night," said Oliver. "I don't think it's anything out of the ordinary to see smoke around here."

"Oi," Fife said suddenly, squinting at Adelaide through the firelight. "Ada, what've you got there on your neck?"

Adelaide clamped her hand over her neck, but not before Lottie saw an ugly red mark that Adelaide's long hair had covered until now.

"I don't know what you're talking about," Adelaide said.

"Yes, you do," insisted Fife, pointing. "You've got to. Lookit! Right there. It's all red, like a blister. Doesn't it hurt?"

"It's nothing."

"It's not nothing! What, did one of those swamp flames get you, too?" Fife swooped his hand down his cheek to show off his own scar. "They can leave some mighty fierce scars. Did it hurt?"

Oliver hurled a pinecone into the fire and got to his feet, skulking into the wood without a word. Adelaide glared at Fife.

"It was an accident," she hissed. "Oliver didn't see me out there in the swamp when we were dragging Lottie out of the oblivion. I caught him by surprise, and when he turned around, his hand just—" Adelaide motioned helplessly to her neck.

Fife straightened up. "Oberon. I didn't know. I swear I didn't."

"You're worse than unrefined, Fife," Adelaide whispered, getting up. "You're just a—a *fool*."

Adelaide disappeared into the forest after her brother.

Fife held a sprig of pine needles that he now savagely ripped down to an ugly switch. Lottie nudged his shoulder.

"Don't worry," she said. "Oliver can't possibly blame himself for—well, for *pigmenting* Adelaide. It was just an accident."

"Of course he blames himself. Don't you think he blames himself for *that*?" Fife pointed at Lottie's arm.

She pushed back her sleeve, expecting to see the imprint of Oliver's hand.

It was gone.

Lottie gave a short gasp. She turned her arm over entirely, but she saw nothing but clean, unmarked skin. The handprint had vanished entirely.

Fife hadn't noticed Lottie's distraction. "He blames himself for everything," he said, "especially when it comes to family."

Lottie hastily pushed down her sleeve and looked back up. "What do you mean?"

"Why do you think Ollie's keen is fluked like it is?" Fife said. "He was born early. Way too early. His mother died because of it."

Lottie felt weak. "I didn't know that," she whispered.

She rubbed her arm and wished that she had never thought an ill thing about Oliver and his poetry.

"I think you should," said Fife. "Just don't let Ollie know I told you, all right? People say it left Mr. Wilfer in a really bad way. Even Ada doesn't ever mention it."

Fife sighed and tossed his switch into the fire. "I'm going to try to apologize, make things up. Will you be all right here?"

"I'll be fine," said Lottie, even though she wasn't thrilled about the idea of sitting alone in the dark forest. Then, before she could stop herself, she asked, "Will you use your keen on him?"

Fife froze. "What?"

"I just guessed, with your keen, you must have the nicest-worded apologies."

"Look," said Fife, "I know you're still weirded out by my keen and all. That's fine. But for the record, there are some circumstances that a self-respecting sprite would never use his keen on. Apologizing? That's one of them."

Fife headed the way of Oliver and Adelaide until he, too, was swallowed up behind branches.

Lottie scooted closer to the fire. She pushed back her sleeve again and stared at the place where the mark of Oliver's handprint had once been.

There was a faint rustling of Lottie's coat against her leg. She drew her eyes away from her arm to her coat pocket. She tugged out Trouble, cupping him close in both hands.

"You've been naughty recently," she informed him.

Trouble gave an unconcerned tweet. He blinked rapidly at Lottie and nudged his beak against her thumb.

"We're almost there, you know," she said. "We'll be in the Southerly Court tomorrow."

He gave a single chirp in response. Lottie yawned.

"If I fall asleep," she murmured, "will you keep watch?"

Trouble's black eyes glistened. He bobbed his head once. Lottie smiled sleepily in return.

Her eyes burned with tiredness, and she sank her nose onto her knees, head whirling with a stew of words and images: oblivion and webs and heirs and keens and seamstresses and her parents' photograph and the Otherwise Incurable and apple trees and a lone white finch.

She was back at the Barmy Badger. Eliot was in bed, sleeping, his uneven snores broken up occasionally by a hoarse cough. Mr. Walsch sat by Eliot's bedside, his head dropped in his hands, and Lottie could not tell if he was sleeping or weeping.

"Mr. Walsch," she said, reaching for the man's slumped shoulders.

It did no good. Mr. Walsch could not hear her. Still, she spoke again.

"I'm sorry," she said. "I *am* coming back, I am!"

Mr. Walsch turned to face her.

But he was no longer Mr. Walsch.

His eyes shone greedily up at her, two silver pinpricks. Then his lips curled back in a snarl.

"She is the Heir of Fiske," growled a voice.

"She belongs to the Northerlies," said another.

"The Heir of Fiske!" both voices said in unison. "The Heir of Fiske!"

Lottie let out a cry and dove into the bed to escape the voices. But it was no longer Eliot under the covers. A cold, sneering face stared out at her from where Eliot had been lying. It was the face of Mr. Grissom.

"I don't understand!" Lottie said, but she could not hear her own screams.

She woke to the sound of voices.

"I still think we should tell her."

Lottie gripped the grass about her face and peered up. It was dim morning. The fire had died out, and dew beaded the sleeves of her tweed coat. Though she was lying on her side, chilled through with cold, Lottie's hand pulsed with something dry and warm. *Trouble.* He was roosting happily on her palm. Lottie's eyes rested on him, and he gave a low, sleepy chirp. She closed her hand gently around the tiny black bird and carefully tucked him into her pocket.

The voices that had woken her now continued. Fife, Adelaide, and Oliver stood only a few feet off, their backs turned to her, talking in hushed tones.

"When we've gotten this far?" said Adelaide. "What good would that do, Fife?"

"I dunno, I just feel guilty about it."

"Oh, honestly," said Adelaide, "someone as unrefined as you talking about *conscience*. None of us should feel the least bit guilty. Father is in real trouble. Oliver and I can't possibly get on without him and neither can you, Fife. Who else is going to teach healing to a halfling?"

"We wouldn't have settled on this," said Oliver, "if we thought Lottie wouldn't be safe."

"If you plead before court, you've got to have something to plead with," said Adelaide. "We all know that. We settled on it at the inn."

"Yeah," said Fife, "but what if Starkling doesn't agree to the trade?"

"He will," said Oliver. "He has to. Otherwise, you know what'll happen to Father. He can't make the medicine from scratch in the time Grissom gave him. He'll be sentenced to death. Either we give up the medicine, or we lose him."

"If it seems like Lottie suspects something," said Adelaide, "one of us can just tell her—"

"No, we'll tell her before then," said Oliver. "I don't like keeping it from her now, but I think that if we explain things when we reach the court, she'll agree. She's got to. Lottie's good. She'll see reason."

Adelaide was the first to turn around at the sound of Lottie's approach. Her frowning face went ashen.

"O-o-ooh," she gasped.

Lottie looked from Adelaide to Oliver to Fife. They were going to let Eliot die.

"It was all a trick."

No one replied. They were going to take the medicine. She would have nothing to bring back, *nothing*. All she could feel was dry despair, and anger.

"You were lying all this time," said Lottie. "You didn't plan to let me save Eliot at all. You're going to give up the Otherwise Incurable to the Southerly King."

"No!" said Oliver, breaking from the circle and reaching out toward her. "It's not like that. Lottie, please understand, it's *our father*—"

"Get away from me," Lottie said. "Don't *touch* me!"

Oliver went still, and Lottie realized too late what she

had said to turn his eyes that painful gray. He closed his shaking palms and lowered his head.

Lottie had thought they'd been friends. She had thought they'd understood each other. Now she wasn't sure if her words could even hurt Oliver. Maybe, even now, he was just playacting at being hurt, just like he had at helping her rescue Eliot.

"See! This is why we weren't going to tell her," said Adelaide.

"Lottie," said Fife. "Let us explain."

Lottie shook her head, trembling. "I trusted you all."

"But could we trust you?" asked Adelaide, holding up the green scarf, still bundled around the precious bottle. "You were trying to take the Otherwise Incurable every chance you got: at Iris Gate, at Ingle Inn, maybe even in Sweetwater! All you could go on about was getting back home. Did you even think about us? Our house overtaken, our father imprisoned, our good name slandered, and all because of *you*. But no, Lottie, from the famed house of Fiske, all you could think about was your stupid friend. There are more important things in this world than your precious Eliot!"

And in that moment, Adelaide's face looked no different from Pen Bloomfield's. Lottie lunged at Adelaide, fists first, and rammed her onto the mossy ground.

"Get off! Get off!" Adelaide shrieked.

"Don't you dare talk about him! You know nothing about Eliot!" Lottie reeled back her fist and aimed a punch at Adelaide's nose.

Before she could bring the fist down, fingers wrapped around her wrist.

"Intervention," Fife grunted, tugging Lottie off Adelaide.

The force of his yank sent Fife and Lottie tumbling. Under the mound of her right elbow and Fife's messy black hair, Lottie could see Oliver standing helplessly by, his hands clutched behind his back. Lottie struggled to free her wrist from Fife and, unsuccessful, she did the first desperate thing that came to mind: she used her teeth.

"Oberon!" Fife howled, letting go. "You've gone mad!"

Lottie staggered up, panting. Then she began to run.

"Lottie!"

She ran faster, faster, accustomed now to leaping around brambles and over logs like a sprite. She ran into the thickening forest, never looking back.

"Lottie!"

On and on, never to forgive them, *never* to forgive them for betraying her, for lying to her. What could she possibly do without the Otherwise Incurable and without Mr. Wilfer? Eliot only had two, maybe three weeks, and she was lost in a strange wood when all she wanted was to leave this horrible world of Southerlies and Northerlies and diseases and healers and false friends.

"LOTTIE!"

She did not turn back.

CHAPTER FIFTEEN

The Southerly Dungeons

LOTTIE EXPECTED every minute to hear a voice at her ear or feel a hand on her back. After all, Adelaide would be able to hear her, and Fife could surely float quickly enough to catch up. She ran on, fought a patch of thistles, sloshed down a slope of mud, but still Lottie heard and felt nothing. So, they had decided to let her go, had they? They probably thought that she would come sniveling back. Well, how little they knew her!

The wood that had been so dark and foreboding before Lottie's dream was now filled with morning light. An unexpectedly warm breeze swirled leaves down Lottie's path, and the branches rang with the early chatter of squirrels. If she had not been so angry, she might have enjoyed it.

Instead, Lottie shouted a word aloud that Mrs. Yates had grounded her for saying a month ago. It did not make her feel much better, so Lottie said the word louder and aimed a kick at a nearby bush, which turned out to be hiding a particularly large rock. Lottie said the word five more times, howling and hopping in pain. Then she limped on, feeling worn and wicked.

The Southerly Court had been close back at the campfire; Lottie had seen it with her own eyes. But that had been before she ran away heedlessly. Now she was smacking into tree branches and untangling her way through shrubberies with no sign of a wall in the distance. Lottie blamed it on her awful sense of direction, and the more she wandered the more her old eight-year-old fear bubbled up. The others could waltz right up to the Southerly King, trade the medicine he wanted for Mr. Wilfer's freedom, and live happily ever after. Meantime, Lottie would be left in Hingecatch Forest, wandering alone while Eliot got sicker and sicker in New Kemble.

Maybe, Lottie began to think, she had been wrong to run away.

Lottie had thought that Fife had been her friend. Hadn't he stitched up her wounds? Hadn't he gone back to his home, even gotten a scar on his face in Sweetwater for her? Or was all of that just pretend, like Oliver's talk of poetry and of the art inside of Lottie and of he and Lottie understanding each other? Lottie had even thought that Adelaide, despite all her nonsense about refinement and sophistication, had begun to like her--she had even halfway apologized to her!—and wasn't that how friends worked, by liking and helping and talking to each other?

Or was friendship different with sprites?

It didn't matter now. Lottie had run away from the others just like she had from the Barmy Badger and from Eliot. Now there was no chance of knowing if they were ever her friends.

Unless Adelaide could still hear her . . .

Lottie turned around. "Adelaide?" she called. "Can you hear me? Fife? Oliver? Anyone?"

The only reply was the distant squawk of a crow. Lottie started to trudge back in direction of their camp. Or *was* that the right direction? All the trees here looked the same.

Her hands were chafed and powdery from cold, and her ankles and shins now ached with cuts and bruises. When she stopped to tie her loose shoelaces, Lottie's hands came up sticky with blood from a scratch that her feet were too numb to feel.

Lottie shoved her hands deep down into her coat pockets. One hand brushed against Trouble. Perhaps *he* could help her. Lottie tugged him out. Trouble's head was ducked, his breast heaving slowly and gently. Lottie brushed one of his wings in an attempt to wake him.

"Trouble?" she whispered. "I'm lost. Can you help me?"

Trouble blinked open sleepy eyes. He released one long, low, mournful tweet.

Lottie sighed. "I guess you don't know this wood any better than I do."

Trouble nudged his head against her palm. He chirruped in what Lottie took to be an encouraging way.

"At least you didn't betray me," Lottie murmured, tucking him back into the safety of her pocket.

As she did, her hand ran up against something small and crinkled. She pulled it out. It was a sweet-so-sour—the one that Eliot had tossed her that last night at the Barmy Badger. If ever Lottie needed an excuse to cry, it was now. She untwirled the neon green wrapper and tucked the sweet-so-sour into her mouth. Then, sniffling, she walked on.

From nowhere in particular, the voice of Mr. Kidd, Lottie's English teacher at Kemble School, popped in and whirled about her mind's ear: *"For the world's more full of weeping,"* said the voice, *"than you can understand."*

> *"For the world's more full of weeping.*
> *Full of weeping.*
> *Weeping."*

"You had it just about right, Mr. Kidd!" Lottie shouted. "Just about –"

A snarl brought her up short. She turned around. Two pinprick eyes were glaring at her.

It was the Barghest.

Only, this was not one of her nightmares. This was Lottie, alone, in a strange wood, with an animal that wanted her dead.

The Barghest snarled again.

Lottie ran.

She heard a long, shrill howl and the fast padding of paws behind her. It would catch up with her, Lottie thought in a panic, in no time at all. Then she remembered. How could she have forgotten?

Lottie stumbled to a stop, whirling around to face the Barghest.

"Stop!"

The doglike creature ground its claws into the dead leaves separating it from Lottie. It let out a high, whining noise.

"D-don't hurt me," said Lottie, stepping back.

The animal licked its mouth and pawed a few steps forward, but there it stopped.

Lottie tried to think quickly. She remembered what had happened in the mulberry bushes behind Iris Gate and in her nightmares: the Barghest had spoken to her.

"I want you to talk," Lottie said. "Can you talk?"

The Barghest whined again; then it opened its mouth.

"Yes," rumbled the Barghest, and its voice sounded the same as it had in Lottie's nightmares, like the crunch of broken glass.

Lottie winced, but kept staring defiantly back into the Barghest's eyes.

"I want you to tell me your business, Barghest."

The creature lowered its head in something like a bow. "I must obey the Heir of Fiske," it barked. "I have followed her with the express purpose of delivering a message from the Northerly Court."

Lottie blinked uncomprehendingly. "Wait," she said. "Do you mean that all this time, you were just going to give me a message?"

The Barghest nodded.

"Then what was all the biting for?" she asked angrily. "You nearly chomped my hands off back in the wood!"

The Barghest bared its yellowed fangs in what looked like a smile. "Sincerest apologies," it said, "but I was ordered to catch your attention in any way possible. Rebel Gem's orders. He sent me from the Northerly Wolds to warn the Heir of Fiske of the dangers of the Southerly King."

"Would you stop calling me the Heir of Fiske?" Lottie said. "And why do you keep doing everything I tell you to?"

The Barghest pawed the ground. "All of my pack made an oath to the House of Fiske that we would obey their every command until the day we died. After the Plague, we thought we were free from our oath. We did not know that any Fiske had survived. Then rumors came into Albion Isle about a child, the daughter of Eloise Fiske and her human. Rebel Gem sent the Barghest to find you. He wants the Heir of Fiske's allegiance."

Lottie shook her head. "I'm not an Heir of anything," she said. "I can't *do* anything. Not even . . ." Lottie trailed off.

"Rebel Gem said that the Heir of Fiske would be reluctant," barked the Barghest. "He said we must give the Heir time, but that in the end, she would join our side."

"Well," said Lottie, "you can tell Rebel Gem and anyone else that he has the wrong girl. I'm a halfling. I haven't got a keen, and I can't command or rule, or whatever else it is that people think I can do."

The Barghest's pinprick eyes dilated into black, watery orbs. It looked, of all things, sad. Lottie only grew angrier.

"I can't fix anyone. If anything, I just end up making things worse!"

She was yelling by the end, and her breath was suddenly short. A bad spell was coming on. Lottie crumpled down in the middle of the path, and tears gushed out and dropped, splat by splat, onto the ground. She could not tell whether it was the bad spell or the sobs that squeezed her ribs until they ached with stupid, useless pain.

Lottie felt something hot and moist against her ear. She hiccupped, clutching at the stabbing in her chest, and looked up. The Barghest had pressed its muzzle to her face, not to bite her, but to nudge its matted fur against her hair. It looked like it wanted to comfort her. Lottie sank her head back into her knees and tried to take deep breaths, fighting against the pain until the bad spell passed away.

"Barghest," she whispered at last, "I think I got you wrong. I think I might have gotten everyone wrong."

"What does the Heir of Fiske order?" growled the Barghest, pawing back a few paces.

"Stop calling me that." Lottie studied the Barghest, whose hulking black frame seemed much less frightening than it had before.

"Do you know the way to the Southerly Court?" she asked.

The Barghest shuddered out a guttural growl. Slowly, it nodded.

"Can you take me there?" said Lottie. "Can you help me find the others?"

"The Southerly Court is not welcoming to the Barghest, but I will take you there if I must." The Barghest crouched down on its hind legs and lowered its head. "You may ride on my back."

Lottie went pale. She was just getting used to the idea that the Barghest did not want to rip her to shreds. Riding on its back was hardly a comforting prospect. Still, her bramble-cut legs were begging for relief and, judging from how quickly she had seen the Barghest run before, she knew how much faster a journey it would be. She flexed her stiff hands, then picked nervously at the bandage on her right wrist. Carefully, Lottie loosened the cloth and peeked underneath. The chafing had healed. She unwound the bandage from her left hand. There was no blood, no gash where the Barghest had bitten her. All that remained was the line of puckered skin that Fife had stitched up the night before. She curled her fingers in on her palm. She pulled herself up, swinging one leg over the Barghest's slick, broad back.

"Hold on to my fur," the Barghest ordered. "Keep low."

Lottie clenched her fingers into the damp fur at her disposal and nodded. "I forgot to ask you, Barghest, if you have a name."

"The Barghest have no names," it growled.

"Oh." Lottie lowered herself against the animal's thick mane. "Then I guess I'll just stick to Barghest, if it's all the same to you."

"Whatever you choose."

The Barghest galloped off for the Southerly Court.

◆

Once Lottie grew brave enough to pull her face out of the Barghest's thick mane, she saw that they were no longer traveling through the forest but across a field. Blank sky stretched across the horizon, and beneath it ran the stone walls of the Southerly Court. Even though there were no longer branches and brambles to avoid, the Barghest still swerved erratically, forcing Lottie to reclutch a fistful of fur at every bump and jostle. She could not understand its unsteady canter at first. Then her eyes adjusted to the morning sun, and Lottie saw that hundreds upon hundreds of jaggedly hewn tree stumps surrounded them, pocking the green grass all the way up to the Southerly Court walls.

"What happened here?" she called to the Barghest, just as it took a great leap over one of the trunks, forcing Lottie to clench her ankles into its belly.

"The Plague," rasped the Barghest. "This was once the apple orchard of the sprite kings. Sprites and humans could come and go between worlds freely here. No more. The Plague poisoned them."

"But they're not all stumps. Look!" Lottie nodded to a lone tree amongst the nearby stumps, then to another, farther out. They looked sickly. "What about those?"

"There were survivors," the Barghest snarled as it ran. "There always are."

"I'm glad," Lottie said.

"You should not be," said the Barghest, crouching to take a new bound. "It is the survivors whose lot is longest and hardest."

The Barghest bounded on, faster than before, and Lottie struggled to keep her watering eyes open against the wind. She could see, as they came closer to the walls, a break in the white stone. A great silver gate stood ahead, open and crowded with the figures of sprites bustling in and out of its hold.

"Are we going through there?" Lottie called over the wild wind.

The Barghest shook its head and veered instead to the left.

"The Southerly Guard will not let a Barghest through the court gates," it called back. "We will go the way other beasts do."

Lottie began to notice a thick, squelching sound as the Barghest ran on. She looked down to find that they were crossing over a watery expanse of mud. The water grew murkier and deeper, too, until it was lapping against Lottie's ankles. Suddenly, the Barghest gave a great leap, and a warm spray of mud splashed into Lottie's face.

The Barghest had come to a stop. Lottie wiped the mud from her face and blinked upward. The Southerly walls were towering just above them, larger and more imposing than ever. The walls, Lottie saw now, were built upon a hill, and she and the Barghest stood at its base. This particular side of the hill was covered in slick muck that seemed to have originated from a wide grate above, built into the face of the wall.

Lottie slipped from the Barghest's back and set her feet down into mushy ground.

"Are we going through there?" she guessed, pointing to the grate.

The Barghest only bounded ahead, finding foothold after foothold on his ascent up the slippery slope. Lottie had a harder time of it and ended up getting her tweed coat muddied to within an inch of its periwinkleness. At last, she squelched to a stop next to the Barghest, inches from the grate. The wall was less than pristine white here, and an unbearable stench surrounded them. The smell reminded Lottie of the time that the house on Thirsby Square had reeked for a full week after Mollie Browne's eviction and before Mrs. Yates had discovered a rotten hard-boiled egg that Mollie had wedged between the sofa cushions as a farewell present.

The grate looked larger than it had looked from the bottom of the hill. Both Lottie and the Barghest could fit through its rusting bars with a little maneuvering. Lottie hoped that she had not upset the Barghest when she had given it a helpful push from behind; it struck her as a very proud creature.

Once they had passed through the thick bars, they sloshed into a dank, dark pool of water that came up to Lottie's shins. Though they were now within the city walls and though the sun was shining down brightly on them, neither of those advantages improved upon the foul smell.

"Is it really that easy to slip into the Southerly Court?" Lottie panted.

"No," replied the Barghest. "We're not in the Southerly Court yet, only Southerly City."

They waded out of the muck and up a silty incline. Lottie just managed to keep down a shriek as something slithered across her green-sneakered foot. But her sneakers reminded her of Eliot, and Lottie felt a new determination as she pulled herself up out of the sewer ditch and onto street level.

All this time, Lottie had been spending every scrap of her energy on trying to get within these walls. She hadn't ever stopped for a moment to consider what the city might actually *look* like. Had she imagined something, though, it wouldn't have been a thing like the scenes that now so solidly smacked her senses. The streets were cobblestone, as they had been in New Albion, but they were narrower here, and rougher, too. Each side of each street was nothing but floor topping floor topping floor of fogged-up windowpanes, short doors, and swinging signs. A spiced, woodsy smell shot through the alleyways and mixed with occasional spurts of smoke from underground grates that Lottie and the Barghest passed in the push and pull of the crowd.

Hoarse vendor calls of "Fresh hummingbeak juice!" and "Boysenberries!" and "Hot flower-bulb soup!" carried through the muggy air. Sprites bustled so thickly around her that Lottie had to grip the Barghest's fur with all of the strength she had left just to stay upright. At least, she thought, she was so squished out of sight that no one would think her and her muddy tweed coat out of the ordinary.

In fact, blending into this crowd would not have been a hard thing to do. Everyone here looked different. Some of the passersby were ridiculously tall, others no higher than Lottie's shoulder. Some had blazing shocks of red hair, others startling mohawks, others unkempt braids. Some were dressed in formal business attire, others in tights and miniskirts, still others in loud plaid prints. All of them were in a hurry, and their frantic energy leaked into Lottie's breath and sped up her heart. When Lottie saw the next deserted alleyway, she pulled the Barghest back by the fur and reeled into it.

"Wait," she gasped. "Now what do we do? Do you know where we're going? How do you know where Mr. Wilfer is?"

The Barghest was whining softly, and Lottie realized that she had accidentally managed to pull out a good clump of fur from its mane.

"Oops." Lottie cringed. "Sorry."

"I do not know where your friends are," the Barghest said, "but I do know the way to the Southerly Court Palace. It is to that place that I am taking you."

"To the Southerly King," said Lottie, nodding. "And the dungeons, where Mr. Wilfer's being held—they're nearby?"

"They lie underneath the palace."

"All right," said Lottie. "Then take me there."

"Do you know what you are going to do once you arrive?"

Despite herself, Lottie found herself laughing. "I haven't got a clue."

"Very well," said the Barghest, who was not affected by this answer one way or the other. "I will lead you to the palace. If I'm not mistaken, this will be the time of day that the king is holding court."

As they pressed on, the crowd grew thicker, the shouts of the vendors faded away, and Lottie had to shove harder against unmoving bodies. Then the talking around her gave way to murmuring, and the murmuring to whispers, until suddenly a complete and eerie silence enveloped Lottie, and all that she could make out were the angry grunts of the people she was pushing past, and then there were no more people to push past at all. Then Lottie just managed to catch herself from tumbling over a thick red rope that separated the silent crowd from a long flight of wide, marble steps. At the top of the steps were ten majestic columns, curled into contortions that Lottie had never seen back in her world, and higher still towered a sunstruck, silver dome. There could be no mistaking it: this had to be the Southerly Court.

The palace steps were lined on both edges by deep stone trenches, and from those trenches shot fountains of water. A landing cut across the very middle of the steps, and from it rose a towering stone figure fashioned in the form of a winged, regal sprite. He held a scepter in one hand, and the inscription at his feet read KING OBERON I. Positioned just in front of the statue was a throne with legs made of silver, spun like holly and sprigged by ruby berries. On the throne sat a sprite that could be none other than the Southerly King himself.

All this time, Lottie had expected the Southerly King to be gray-haired and wizened by years of rule. But the king's face was young and smooth. Though not one wrinkle creased his features, dimples cut into his cheeks in what looked like a perpetual, languid smile. His eyes were thickly lashed and a warm brown, like cocoa. Around his flawless face hung long locks of blond hair that Pen Bloomfield's minions would have killed to possess. This king did not look harsh at all. He also did not look a day past twenty-two.

Then the king raised his hand.

Lottie gasped. His fingers were shriveled and thin, browned with sunspots and bulging with veins; they shook as the king held them aloft. They were the fingers of an inconceivably old man. Something was wrong. Something was terribly wrong with the king.

On the palace steps, a row of red-cloaked sprites surrounded the king. Each guard held a large, wooden mace, except for the two who were currently dragging a limp figure before the throne. The Southerly King had raised his pruny hand, Lottie now saw, because he was speaking into the eerie silence around her. He was giving some sort of order.

". . . to be hanged by the feet until unconscious, then dipped into the sulfur baths, drawn, and quartered."

Lottie stiffened. This wasn't just an order. This was a sentence. A death sentence.

The king lowered his hand, and the two red-cloaked guards who held the limp figure bowed their heads at the king's words. The guards turned around, and Lottie's gasp was drowned in a sudden roar of cheering and applause from the crowd.

The sentenced prisoner in the guards' arms was a boy not much older than Lottie herself. He did not scream any protestations or wriggle about. His limbs and mouth seemed to have all gone slack. The only sign that he was conscious at all was a look of absolute horror burning in his eyes—eyes set in a perfectly expressionless face.

"Wait," the king shouted over the roar of the crowd. "Aren't we forgetting something?"

The guards halted. One of them stooped to take something out of the boy's pocket. He handed the object to another guard, who approached the king's throne, knelt, and passed something small and fluttering into the king's hand. It was the boy's genga. The swallow's frantic chirruping bounced off the palace columns until, abruptly, there was a *crunch*. The chirruping stopped. The king opened his fist, and a brown lump fell from his hand back into the cupped palms of the guard.

"Carry on," said the Southerly King.

Again, the guards began to pull the paralyzed boy away.

"Oh!" cried the king. "Did I say quartered? I meant *fifthed*."

The crowd erupted into another deafening roar of approval. Lottie felt the Barghest shudder against her leg.

"Fifthed!" chanted a group of boys next to Lottie who looked uncomfortably like the boy who had just been sentenced to death. "Fifthed! Fifthed! *Fifthed*!"

From his throne, the Southerly King daintily crossed his ankles and produced a dazzling smile worthy of an orthodontic ad. Lottie could see, though, that the king's old hand was impatiently tapping against his armrest, one emaciated finger at a time. After minutes of undiminished cheering from the crowd, the king raised the ugly hand, and silence descended once more.

"Truth be told, my faithful Southerlies," the king announced in his songbird of a voice, "I've grown bored with the petty cases of this month. It's high time for a trial of real import, wouldn't you agree?"

The crowd gave its roaring affirmation.

"Then let this serve as an invitation," the king said, "to a case of particular public fascination: the sentencing of one Moritasgus Wilfer, former Head Healer and now confirmed traitor to the Southerly Court!"

A mixed eruption of boos and cheers.

"I have more to tell!" the king shouted over the din. "Just this morning, there has been a thrilling development in the case. The fugitives of the Wilfer household, who had heretofore evaded capture, have at last been apprehended. They, too, will stand trial before the throne to receive their sentences."

Lottie felt as though her stomach was melting into wax. They had been caught. Oliver, Adelaide, and Fife could not have made it more than a few feet within the city walls before they had been arrested by the Southerly Guard. The king was not going to hear their petition or make any trade after all; he was going to *sentence* them.

"The trial shall be held tomorrow, on these very steps, at noon sharp. I would suggest an early arrival for all of those hungry to see justice exacted upon a foul and seditious wretch."

The crowd burst into a brain-rattling roar of excitement. Then the noise fell off into conversation, murmuring, laughing, and whistling as the sprites dispersed to their daily routines. The Southerly King's announcement was over. He himself had disappeared from view, and his guards were toting his throne up the steps and into the safety of the palace through its great marble doors.

"Ow!" Lottie swatted at something that had hit her right at the bridge of her nose. Her eyes refocused on the offending object, which was still fluttering in front of her.

It was a finch. A white finch.

"Oliver!" The name passed Lottie's lips as a reflex.

Dizzying joy and relief swelled in Lottie at the sight of Oliver's genga, Keats. This had to mean something good, didn't it? It must mean that Oliver was somehow all right.

By an instinct that Lottie did not recognize as her own, she lifted her forefinger for Keats to perch upon.

"A finch," barked the Barghest, "from the house of Wilfer. What message has it been sent to deliver?"

"Did Oliver send you to me?" Lottie asked the finch.

Keats bobbed his tiny head and cheeped once. Lottie took this as a *yes*.

"Are he and the others all right?"

The finch quivered his head back and forth. He cheeped twice, lower than before. This, Lottie realized grimly, meant *no*.

"Are they locked up?" she asked. "Are they in the dungeons with Mr. Wilfer?"

A bob and a cheep.

"Take us to them!"

Keats twittered excitedly and swooped off Lottie's finger in a dive. He reappeared a moment later in the near distance, over the heads of the crowd, his wings gleaming in the sun like a beacon.

"Come on, Barghest," Lottie said, scratching its ear encouragingly. "Let's go."

The Barghest obeyed the order. They set out again into the press of the crowd. They had been standing, Lottie now saw, in a great cobblestone pavilion that fronted the Southerly Court Palace. It was an impressive sight: all columns, fountains, marble, and stone. It bespoke wealth and power and was nothing like the surrounding alleys that Lottie now plunged into. These alleys were winding and crowded, billowing with smoke and noise. The streets bent severely, zigzagging in almost impossible ways, as though the sprites who had first laid them out had done so with their eyes closed, and after having been spun around in circles. Balconies hung overhead in steep slants that blocked out the sun. Silver pipes jutted out from under windows, and as Lottie passed by a shop marked ROYAL LANE LAUNDROMAT, one of those pipes poured out blue-colored steam and the fresh scent of cotton. More vendor shouts echoed: "Fresh honeysuckle straws!" and "Hummingbird dung!"

More than once, Lottie lost sight of Keats, and each time she did—even if for only a mere second—hot dread seized her. But just when Lottie's feet slowed in hesitation, the genga would reemerge, five or even ten heads away, and swoop on.

Then Keats gave a very sudden swerve that would have been inconceivable in a gridded neighborhood like the respectable Thirsby Square. The alleyway yanked back on itself in an acute diagonal, sloping downward so instantly that it threw Lottie off her balance and propelled her down at an alarming speed until she smacked straight into a door.

Lottie backed away, rubbing at her sore shoulder, which had gotten the brunt of the impact. Keats hopped from the door's silver handle to its lintel.

"This is it?" said Lottie, craning her neck up to see that somehow, indeed, Oliver's genga had led them to a solid stone wall that belonged to some back portion of the Southerly Court Palace itself.

Keats chirped expectantly at Lottie.

The Barghest pawed at the door's threshold.

"It is enchanted," it growled. "Only the king's Guard can enter such a door."

"I don't suppose that 'Vesper Bells' would work at a time like this?" Lottie suggested with a nervous laugh.

The Barghest did not laugh. There were no vines here to obey Lottie's command. She looked around the deserted alley for some other sign of entrance, but there was the door and the door alone.

"Well, this is stupid," Lottie observed. She gave Keats a cross look. "What good is a door if we can't go through it?"

And simply because there was nothing else to do, Lottie gave a great yank at the door handle. For one fantastic moment, Lottie really thought that there must have been some enchantment-breaking magic in her touch and she had been the one to open the door. But then the door was flung open farther, much farther than Lottie's yank warranted, and sent her staggering into the wall. She just managed to swallow a cry of pain as a red-cloaked guard came sauntering out and leaned back against the door hinges. He took out a thin pipe and lit it up. He paid no mind to Lottie or the Barghest crouched at her side. Keats was nowhere to be seen.

The Barghest raised its eyes to Lottie. They were both shielded for now in the crook behind the open door, but Lottie knew the guard's smoke break would not last forever. She crouched and slipped her mouth into the floppy fold of the Barghest's ear.

"Distract him," she whispered.

The Barghest gave a low rumble that sounded surprisingly cheerful. Lottie sucked in one thick, steadying breath. She readied her feet for a swift run. Then she nodded to the Barghest, who grinned and leapt around the door with an inhuman, shrieking howl. The startled shout of the Southerly guard rose to a terrified cry.

As Lottie edged quickly around the door, she glimpsed spattered crimson and a flurry of dark fur. She did not think on these things. She ran past the screaming guard and into a dark hallway. The door slammed behind her, shutting out both the Barghest and the noise. Lottie ran on, her sneakers sliding on slick, silver tiles. In fact, the entire hallway—floor, walls, and ceiling—was made of pure silver. Lottie's breath hitched when she turned the corner and found herself face-to-face with another sprite—which turned out to be nothing more than her distorted reflection. There was no one else in the hallway, or at the next bend, or the next.

"Come on," Lottie whispered, keeping on the alert for some sign of where she ought to turn, but more than anything for a sign of white wings. "Where did you go, Keats? Where do *I* go?"

There was no reply, not so much as a twitter. So Lottie ran on. It was a terrible feeling, to run in those halls alone and with no sense of direction. The space was narrow and the ceilings short, and the twists were more ridiculous than the twists of the city alleyways. Lottie decided that Southerlies must have an affinity for sharp turns.

Lottie ran around another blade-sharp corner, and her breath caught again at the flash of something in the silver. *Just your reflection, you loon,* she reminded herself, and then she proceeded to collide into what was not just her reflection, but really another sprite. Not just any other sprite, but—

"Fife!"

"Lottie?" Fife's hair was standing straight on end. He tugged a fallen Lottie back to her feet, and he spoke in a loud whisper. "Lottie! What are you doing here?"

"Looking for you all. Oliver's genga led me here, and then the Barghest helped me to—"

"What? Whoa, *whoa*, what? A *Barghest* is with you?"

Lottie nodded fervently. "But that's not important right now. What are you doing here? What is this place?"

"The Southerly dungeons," said Fife. "Or the start of them, anyway. It's a maze down here."

"But how come you're free?"

Fife smirked. "I sweet-talked my guard. It's incredible how quickly you can flavor a hardened old crust into a sympathetic stew of goo."

"You used your keen?"

"Astutely deducted," said Fife, shifting his feet in an antsy, half-hovering bounce.

"And the others?"

"I've been trying to find some sign of where they've been locked up, but I might as well be looking for a grain of Piskie Dust in a snowstorm. Surprisingly few guards to worry about, though. That's one perk of the dungeons: they're so well made that they keep 'em severely underguarded."

"We can look together," said Lottie. "Where to?"

Fife pointed to a fork in the hallway down which neither of them had run. "That way."

Fife took Lottie's hand, and as his fingers curled into the gaps of hers, Lottie's feet left the ground.

"Unless you'd rather run?" Fife said, looking over at her uncertainly.

"No." Lottie flapped her free arm, balancing herself into an upright hover. "This is faster."

"You bet it is," said Fife. "Just hang on."

They swished down the jagged halls, surrounded at every turn by a company of reflected Fifes and Lotties.

"Have you seen Mr. Wilfer?" Lottie asked.

Fife shook his head. "We didn't even get past the main gate. The Guard was waiting for us. They took us to make our plea before the king, just like Mr. Ingle said they would. Then King Starkling laughed at us all like a regular bully and threw us down here."

"Even when you offered him the Otherwise Incurable?"

Fife hesitated. Lottie saw his tongue peeking out from the side of his mouth.

"Don't use your keen on me! Just *tell* me."

"Fine," said Fife. "Yes, we gave the medicine up. But Lottie, just listen—"

Lottie shook her head. She knew what Fife was doing: he was trying to change her mood, change her mind. So she would change the subject.

"Is Mr. Wilfer safe?"

"As far as we know," Fife said, still looking uneasy as they swooped down another hallway. "The king's keeping him somewhere down here. He claims that he's got Mr. Wilfer working on a new version of the Otherwise Incurable, but everyone knows that's a sham. He's through with Mr. Wilfer. He's going to sentence him tomorrow."

"I know," said Lottie. "He said so at the trial today."

Fife shuddered.

"The king said that *all* of you were going on trial—Mr. Wilfer and the 'fugitives,' too."

They skimmed another turn, and Lottie saw in their reflection that Fife was giving her a good sidelong stare. At last he said, "You came back for us."

"Astutely deducted."

"Ollie said you would." Fife hesitated. Then, "Lottie, about what happened back in the wood: you need to know the rest, about what Mr. Wilfer told us beforehand."

"Why?" said Lottie. "What did Mr. Wilfer tell you?"

Before Fife could answer, something cold slapped against Lottie's neck.

It was the flat of a sword, and it was in the hand of a red-cloaked sprite whose assessing eyes were all too familiar.

"Please continue," said Grissom. "What *did* Mr. Wilfer say?"

CHAPTER SIXTEEN

The Missing Ingredient

FIFE DROPPED Lottie's hand, and immediately the weightlessness left her body. She fell to the floor and out of reach of Grissom's sword.

"Run!" yelled Fife, but Lottie could see from where she lay that it was no use. There were two red guards closing in from the other end of the hall, their maces raised. Grissom had them surrounded.

"Worthy effort," Grissom said with an unkind smile, "but surely it crossed your mind that the king's Guard includes sprites with the most acute hearing."

"Not the one at your back door," Lottie said, struggling to her feet.

Grissom's smile faltered.

"So . . . ," said Fife, slowly licking his lips, "aren't you tired of hunting down a handful of obnoxious *children*? Much better to let us go, don't you think?"

Lottie eyed Fife. He was trying to use his keen on Grissom, all stops out. Lottie wondered if it could possibly work.

Grissom's smile returned. "I can smell the manipulation on your skin. You can stop trying."

No. No, it could not possibly work.

Grissom continued, "You, halfling boy, will be taken back to your cell and—now that you've so flagrantly displayed your keen—placed there with a guard who won't be susceptible to your trickery."

Grissom motioned to the two red guards behind them, who clamped their hands on Fife's arms.

"Hey!" Fife cried. "Easy on the limbs, you oafs." He smiled weakly at Lottie as the guards dragged him off. "Chin up, Lottie Fiske. It might not all end in tears and fifthing!"

"That boy is more of a fool than his mother ever was," said Grissom, who had meantime caught Lottie by the wrist. "And so are you, Lottie Fiske."

Lottie glared unflinchingly at Grissom. "My mother wasn't a fool. She had a marvelous heart. Which is more than you can say for yourself."

"I," said Grissom, digging his nails into Lottie's veins, "am soon to be the king's most trusted right-hand sprite."

"Because that worked out so well for the others?"

Fife's flippancy must have worn off on Lottie, because the taunt had rolled like butter off of her tongue in spite of the knot in her stomach. The ugly look that appeared on Grissom's face in response gave Lottie a proud thrill.

"You," Grissom said, "have an appointment with the king."

He jerked Lottie down a new hallway. At the end of this hall, unlike in all the others, was a spiraling staircase. Lottie and Fife had been only seconds away from an exit when they were caught. She felt like crying.

Lottie stumbled up the stairs under Grissom's hard grip until they reached a door that opened into a new hallway. This place was nothing like the silver dungeons.

Its ceilings were higher even than those of Iris Gate, and it was bordered on both sides by nothing but long, glossy black panels. The only light came from the ground, where two rows of stumpy black candles edged a velvet runner. Their flames flickered wildly as Grissom pulled Lottie to the very end of the hall. There, he swept aside a golden tapestry and knocked on the door hidden behind it.

"Enter," said a voice beyond the door.

Grissom pushed Lottie inside.

"I have her, Your Majesty," Grissom said.

They were standing before the same silver throne that Lottie had seen on the steps of the palace, and the Southerly King sat there just as he had that afternoon. He smiled so benevolently at Lottie that she nearly forgot why her heart had been thum-thrumping so unbearably just moments before. Then she remembered the chants of "Fifthing!" from the crowd. She remembered the crushed genga in the king's bare, sunspotted hand.

"Here she is!" the king said merrily. "The Heir of Fiske, come to pay a long overdue visit."

He smiled tenderly at Lottie, as though she were a lost kitten. "Grissom, fetch the girl a chair."

Grissom scraped a chair behind Lottie, but she did not move.

He is bad, Lottie reminded herself. He has done wicked things.

It was difficult, she found, to remember these warnings when she looked at the king's gentle face.

"Sit," said the king.

Lottie wiped at her eyes and took a seat. She could hear Grissom's ragged breaths behind her, and even though it was uncomfortable knowing a bad man was standing just behind her, she decided it would've been less comfortable still to be left alone with the Southerly King.

"My throne room must seem terribly overpowering to a slip of a halfling like you," the king said. He set aside a crystal goblet of wine he had been holding.

Lottie glanced around. Tall candles burned on tall candlesticks. There was a shelf lining one end of the room, and on it sat a row of various glass jars. The one nearest to Lottie was filled with a pale blue powder. *Royal Piskie Dust,* read its label.

"It's very . . . large," Lottie said.

King Starkling noticed Lottie staring at the jar of Royal Piskie Dust. He gave a pleased smile.

"That," he said, motioning toward the shelf of jars, "is my collection of the most prized concoctions in all of Albion Isle. Piskie Dust is just one of those coveted items. A mere handful, and *swoop!*—you're transported to wherever your heart desires. Excellent substance, Piskie Dust. Go on, ask me for some."

Lottie understood. He wanted her to give him a command.

"You think that I'm a threat," said Lottie. "I'm a Fiske, and some people think that Fiskes will rule the Isle again. You're scared that I'm after your job. That's what it's about, isn't it?"

The king folded his hands on his knees. They were more gruesome on closer inspection than they had looked from the palace steps—blackened and browned and unthinkably wrinkled.

"Oh, dear heart," he said. "It's not nearly so simple as that. Though yes, of course, it was rather inconvenient when I found out that the Plague I brought to the Isle hadn't killed all the Fiskes, as I had intended. Life does keep you on your toes."

Lottie went cold. "That's not possible," she said. "You couldn't have made the Plague. It's a sickness. Sicknesses just happen."

"Of course I didn't *make* the Plague," the king said indulgently. "No, that disease is very old. Ancient. I said *brought* because I brought the Plague up from *my* world."

Lottie's throat turned papery. With difficulty, she asked, "You came here from *Earth*?"

The king *tsk-tsked*. "No, not from Earth. The *other* place."

"You're not a sprite," Lottie whispered. "That's what's wrong with you. You're not from here at all."

The king slid back the silken sleeves of his robe to reveal arms as foul and wrinkled as his hands. These were not just old arms. They were not the arms of a human or a sprite. They were scaled like a fish's, and bones poked out of them at all the wrong junctures.

"See what's become of me?" the king sighed. "Each day my magic weakens, and I revert to my natural form. The moment I realized the toll that living in Limn was taking on my health, I of course put the court's best healer to work. But how could I have suspected that this healer would also be harboring the final ingredient to my cure?"

He approached Lottie's chair with a smooth gait, knelt at her side, and took her hand. His fingers felt like damp, shriveled turnip greens. Lottie could not stop a shudder from rattling down her spine. "Moritasgus didn't tell you about the final ingredient, did he? Your friends may have been quick enough to snatch their father's medicine from me, but what about his notebook? How very silly of him to have filed the final ingredient away in his papers and not told you."

Lottie's heart fell. Grissom had gotten his hands on Mr. Wilfer's scrapbook for the Otherwise Incurable.

"Would you like to know what that ingredient is?" the king asked. "*A sliver of skin from a living human halfling.* Very convenient, for look what's sitting before us: the only known human halfling to exist! I'm sure you'll rest easier knowing that your otherwise good-for-nothing parentage is good for *something.*"

The king produced something from the folds of his robe. It was a square vial filled with bloodred liquid. He unstoppered the vial. He looked as serene as ever.

"No," whispered Lottie. "No, that can't be right."

"The whole business is regrettable, isn't it?" the king said sympathetically. "But have no fear, last of the Fiskes. It will all be over soon.

"Now," the king said, nodding toward Grissom.

Lottie did not have time to think before Grissom's meaty hand had braced her back against her chair. Something sharp and unyielding scraped across her right arm. Lottie did not cry or scream, but only looked in bewilderment at the thin scalpel that Grissom held aloft. On its tip rested a perfectly rectangular, tissue-thin slice of Lottie's freckled skin. The graze had not been deep enough to even draw blood.

Grissom released Lottie from his grip. He walked the scalpel over to the king, who stood waiting with the open vial of Otherwise Incurable. Grissom took the vial, tilting its lip and maneuvering his scalpel with practiced precision. The skin folded and fit into the vial's mouth. Then, with a single push from the scalpel's tip, it dropped into the red liquid below. The skin shriveled instantly and disappeared. There was an awful silence.

Slowly, the Otherwise Incurable began to swirl and froth. Then, just as slowly, the potion stilled, and its anxious red gave way to a deep, serene blue. The king's face shone with a radiant smile.

"So," he said. "You were right, Grissom."

Lottie looked on in confusion. Why wouldn't Mr. Wilfer have asked her for a little skin days ago, when she'd first arrived? She could have given it to him. She could have *saved Eliot*.

The king turned to Lottie. He raised the vial in her direction. "To what shall I drink?" he asked. "Perhaps to the memory of Fiskes past, hm?

"To Fiskes!" the king cried, and he raised the vial to his lips.

Lottie would never know what force it had been that then moved in her, launching her from her chair. She only knew that the king held in his hand the only, the *last* chance of curing Eliot. Lottie leapt across the room at a startling speed.

"Get your hands off it!" she shouted, and she made a grab for the Otherwise Incurable.

This was not one of those moments when the whole world goes still and everything seems to happen in painful slow motion. In fact, for a full confused moment, Lottie did not even realize that she had knocked the vial from the king's hand or that it had fallen and shattered on the floor, or that its contents had fizzed away. She did not realize what had occurred until she felt a blow across her face.

"You *wretch*!" shrieked the Southerly King.

His face had become a hideous thing. It had transformed as though it were a boiling stew of thick tar. Beneath bubbling skin, Lottie saw the raw jaw and reddened teeth of a creature entirely unlike the beautiful visage of the young sprite king. *This* was the creature that the Southerly King was slowly turning back into.

Strong fingers clamped onto Lottie. A half dozen red-cloaked guards had burst into the room, and two of them now dragged her out by her hands and hair.

"Take her to the dungeons!" the king screamed. "She'll be executed with the lot of them! She'll be executed first and worst!"

Lottie only stared in quiet horror at the broken shards of Otherwise Incurable. She had destroyed Mr. Wilfer's life's work. Her only hope for Eliot lay shattered on the throne room floor, and she had been the one to shatter it.

CHAPTER SEVENTEEN

Royal Piskie Dust

THE SOUTHERLY GUARD dragged Lottie down the palace hall. She did not kick or scream; she did not fight. She had lost Eliot's cure. She had lost everything. The shock had left her limbs numb and useless, and the guards had to drag her to her feet and march her down the spiraling staircase, down once more into the silver dungeons.

As they walked the dungeon halls, one of Lottie's guards flinched and dropped his mace. He appeared to be in some sort of pain.

"It's the king's blasted shouting," he explained to the other guard as he retrieved his fallen weapon. "Loud enough to raise the dead."

The second guard shook his head. "The king never loses his temper."

The first guard fixed Lottie with an appraising stare. His complexion was ruddy, and three metal rings pierced his nose.

"What did you *do*?" he asked.

Lottie just stared back at her guards with lifeless eyes.

"Think the rumors are true, Dorian?" said the other guard. "Think she's a Fiske?"

"'Course not. The Fiskes are all dead."

They pushed Lottie deeper into the dungeons' winding halls, but as they did so, Lottie felt a finger at her right wrist. The guard named Dorian was pulling up the sleeve of her coat. He was looking at the topside of her arm—where the mark of her court allegiance ought to have been and where instead was only bare skin.

Lottie glanced up. Dorian had been staring at her, but he abruptly averted his eyes. He gave Lottie a strong jab in the shoulder blade with his mace.

"Walk faster," he ordered.

They approached two other red-cloaked guards who appeared to be doing nothing more than loitering in the hallway. But as Lottie's guards ground her to a halt, she saw that a door was cut into the wall here. Its edges were no thicker than the ridge of a dime, and they formed a thinly sliced square of silver wall. It was no wonder that she and Fife had not seen any cells while floating through these halls; the doors to the cells were as good as invisible.

The sprites guarding the cell nodded to Lottie's guards and then parted to grant them access to the door.

"Has the wisp halfling given you any more trouble?" Dorian asked them.

"None, Guard Ingle," said one of the guards. "We've been listening and tasting with due attentiveness."

"Very good," said Dorian. "You're both relieved of your posts. Tavish and I have been sent to replace you."

Tavish looked up in surprise. "Have we? I hadn't heard—"

"Because it was an order given directly to *me*," Dorian interrupted with a commanding glare.

Tavish, the decidedly younger and meeker of Lottie's guards, went quiet. The other guards looked only too happy to be off duty.

"The king sounds none too pleased up there," one of them remarked.

"I'd suggest taking the side hall up to Guard quarters," said Dorian. "In fact, I'd avoid the king's wing of the palace this entire evening if you can help it."

Dorian clapped the guards on their backs in a gesture of familiar camaraderie. They grinned and sent back mock salutes as they left. Then Dorian turned to Tavish.

"Stand watch," he said, "while I confine the prisoner."

Dorian clenched his fingers into Lottie's back. "You'll be held here," he said, sweeping his hand over the dungeon cell door in a strange but fluid pattern, "until your trial tomorrow."

Then he leaned in close to Lottie and whispered into the cover of her hair, "I'll be listening."

The door gave way, and Dorian threw Lottie inside. The first thing she saw was a flash of chestnut brown hair. Then arms wrapped around her neck. The door heaved shut behind her, and Lottie heard Adelaide's voice in her ear.

"Thank Titania. We thought you were dead!"

From over Adelaide's shoulder, Lottie saw that this "we" included Oliver, Fife, and Mr. Wilfer himself. Shame flooded through her.

"I ruined it!" Lottie cried, yanking herself out of Adelaide's embrace. "Don't *hug* me. I've broken the vial, and I've lost the medicine. The Otherwise Incurable is gone." She turned to Mr. Wilfer. "It's all my fault!"

"We know," Adelaide said softly. "I heard all of it."

"Lottie, do calm yourself," said Mr. Wilfer, taking Lottie by the shoulders. "You think I care about that medicine more than your well-being?"

"It was your life's work," wailed Lottie. "It could have saved you from execution!"

"But it didn't," Mr. Wilfer said calmly. "Did it? Believe me, Lottie, Starkling has been waiting to kill me for some time now. The only thing preventing him was the simple fact that I was the finest healer of my age. None of my colleagues could boast a recipe for Otherwise Incurable. Not, that is, until Grissom grew greedy. Then, as you see, I became expendable."

"You became expendable because of me," Lottie insisted. "You were kidnapped for rescuing *me*."

"Lottie," said Mr. Wilfer. "I want you to listen to me closely. I've chosen this path. The day that King Starkling told me he'd heard rumors of the existence of a living Fiske, that he meant to find and kill the child of Eloise and Bertram Fiske, a girl to whom I'd sent birthday gifts all her life, I knew the time had come for me to do something that I hadn't had the courage to do before: rebel."

"Hear, hear!" cried Fife, clapping loudly.

Oliver was staring at Lottie with warm amber eyes. "You," he said, "have done a braver thing than all the Worthies did."

Adelaide sighed. "What Oliver means—"

"It's okay," Lottie said, smiling sadly at Oliver. "I think I know what he means."

"Keats is sorry that he lost you," Oliver said. "He got scared outside the dungeons and came flying back to me. You don't know how glad we all were to hear that he had found you, that you were okay."

"Then after what Adelaide heard up there in the throne room," said Fife, "we thought the king might have killed you on the spot."

"He's going to kill us anyway," whispered Adelaide. "He's going to have us all executed as traitors."

That was when Lottie remembered the guard Dorian and what he had whispered in her ear. That whisper suddenly made sense.

"Listen, everyone," she said, waving frantically and lowering her voice. "I think there might be a spy outside. A spy for the Northerlies. Someone on our side."

Mr. Wilfer stepped back in surprise. "Whatever makes you say that, Lottie?" he asked.

"His name," she said. "One of the guards called him by his last name, *Ingle*."

"You mean like *Mr.* Ingle?" asked Fife.

Lottie nodded. "I think so. Don't you remember what Roote and Crag told us in the forest? That Mr. Ingle had a nephew in high places. Mr. Ingle told me so himself. Well, I think this might be the one. He told me he'd be *listening* to us." She pointed to Adelaide. "He's got a hearing keen, I think, like yours. Which means—"

"—that he can hear everything we're saying right now," finished Adelaide. "But what about the other guard?"

"He has another sort of keen," said Lottie. "The king's screaming was only bothering the Ingle guy."

"So," Oliver said slowly, "this spy is waiting outside for us to make a plan?"

"A plan of escape!" said Fife.

"Is that it, spy?" said Adelaide. "Are you just waiting for us to come up with a plan you think won't get us all fifthed in the process? All you've got to do is give me a whisper." She tensed for a listen, then nodded. "Yes. Yes, that's what he's waiting for."

Fife rubbed at his neck. "What kind of escape plan will get us out of the dungeons? This place is a maze."

"But Dorian could help us with that," said Lottie. "He's a guard, so he knows his way through the dungeons. What we have to worry about is running into trouble on our way out."

"Dorian?" Fife snorted. "What a stupid name. Only great-grandfathers are named Dorian."

Adelaide smacked Fife. "Can you focus for half a second? Our lives are at stake! Anyway, I think Dorian sounds sophisticated. It's charmingly old-fashioned."

"So, Lottie," said Mr. Wilfer, who Lottie thought was being frustratingly calm in light of their present predicament. "What do you think is a feasible plan of escape?"

"I've been thinking of something," said Lottie, "but it might be a terrible idea."

"Tell us," encouraged Mr. Wilfer.

"Well," said Lottie, "in his throne room, the king has a collection of rare concoctions. One of the jars is full of Piskie Dust."

"You mean," said Fife, "you want to dust us out of here?"

"Well, why can't we break in, throw a little dust on ourselves, and be out of here?" said Lottie.

"That could work," Oliver said. "Couldn't it?"

Mr. Wilfer nodded slowly. "It certainly could. But how will we get to the throne room undetected?"

"Adelaide can help us there," said Lottie. "She can use her keen to tell us where the king and his guards are."

"There are three guards in the throne room, by the sound of it," said Adelaide, "but the king's in another wing of the palace. He's been throwing things around for the past minute." She winced. "It's loud."

Lottie nodded. "So, three guards to take on in the throne room, if we go now."

"What are we supposed to do, fight them off?" said Adelaide.

"You bet we're gonna fight!" Fife said. "Our lives are at stake, Miss Priss."

"We'll have Dorian with us, too," said Lottie, "and he knows the guards. If they see him leading us, it should confuse them, maybe even take them a few minutes to figure out what's really going on."

"I think it's a good plan," said Oliver. "The king would never expect for us to be let loose, and definitely not in his own throne room. If we're quick about it, like Lottie says, and if this Dorian really does help us, there's a chance that we could make it."

"And if we can't?" whispered Adelaide.

"We've got nothing to lose," Fife said grimly.

"But Dorian," said Oliver. "He has something to lose. Revealing his identity this way could cost him his head."

The cell door swung open. Dorian was looking in, and his fellow guard lay unconscious at his feet.

"That's a risk spies sign up for," he said. "Now get out, and let's get moving."

⚜

They piled into the hallway, Dorian in the lead. Though Lottie had been down these halls twice already, she felt just as daunted by the distorted reflections and dozens of identical turns. She wondered how the king's guards ever managed to learn their way around. Dorian, however, did not pause or falter for a moment. He led them straight to the spiral stairs. At their base, he turned.

"There are four guards in the hall above," he said, "and the three in the throne room."

"I hear five in the hall," said Adelaide.

"Four *guards*," Dorian said.

"Lead us up," Mr. Wilfer whispered, "and we shall deal with whatever surprise lies in the hallway."

They climbed the stairs, Lottie just behind Dorian. When they reached the top landing, Dorian pushed open the door to the palace hallway.

Four guards stood crowded at the entrance, waiting for them.

"What's this, Dorian?" said a burly voice. "Taking an unauthorized stroll?"

Lottie could not make out what happened next. Arms tugged under hers. There was a sudden, confusing jumble of loud thuds and growls. She felt wet fur brush across her legs. She saw a flash of deep red cloaks and deeper black hair. She was knocked down. She heard Adelaide scream.

Then everything came into focus again, and Lottie was lying facedown with a mouthful of velvet rug. She pushed herself up, coughing, and found her shoulder seized in the hand of one of the guards. The guard hoisted Lottie up, pressing her back hard against the wall. He jabbed the cold, blunt end of his mace under Lottie's chin.

"You there!" he barked back to indistinguishable shapes. "Wilfer! Let him go, or I swear I'll—"

Then his mouth went a funny shape. The mace fell from Lottie's neck. The guard gagged and shuddered, his face blooming a shade of sickly orange, then green, then deep charcoal. His eyes rolled back into his head, and he slumped off Lottie, unconscious but twitching, his discolored face turned up toward his attacker.

"Oliver." Lottie rubbed her throat, trembling. "Th-th-thanks."

Oliver's eyes were a frightening shade of red. He was still staring at the unconscious guard. Slowly, he nodded.

"Come on," he said.

Lottie stumbled to her feet, grabbing Oliver's elbow for support. She looked around. Two crumpled guards lay on the floor, and a Barghest—*her* Barghest!—stood panting over them. A fourth guard was still standing, locked in the arms of Mr. Wilfer.

"Don't look!" screamed Adelaide, dragging Lottie to her feet. "Just go!"

The candles in the hall sputtered out as Lottie and the others ran past, straight for the golden tapestry that hid the throne room doors. The Barghest scampered ahead of them. The tapestry swung back, and the three guards that Adelaide had predicted piled out just in time for the Barghest to leap on one of them, dragging him down in a howling heap. The fallen guard's mace swung out of his hand and cracked into another guard's ankles. He screamed and buckled to his knees.

The remaining guard stood facing them, his mace shaking in his hands.

"Don't come any closer," he said. "I'm warning you, the rest of the Guard will be here soon enough."

"But they aren't here now," said Dorian, swiftly plunging a fist into the guard's stomach.

"You're a traitor," the guard grunted, stumbling back.

"We're both bad guards," Dorian agreed, lobbing a punch at his eye. The guard dodged the blow and lifted his mace over Dorian's head. But before the blow could fall, another mace clonked the guard's head from behind. He collapsed, senseless, revealing a hovering, triumphant-looking Fife.

"Nice mace, that," Fife commented, tossing the weapon aside.

"Thanks," Dorian said curtly. He pushed open the throne room doors.

Lottie hurtled straight to the shelf of rare concoctions. The jar marked ROYAL PISKIE DUST was right where she had remembered it, a third full of powder the color of robin's eggs. She lifted the jar down with both hands and unscrewed its lid.

"Wait!" cried Adelaide. "Wait for Father!"

Mr. Wilfer stumbled into the room with the Barghest.

So did Grissom, and a dozen red guards just behind him.

"Draw close," Mr. Wilfer ordered the others. Then to Lottie, "Throw the dust! *Now!*"

Lottie heaved the jar up with all the strength she had. The Piskie Dust did not come out at all like Lottie had expected, like an emptied pack of sugar. Instead, it remained suspended in midair, and then it shifted upward in a swirling spiral of blue. The spiral flung outward, wrapping around her in a powdery vapor.

Lottie opened her mouth to shout a destination. Then her lips froze. She hadn't taken the time to think of *where* to take them. She hadn't thought of a place to say! Piskie Dust whirled into Lottie's mouth, sending her into a coughing fit.

"NO!" shouted Grissom, leaping toward their circle.

Then an image flashed in Lottie's mind: her green apple tree. That was where they needed to go!

"Tree!" Lottie coughed out. *"Apple tree!"*

The dust swirled faster, blowing so hard into Lottie's face that she had to shut her eyes. When she opened them again, she was standing outside.

But they had not been transported to her apple tree in Thirsby Square.

They were in a heap of vines, standing before the sickliest apple tree that Lottie had ever seen. The Piskie Dust had only taken them just outside the Southerly Court walls, to the plagued orchard.

"No," said Lottie. "This wasn't what I meant!"

She stumbled back, her foot lodged in the tangled curl of a vine. Mr. Wilfer steadied her by the shoulder. Fife and Adelaide were stooped nearby, and Oliver was pulling himself out of a tangle of ivy. The Barghest lay at Lottie's feet. He was bent, as though in a reverent kneel, before Dorian.

"Dorian Ingle," the Barghest rasped, pressing his muzzle into Dorian's outstretched hand. "Servant of Rebel Gem, it is an honor to be at your service."

"I—I—thank you," Lottie sputtered. "Thank you for saving me. For saving all of us."

Dorian nodded. "My uncle sent his genga to court after his house was raided by the Guard a few days back. He said to be on the lookout for his friend Moritasgus Wilfer, and for the last surviving Fiske. It wasn't until the Barghest found me that I knew just what sort of danger you were in."

"Danger that you're still in," said Mr. Wilfer. "We must move quickly."

Lottie knew what had to be done. She'd seen it done before, and a tug—soft but insistent within her—guided her hand by instinct. She reached deep into her pocket and curled her hand around the warm bundle that was Trouble. Carefully, she lifted him out, placed her lips against his downy black feathers, and whispered, "Take us home."

Trouble did not hesitate. He flew directly to a branch hanging just over Lottie's head. The branch was pallid, its branches peeling with the ravage of sickness. Lottie pulled it down as carefully as she could manage. Then, gently, she pocketed Trouble in her periwinkle coat.

She was not so shocked this time as she had been in Thirsby Square when she heard the violent groaning and watched the apple tree writhe its splintering bark into an opening.

"*Quickly,*" said Mr. Wilfer.

Adelaide stepped inside, and Oliver and Fife filed in next. Mr. Wilfer stood guard at the tree's entrance; he motioned for Lottie to step inside.

"Grissom!" she said, the thought sudden and awful. "We can't go back to Thirsby Square. He knows where I live."

"Don't trouble yourself with that," said Dorian, smirking. "I know what route he'll take, and I'm not the only spy in the Southerly Court. You're with me, aren't you, Barghest?"

The dog bent its head in assent.

With a gracefulness that would have put even

Adelaide's best curtsy to shame, Dorian swept a leg over the Barghest's back and gripped its mane.

"Only remember," said Dorian, "two Northerlies just saved your life, Heir of Fiske. You owe our court a life debt. Think on that while you are in Earth."

Then he bent and whispered something into the Barghest's ear. Before Lottie could say a word more, the Barghest grunted and set off in a rough bound toward the court walls.

"Come, Lottie," said Mr. Wilfer. He climbed into the apple tree and beckoned to her. "We cannot linger here."

Lottie shook herself. "Sorry. I'm coming."

She took a step, and something clutched her foot.

A hand had emerged from the vine-covered ground, pinching into the hollows around Lottie's anklebone. Her leg buckled in pain, and Lottie fell. She tried desperately to shake off the hand, but its bony fingers only clenched harder. Their owner now sat up from where he had been buried in the vines.

Lottie had not spoken fast enough in the throne room.

"Finally," said Grissom. "I've got you all to myself."

"Let her go!" Oliver shouted.

"Grissom," said Mr. Wilfer, gripping the threshold of the apple tree, "your quarrel isn't with the girl."

"Fair enough, Moritasgus," said Grissom. "But considering none of *you* can step across that enchanted threshold, I'll bide my time with the Heir of Fiske."

Grissom shoved Lottie's ankle from his grip so that she fell painfully to the ground, the air knocked from her lungs. Then he rose to his full height, towering over her, and kicked her in the ribs. A hot pain tore through Lottie. She screamed, clutching at her side.

"You thought it would be that easy? That you could defy the Southerly King and traipse off to Earth scot-free?"

Lottie did not answer. She could not. The pain in her ribs was claustrophobic. And on top of it there was a tightening, thickening sensation in her chest that she had known since she was a little girl. Lottie squeezed her eyes shut and tried to steady her breathing.

"Grissom, stop this!" Mr. Wilfer shouted from the tree, but Grissom only sneered in his direction before turning his full attention back to Lottie.

"Typical," he said. "Fiskes have always been known for their duplicity—fraternizers with wisps and Northerlies alike. Your mother was the worst of them all, consorting with the filth that reside in Earth. Of course you have none of the Fiskes' keen. Not with that excuse for a father."

Lottie tried to speak again, but her throat had seized up in the same tightening strain that raged in her chest.

"What's that, halfling?" said Grissom with a mocking smile. "What are you trying to say? Why don't you get up and tell me?"

Suddenly, Lottie's bad spell was fading, and a new sensation had begun to grow in her chest and burn like acid against her rib cage. Lottie did not feel frightened anymore. She only felt angry. The sensation boiled in her blood and strengthened her bones, pushing Lottie up to her knees. She gripped the ivy beneath her, panting. Her throat warmed and loosened, and words unbundled from her mouth.

"Vesper Bells."

The ivy burst into motion. Vines snaked up Grissom's legs, cinching tight. They crawled up his potbelly and strapped his arms down to his sides. Grissom's eyes went wide with terror. A vine shot under Lottie's foot and she lost her balance, tumbling back toward the apple tree, where Mr. Wilfer caught her and pulled her inside.

"How?" Grissom screamed. "No! *No!*"

Vine and leaves swallowed up Grissom's shouts, and his body went rigid under the winding, thick shoots of the Northerly vines. Mr. Wilfer tugged Lottie deeper into the apple tree, and the bark sealed up and cast them all into darkness.

CHAPTER EIGHTEEN

A Bad Spell

"THAT," SAID FIFE, "is going to leave some permanent psychological damage. Ouch! What, Ada? It *is*."

"You all right, Lottie?" said Oliver.

"I'm f-f-fine," Lottie sputtered, "but is Grissom ?"

"The Northerly vines are relentless," Mr. Wilfer answered her unfinished question. "It will take the king a long time to free Grissom from those vines—if he chooses to free him at all."

Lottie gulped. "So what do we now?"

416 THE WATER AND THE WILD

"You must think, Lottie," said Mr. Wilfer, "of the best place to go in Earth."

"The Barmy Badger," Lottie said immediately. "Eliot."

Then something very important occurred to Lottie.

"Wait! There's no tree—"

But an aching sensation had already started in Lottie's legs, and she suddenly felt like she was in the palm of a giant who was slowly squeezing her to death, snapping her bone by bone. She had gotten it wrong, but it was too late to change now. So Lottie kept on thinking of Eliot's painted room. She thought of ye ol' porthole. The squeezing stopped. Lottie felt weightless and thoughtless for a second. Then came the *whoosh*.

"Well, we're going *somewhere*," Mr. Wilfer called encouragingly. "Get ready for the flip. Oliver, keep your hands tucked in!"

Lottie thought that turning a somersault in midair had been painful enough when she had ridden with Adelaide, but this time her knees whacked into someone else's back, her nose bonked against someone's foot, and some of her own hair flew into her mouth. Then all five of them dropped to the ground. Everyone was upright and looked perfectly unflustered. Everyone but Lottie, who was sprawled on the floor. Fife broke the silence.

"Nice work," he said.

Adelaide poked him hard in the side. "Shut up, you imbecile. Can't you see that she's shaken up?"

"Well, who wouldn't be?" said Fife. "She just took down the whole Southerly Court!"

Adelaide and Fife continued to argue in loud whis-pers, but Lottie wasn't listening. She had not made a move to get up. She remained still on the floor as the elevator continued on its gentler ascent. Mr. Wilfer knelt by her side.

"How are you feeling, Lottie?" he asked. "May I?"

Gingerly, Mr. Wilfer touched the place where Grissom had kicked Lottie in her side. Lottie watched him quietly as he pressed his fingertips up and down her ribs. A strange look crossed Mr. Wilfer's face.

"That doesn't hurt?"

Lottie shook her head. "No. It feels fine now."

"A kick like that should've fractured the bone," said Mr. Wilfer. "I don't understand it. Excepting your head-ache, you're in perfect condition."

Lottie blinked at Mr. Wilfer in surprise. "How do you know about my headache?"

Mr. Wilfer removed his hand from Lottie's side, and she suddenly understood.

"That's your keen, isn't it?" she said. "You touch people, and you know what's wrong with them."

"*Right* with them, too," Mr. Wilfer said. "Anything physical there is to know, good or bad, I know from a touch of my hands. I didn't become the land's finest healer by sheer force of will. A good healer must have an equally good keen."

"Mr. Wilfer?" Lottie whispered. "Why didn't you tell me that first night about being a Fiske? Or that I was the final ingredient to the Otherwise Incurable? Why didn't you *tell* me?"

Mr. Wilfer raised a brow. "For the same reason I instructed Adelaide and Oliver that, should I be taken captive and should they run into trouble—two things I feared were very likely—they could never give you up. I told them that, if they had to bargain for their lives, they must use the Otherwise Incurable."

Lottie frowned at Mr. Wilfer, then at Oliver, whose eyes were a light, timid violet. "You mean, you *told* them to give up the medicine?"

"When Adelaide and Fife and I first talked to Mr. Ingle at the inn," said Oliver, "he told us we'd have to make a bargain with the king. It was either you or the medicine, and we weren't about to turn you in. We weren't trying to betray you, Lottie. We were just trying to keep you safe."

"Sorry to interrupt," said Fife, "but should we be concerned that this tree of ours is noisier than usual?"

Lottie stopped to listen. Fife was right: there was a terrible screeching noise coming from above their heads, and it was getting louder and louder and louder until the very floor began to shake from the sound of it.

Then the screeching stopped. The tree splintered open, and Lottie, who was leaning against the wall there, fell out, backside first, into a damp clump of grass. She was outside, it was nighttime, and it was raining. Electric streetlights buzzed over her head, and she could hear a television blaring from a nearby house. She was in her world, in New Kemble, and she was sitting in the back garden of the Barmy Badger.

"That doesn't make sense, though," said Lottie. "There isn't an apple tree in Eliot's backyard."

The others filed out of the tree, much more elegantly than Lottie had done, and the tree whorled shut behind them. Rather than remain upright, the tree trunk shrunk, growing smaller and smaller still, falling closer toward the earth until it disappeared into a patch of shrubbery.

"Look!" cried Adelaide. She pushed back the shrubbery and pointed. "It's just a seedling."

"That would explain those fantastic noises on the way up, then," said Fife. "Those were small roots to shoot through."

Lottie and the others crowded around Adelaide. Just as she had said, the smallest sapling of an apple tree had emerged from the Barmy Badger's unkempt garden.

"It's from the day that Eliot and I ate apples on the rooftop," Lottie said in wonder. "I warned him that he might accidentally plant a tree!"

Lottie glanced up at Eliot's window now, half expecting the light to be on, or even Eliot to be looking out of ye ol' porthole. But the window was dark. A rush of fear seared through Lottie, then grief. She had no cure. She might even be too late to watch Eliot die.

She stumbled up the back steps of the Barmy Badger and rapped hard on the door. Rain was soaking everyone's clothes. Fife's normally static-shot hair was wetted to his face, and Adelaide's teeth were chattering.

The back door swung open, and Mr. Walsch poked his white-tufted face out. When he saw Lottie, his mouth went round.

"My dear child," he croaked. "We've been so worried!"

"Mr. Walsch!" cried Lottie. "Is Eliot all right?"

The old man shook his head. "He's in a very bad way. Very bad. Took a turn for the worse last night. This whole business of you being gone came as quite a shock. We had no idea where . . ."

"But I'm back!" Lottie said, hugging Mr. Walsch. "I'm back now, and I've got to see him."

Mr. Walsch seemed distracted. He was peering over Lottie's head at the strangers standing in his doorway.

"Oh," said Lottie. "These are my friends, Mr. Walsch. May they come in?"

Mr. Walsch nodded feebly. Oliver, Fife, Adelaide, and Mr. Wilfer all huddled inside, looking every bit as dazed as Mr. Walsch had been to discover a crowd on his back doorstep after shop hours.

"Is he awake?" Lottie asked, but she ran up the stairs without stopping for an answer.

Lottie flung herself into Eliot's room. He was lying in bed, eyes shut and covers rumpled. His glasses were set

aside on the nightstand, and his shaggy hair was damp
about the forehead. Notepads, pencils, tissues, and scrap
pieces of paper littered Eliot's narrow bed, and the faint
smell of paint still hung in the room.

Lottie had imagined this scene more than once since
she had run through the burning gardens of Iris Gate,
stumbled through Wandlebury Wood, dropped into a
wisp yew, sat on a chair made of Northerly vines, and faced
down the Southerly King. Still, now that the moment had
come, it was far sweeter and far more painful than Lottie
had thought it would be. She took Eliot's sweat-clammed
hand in hers.

"Eliot," she whispered. "I've come back."

A floorboard creaked behind Lottie. Mr. Wilfer stood
at her side.

"I'll fix tea, shall I?" Mr. Walsch offered from the
doorway. He cast one befuddled glance at a sleeping Eliot,
then Mr. Wilfer, then Lottie, and then shut the door on
the three of them.

"I've ruined everything," Lottie whispered. "It
doesn't matter if the Otherwise Incurable had one ingredient missing or a hundred. All of it's gone for good."
She glanced up, foggy-eyed. "I just don't understand

why you didn't tell me that *I* was the ingredient all along. I could've given you some of my skin the moment we met. I could've brought the medicine back to Eliot that night, and he'd be cured."

"No," Mr. Wilfer said softly. "He wouldn't be."

Lottie sniffed. "What?"

Mr. Wilfer let out a long, weary sigh. "There's no such thing as a cure for the incurable, Lottie," he said. "The Otherwise Incurable was a fake. I was sorry to deceive you, but all my art could not cure the king. The Otherwise Incurable was simply a way to delay my execution."

"But—" Lottie stared at Mr. Wilfer in disbelief.

"I knew he would kill me when he found out I had failed. I also knew that he would stop at nothing to find and kill *you*. The House of Fiske may not have ruled our world for ages, but your name still made you a dangerous threat to his throne. That is why I made up the last ingredient in my notebook. That is why I handed it over to Grissom when he arrested me. I let the king believe that the final ingredient for his cure was something that only you could give him, and only while you were alive. That way, if he somehow got ahold of you and not the Otherwise Incurable, he would have you locked up—not fifthed."

"You lied to the others, too," Lottie said. "You told them that the Otherwise Incurable was real."

"My only intent," said Mr. Wilfer, "was to keep you safe."

Lottie felt lightheaded. She gripped the side of Eliot's bed to keep her thoughts intact. All this time, she had worked and traveled and fought for something that had never even existed.

"Why didn't you tell me that to begin with?" Lottie was still whispering for the sole reason of not waking Eliot, but anger clattered fiercely in her chest. "Why did you drag me away from Eliot when he needed me most and send me running all over the Isle?"

"There were, if you remember, extenuating circumstances," said Mr. Wilfer. "Small matters involving your personal safety and attempted kidnapping and a medicine that the Southerly King wanted very badly. Would it have done you or Eliot any good if I'd allowed Grissom to steal you away?"

The anger clattered more loudly within Lottie. She knew that the answer to Mr. Wilfer's question was no, but she did not dare give him the satisfaction of saying it out loud.

"I took a risk," said Mr. Wilfer. "Perhaps it was poor timing, perhaps poor judgment on my part, but I did what I thought best at the time. I wish I were a better healer than I am, Lottie. I wish I could save your friend's life. You have been so brave in the attempt to do so. I know that goodbyes are not easy, but—"

"Stop," Lottie said, choking on a sob. "Stop it. I don't want to say goodbye to Eliot. I can't."

Lottie shrugged Mr. Wilfer's hand off her shoulder. How *dare* he? Fury was making her eyes tear and her heart pound in her chest. Her lungs were constricting, her throat burning as though a bottle of vinegar had been emptied into it. It was a bad spell for certain.

No, goodbyes were not easy. Saying goodbye to Eliot would be the hardest thing imaginable. Lottie closed her eyes, tears rolling down her cheeks, and remembered Oliver dancing the Sempiternal.

Not supposed to be easy . . .

Lottie hunched against the pain. Sometimes it seemed that this pain was the only constant in her life. *The bad spell after Grissom's kick, the bad spell when the Barghest attacked, the bad spell in the pub, after*—the familiar pain welled within her, hot and piercing. It was sharp, and sharper still. It was . . . *keen*.

Lottie straightened suddenly.

She grabbed Eliot's hand in hers and shut her eyes. For once, just once, she let the bad spell have its way, constricting her chest in a twisted knot past bearing.

And then the pain was there but not there. It was a deep river inside her, but she was balanced above it, as though on a weightless web. The tightening sensation shifted out of her chest and burned its way down Lottie's arms, cooling as it sank down into her fingertips, and vanished altogether into Eliot's soft palm.

The bad spell had passed. Eliot stirred awake.

". . . Lottie?"

"Eliot!" Lottie threw her arms around his neck. "Eliot, I'm sorry. I'm *sorry*."

Eliot blinked blearily at Lottie. His chapped lips broke into a smile.

"What," he coughed, "are you talking about? I figured we'd already made up by the time you slammed the front door."

Lottie grinned back as tears trickled down her cheeks and over her lips.

"I had a dream about you," said Eliot. "Two, in fact."

"I did, too."

"Hey." Eliot reached out to stop one of Lottie's tears with his thumb. "What's this about? I'm feeling a lot better, you know."

This time, Lottie knew with a surging hope that Eliot wasn't lying. He was even *looking* better. She ventured a glance up at Mr. Wilfer.

"What—what just happened?"

"I can hardly say how," whispered Mr. Wilfer, "but something very wonderful."

Gently, Mr. Wilfer touched Eliot at the elbow. Then, as though shocked by electricity, he pulled back his hand. His face was full of awe.

"Hello there," Eliot said brightly, nodding to Mr. Wilfer and reaching for his glasses. Then, turning to Lottie, he whispered, "Who is this?"

Lottie looked at Mr. Wilfer and then back at Eliot. Where did she begin?

"This, Eliot," said Lottie, "is the letter-writer."

Epilogue

A GREEN APPLE TREE no longer grew in the heart of Thirsby Square. The neighbors decided that the tree must've been struck by lightning during that fearsome thunderstorm at the end of September—the very night, if they remembered correctly, on which Lottie Fiske had disappeared.

No one, not even Pen Bloomfield and the gossips at Kemble School, knew why or where Lottie Fiske had gone, but Mrs. Yates found a letter in her mailbox a week after Lottie's disappearance. The letter came in an envelope with no return address, and its message was simple:

This is better. —L

Quotations in order of appearance

P. 64 "My face in thine eye, thine in mine appears, / And true plain hearts do in the faces rest;" (John Donne, "The Good-Morrow")

P. 66 "Myself unseen, I see in white defined, / Far off the homes of men," (Robert Frost, "The Vantage Point")

P. 125 "From what I've tasted of desire / I hold with those who favor fire." (Robert Frost, "Fire and Ice")

P. 131 "Others, I am not the first, / Have willed more mischief than they durst: If in the breathless night I too / Shiver now, 'tis nothing new." (A. E. Housman, *A Shropshire Lad*)

P. 184 "As I ponder'd in silence, / Returning upon my poems, considering, lingering long, / A Phantom arose before me with distrustful aspect," (Walt Whitman, *Leaves of Grass*)

P. 225 "One impulse from a vernal wood, / May teach you more of man, / Of moral evil and of good, / Than all the sages can." (William Wordsworth, "The Tables Turned")

P. 227 "Can I see another's woe, / And not be in sorrow too? / Can I see another's grief, / And not seek for kind relief?" (William Blake, "On Another's Sorrow")

P. 263 "There is a magic made by melody: / A spell of rest, and quiet breath, and cool / Heart, that sinks through fading colors deep" (Elizabeth Bishop, "I Am in Need of Music")

P. 294 "We are called—we must go. / Laid low, very low, / In the dark we must lie." (Alfred, Lord Tennyson, "All Things Will Die")

P. 315 "We are not prepared / For silence so sudden and so soon; / The day is too hot, too bright, too still, / Too ever, the dead remains too nothing." (W. H. Auden, "Nones")

P. 328 "But bid the strain be wild and deep, / Nor let thy notes of joy be first:" (George Gordon, Lord Byron, "My Soul Is Dark")

P. 336 "I sigh the lack of many a thing I sought,

. . . .

And moan the expense of many a vanish'd sight:" (William Shakespeare, "Sonnet 30")

P. 399 "I have done one braver thing / Than all the Worthies did," (John Donne, "The Undertaking")